PRAISE FOR KRISTINE GRAYSON NOVELS

"With her series of magical romances, Kristine Grayson has carved out her own special and unique place in the romance genre."

— *ROMANTIC TIMES*

"The reigning queen of paranormal romance."

— *THE BEST REVIEWS*

"…[Kristine Grayson] will have a long and glorious career."

— *THE ROMANCE READER.COM*

"Kristine Grayson gives 'happily ever after' her own unique twist!"

— KASEY MICHAELS

PRAISE FOR CHARMING BLUE

"A beguiling mystery is matched in power by the palpable and forbidden attraction between Jodi and Blue, making this one of the best series installments to date."

— *PUBLISHERS WEEKLY*

"If there's one word that sums up this book, it's originality."

— *LONG AND SHORT REVIEWS*

"The mixed-up fantasy world and mystery of *Charming Blue*, the fourth installment of Grayson's Charming Books, is a compelling read, with engaging characters and a plot that will keep you turning pages."

— RT BOOK REVIEWS

"*Charming Blue* by Kristine Grayson is an intriguing book with a plot that brings back my love of fairytales since I was a little girl. 5 Stars, Reviewer Top Pick."

— NIGHT OWL REVIEWS

"I loved the world this book was set in"

— A BUCKEYE GIRL READS

"*Charming Blue* will appeal to a wide range of readers – it's a great mix of fairy tale, romance, paranormal, and mystery. The characters are interesting, with compelling problems, and there's a touch of whimsy with the magic involved."

— BOOK TRIB

TIDINGS OF COMFORT AND JOY

THE SANTA SERIES

KRISTINE GRAYSON

Tidings of Comfort and Joy
Copyright © 2019 by Kristine Kathryn Rusch
Published by WMG Publishing
Cover and layout copyright © 2019 by WMG Publishing
Cover design by Allyson Longueira/WMG Publishing
Cover art copyright © pavel_kolotenko/Depositphotos
ISBN-13: 978-1-56146-196-7
ISBN-10: 1-56146-196-2

TIDINGS OF COMFORT
AND JOY

PART I

THE GODDESS OF ALL MACHINES

CHAPTER 1

The first thing Dallas Demaris would have told anyone who asked was that she loved the office building. Really, really loved it. Set on a cliff overlooking the ocean in Malibu, California, the office building had everything she had ever wanted in a work space. It had:

•Floor-to-ceiling windows everywhere, to soak in the sunlight and maximize the views.

•The view, which was of:

The ocean—and not some gray, scary, violent, *cold* ocean, but the ocean the way it should look, all blue and sparkly and inviting.

The sky—which was generally blue and sparkly and inviting as well.

The beach—which was pristine (except where it wasn't), and if she squinted just a bit (past the ships and the outlines of oil rigs) she could almost imagine the world as it once was, all pretty and ready...to be ruined by human beings.

•A soft carpet, which enabled her to stand and look at the view for a long period of time.

In truth, the office was beautifully designed, with workspaces that flowed. Each workspace had its windows. Even the corridors had views. Whenever she stepped off the elevator (which, sadly, did not have

3

views), she was greeted by a bank of windows, revealing some part of the Southern California coastline.

The entire working part of the building faced westward. The rest of the building was built into that cliff face, and the storage parts of the building were the ones on the cliff-face side.

Presciently, the building was made of concrete so even when the scary wildfires scraped across Malibu—and they did, far too often for her taste—the office would survive or would *have* survived, even if it hadn't had magical protection, which it did.

It also had been retrofitted for earthquake protection, by the mortals who were following mortal law, which simply made the building safer through a non-magical event. The building had always been protected against a real earthquake, but mortals didn't recognize magical protections, hence the retrofitting.

Mortals also didn't realize what this building was, and that was by design. Most people saw a rectangular gray and glass building rising out of the cliff face, thinking the office was just another wealthy person's home or big company's monument to excess, instead of a working office, filled with mostly disgruntled employees who, for some odd reason, would rather have been elsewhere.

Dallas didn't want to be anywhere else for any reason. She loved the warmth. She loved the sunshine. She loved the beach, the ocean, and even those tinder-dry mountains behind that cliff.

She had been lucky enough to score (an exceedingly expensive) rental nearby, but even back in the days when she had to drive to work, she didn't mind the traffic in the greater Los Angeles area. She figured it and the smog and the congestion were a small price to pay for getting to work in one of the prettiest places she had ever seen.

The second thing Dallas would have told anyone who asked (and really, no one ever did) was that she loved the work. She'd been doing it for nearly two hundred years now, trying to make machines compatible with magic, and when that didn't work, inventing machines that were. She had a knack for making devices bow to her whims.

It had taken her a greater part of the last century to figure out how to make magic and computers compatible, but she had done the deed well enough that most of the magical could now carry cell phones without having them explode on a daily basis.

Sure, she wasn't able to make magic and tech completely compatible —not mortal non-magical tech—but she could invent tech that had magic as its base.

Her brain was filled with fiddly little details of all kinds of science and magical history, waiting for each fiddly little detail to serve its purpose in the grander scheme of things. She wasn't sure what that grand scheme was, but she knew—deep down—that she was part of that grand scheme.

And one day, she would figure out how, exactly, she fit in.

But—and anyone who was paying attention would know that there was a *but* coming, wouldn't they?—her job wasn't ideal. She was the only woman who worked in the office, not because she was the only woman who could combine tech with magic, but because she was the only woman who had actually bullied her way into this place.

Or rather, obliviously barged her way in. Because Dallas obliviously barged her way into a lot of success over the centuries. She simply didn't take no for an answer. She also refused to believe that her brain was inferior to anyone else's—man, woman, transgender, standard magical creature, non-standard magical creature, or something brand-spankin' new.

And since she took that attitude toward life, she figured most of the pushback she got on the things she did was because she was brilliant and ahead of the curve, rather than because she was a woman.

Although today, standing inside the corporate meeting room of the office, it was hard to ignore the fact that she was being chosen for this new job not because she was the best person for the job, but because she was a woman—or rather *the* woman—and the men who ran the place wanted her the hell out of here.

The men who ran the place had been in charge for a Very Long Time. Before the office was built into this cliff face sometime in the last century. Those men—and there were a dozen of them—weren't in Malibu because they loved it. They still considered Malibu a backwater of the first order, since all but two of them were European.

In truth, they couldn't get more out of touch. The director, Waldo Ranklesworth, flew home to England every evening. Literally flew. He didn't like to spend any more time in the Colonies, as he put it, than he had to.

Ranklesworth was round. His face was round, his torso was round, and his stubby little legs were round(ish). He had had a mustache since the nineteenth century, and it had finally turned white to match his thick head of hair. That mustache had either dug deep grooves into his jowls or had forced his skin into jowls—Dallas couldn't really tell. His bushy eyebrows sometimes brushed against his eyelashes, creating a tangle that he had to rub away like a child rubbing sleep out of his eyes.

Dallas had had trouble taking Ranklesworth seriously from the moment she met him. His pinched tone and his accent, liberally borrowed *from* Oxford but not *of* Oxford, didn't help.

He tended to hire men similar to him, following the mandate of the company, which was that most Western languages and cultures be represented. He wouldn't have been able to handle the office if it had to handle Asian cultures, African cultures, and Middle Eastern cultures. He had been heard to argue that the Eastern European cultures weren't really European at all.

If Dallas were militant—and she wasn't, not really, because it interfered with her work—she would have been some kind of whistleblower. Although she was never entirely sure who Ranklesworth actually worked for, or what the hierarchy of the office was once you got outside of this particular building.

Dallas had always been happy to do the almost-impossible assignments the men around the table had given her, because she liked a challenge. When she first started here, before there were even roads heading to the beach, she had believed the men gave her the biggest challenges because she had the biggest brain.

Slowly, she realized, they had given her the biggest challenges because they couldn't figure out any other way to get rid of her.

And really, it was the other men at the table who had taught her that. Not the ten Ranklesworth clones, who all had varying degrees of roundness, mustachedness, and thick-white-hairedness, but the rotating seats of the two Americans.

At first, those two men were also round and mustachioed and white-haired (one illegitimately, using magic to make his bald pate look just like Ranklesworth's head). Those two men had both come from the East Coast, from "good" families, and got tired of Ranklesworth's snobbery, moving on and up, as the men liked to say.

But then orders came from on high for some diversity in the office, and that at first meant men from the Middle West and California itself, not that it worked out for them either. And then the 1960s happened, and diversity took on a new meaning, and so did the levels of passive-aggressive viciousness. The two American seats usually went to a man of color, who would get angry at The Way Things Were Done, and would usually try to recruit Dallas to help foment some rebellion, and she would beg off, usually because she had the latest interesting job, and the rebellious Americans would move on, for reasons she never entirely understood. (Except she knew that they hadn't been fired.)

She put up with the passive-aggressive bigotry, and the frosty tones, and the arch comments about everything from her gender to her accent to her clothing, because she loved the work, although she had to admit that she had come to dread finishing the latest task, because that would mean another meeting with Ranklesworth and his team.

This meeting was no different. She knew that she wouldn't be praised for proving yet another impossible task to be possible, but she would like Ranklesworth and his team to at least put a chair at the table for her, so she wouldn't stand like an angular, overly tall, badly cast supplicant out of a high school production of *Oliver!*

Because that was another of the problems. In addition to being the only female mage in the building, she was also the tallest, thinnest person here. Six-two when she was barefoot, taller when she wore her favorite pair of leather-tooled cowboy boots, she was also the only person who still had actual color in her hair.

And that color happened to be a rich, dark amber—not flaming red, really, but not brown either. One of those colors that women usually bought out of a bottle. Dallas never messed with it, not even as strange hair colors like hot pink and green came into vogue. She usually wore her hair pulled away from her face, although today, she let it down, because something about these meetings made her want to seem more female rather than less.

Her eyes were that same amber and her skin wasn't much lighter. If someone had done a genetic test of her past, they would have found every single category of Texan in her DNA—from Comanche to Spanish to Mexican to white. She hadn't lived in Texas in more than a hundred and fifty years, but she carried it with her, in her dress (she favored bolo ties when forced to wear a tie), her accent, and her DNA.

She clearly did not fit in, and she wasn't quite sure why the men hadn't told her that from the beginning. She liked to think it was because they were stunned by her presence—an uppity woman of uncertain background who could outperform them on every single task. They kept trying to best her, and they never could.

One of the Americans hired a few decades ago told her they kept her because she ticked every diversity box. And she had raised her eyebrows at him: *When you can solve problems as easily as I can*, she had said, *I will accept your theory.*

He had been gone long before that theory could ever be tested.

Still, as the world changed around her, she wondered why she stayed here. Maybe there was a bit of ego involved for her as well. She liked besting the bigots. She liked proving to them over and over and over again that she was the best at what they all did, and that they could never find a job that was impossible for her to do.

Although this new job had an odd feel, right from the beginning.

First, the men were laughing as she came through the door. The nine Ranklesworth clones had a rather gusty way of laughing, all nose and closed-mouth hilarity. The two Americans (as she still called them, even though she really should have used their names) actually giggled, which wasn't really a good look on them when they were trying to be as fusty as their colleagues.

They were holding green-and-red folders that looked out of place three days before the beginning of the Fourth of July holiday (Ranklesworth insisted on celebrating every holiday, even when the holiday celebrated his country's defeat). She had a feeling that the men thought that this time—*this time*—they had finally found the project that would defeat her.

Since they thought that every single time they brought her a project, and she always proved that she was more capable than they thought, they shouldn't have been so mirthful. And they usually weren't. They usually watched her with beady-eyed uncertainty, trying to figure out if they had found the right project to get her out of the company.

This time, though. This time, they seemed certain of it.

She clomped into the room, her boot heels slapping on the polished concrete floor. She had long ago stopped asking that another chair be brought into the room. Instead, she stood, towering over them as if she were the one running the meeting.

On this day, she had chosen to wear a rather flirty, sky-blue skirt, with ruffles along the hem, and a sedate ivory blouse over it. That blue skirt said *female* in ways she couldn't, and that ivory blouse showed off not just the assets that Ranklesworth had once commented on (inappropriately, but before the mortal laws changed to disallow that sort of thing), but the assets that she was actually proud of—her toned arms and her surprisingly narrow waist. (Surprising to her, because she loved to eat. So she would enjoy the narrow as long as she could maintain it—without magic.)

The laughing stopped when she stopped at the head of the table—or rather, the foot of the table, since Ranklesworth was directly across from her.

Half of the Ranklesworth clones looked at her as if they had never seen her before, and the other half looked at her as if they couldn't wait to see her brought down. The two Americans had stopped giggling, and weren't looking at her at all. They were examining those strange red-and-green file folders.

"Well, nice of you to join us, Miss Demaris," Ranklesworth said, with an emphasis on the *Miss*. He hated calling her by her last name, something she had insisted upon during their very first meeting, more than 100 years ago.

Mr. Ranklesworth, she had said primly, *I do hope you run this office in a professional manner. I expect to be addressed the way you'd address any other colleague, with an honorific, instead of using my given name. Unless this company uses everyone's given name...?*

He had flushed, but had called her Miss Demaris ever since. With an emphasis on the *Miss* to let the others know that she was female, yes, and also unmarried, which, apparently, he found to be as irregular as her female status.

His tone on this day implied that she was late, which she was not. The meeting was scheduled for the top of the hour, which was still five minutes away. For decades, he had played this passive-aggressive game with her of letting her know the incorrect time for a meeting. He had always done the same with the Americans, but on this day, apparently, they had gotten the right memo.

She had stopped worrying about it. Mr. Ranklesworth couldn't fire her, much to his chagrin, since the company had deemed her one of the most important employees it had ever had. She had had that designation since the dawn of the combustion engine, and it had only become more important in the years since she solved the computer and handheld device problems.

The company had called her to their London office just once, and there, a wizened little man who actually looked like a wizard should look had offered her the job of Director—Ranklesworth's job—but she had declined. She knew that she wasn't good at bossing people about. She was much better at making sure machines and magic worked well together, and she had said so.

The wizened little man—whose name she was not allowed to know —had nodded, and had tried to grin, even though his grin got lost in the folds of his face.

Ranklesworth is jealous of you, and will do anything to get rid of you, the wizened little man said. *Rest assured that will never happen. But you will be subject to his whims if you don't replace him in the job.*

She thought she could handle the whims. After all, she had been handling them for more than a century now.

But occasionally, they grew tiring. Like today.

"This is our new job," Ranklesworth said, waving the red-and-green folder. "The command comes from on high. I tried to turn the work down, but wasn't allowed to. We are stuck with this project—or rather, you are, since you're our go-to gal."

She didn't wince when he said that. He'd adopted it over the last fifty years, and it still grated. It sounded like he was making fun of her accent and her gender whenever he said it. (And her competence. Always her competence.)

"May I have a folder?" she asked as she swiped a folder out of the hands of the nearest Ranklesworth clone. They were conveniently one folder short, which was a stupid trick they had played more often than she cared to think about.

The folder was thick with materials. All of the jobs arrived in the office on paper. She had arranged a way to get email and had a computer that could print out anything the group needed, but no one ever asked. The entire company preferred to use old-fashioned delivery services to deliver jobs in black embossed British letter-sized boxes embossed with gold foil.

She found those pretty a century ago, quaint sixty years ago, and tiresomely stuck in the past now.

An embossed candy cane was printed in the lower right hand corner of the front of the folder. There were no other words on the front at all.

She opened the interior, and some red, white, silver, and green sparkles plumed out, accompanied by a cheerful little tinkle of music, as if she were in a cartoon and she had just received a magical gift.

She sighed, and hoped she wouldn't be tainted by any unwanted magic. She would have to check later.

The first page floated upward and created a lovely snow-filled scene, slightly larger than the folder itself. The scene included one of those fluffy snowfalls that everyone (except her) agreed was the perfect snow-fall—big fat flakes that floated lazily down and landed on snowdrifts as if directed there by some algorithm.

Shoved deep in the snowdrifts were gigantic candy canes that served as some kind of gate, and beyond it, barely visible through the lovely snowfall, were the words *Claus & Company*.

She closed the folder on the image. It vanished, leaving the crisp scent of new-fallen snow behind.

"What is this?" she asked, even though she had a hunch she knew. They had brought her jobs like this before, in which she had lost half a productive day watching some advertising gimmick, instead of learning what the job was. Those gimmicks always put her behind.

"You," Ranklesworth said in a tone even more plummy than usual, "are going to the North Pole."

She let out half a laugh and set the folder on the table. "Yeah, sure. Let's cut through the hazing, and get to the actual job, shall we?"

The two Ranklesworth clones sitting closest to him started to snicker. That wasn't a good sign.

"That is the actual job," Ranklesworth said, his lips puckered ever so slightly, as if he was trying to hold back an uncharacteristic smile. "You are going to the North Pole to fix their computer system."

"The North Pole," she said. "The geographic North Pole? The one with the constantly shifting ice that makes it impossible to live there?"

Ranklesworth let out a noise that sounded suspiciously like a raspberry. He was too dignified to release an actual raspberry, wasn't he? And wasn't a raspberry an American sound of disgust, not a British one?

"For the sake of the magical universe," he said when he got his puckered lips under control, "I would never send anyone to the—what did you call it? The 'geographic North Pole.' That's as uninteresting to me as the 'real' Mount Olympus. No, Miss Demaris. I am sending you to the *actual* North Pole. Santa's North Pole. I want you to fix his computer system."

"Santa isn't real," she said, and everyone in the entire room swung their heads toward her as if she had just said that magic wasn't real.

"I assure you," Ranklesworth said, "Santa is real."

"Well," Dallas said, "if he is real, I have issues with working for him. He allows children to go to sleep in need every night. He doesn't give out gifts to a goodly portion of the world. And he seems to favor the wealthy over everyone else."

"I don't really care what your political beliefs are, Miss Demaris," Ranklesworth said. "The fact is that his computer system is malfunctioning and he needs a magical/machine tech. I must tell you that all of the Christmas holiday is on our shoulders here. If we fail—well, if *you* fail—no child will get a visit from Santa Claus this year."

The laughter had left the room. The men were all staring at her nervously. And if Ranklesworth was telling the truth, then this might actually be a job that could get her fired if she failed.

"No," Dallas said.

"No?" Ranklesworth asked.

She nodded. "No," she repeated.

"No what?" he asked.

"No, I will not take this job. I despise snow and cold. I refuse to go anywhere that has candy canes for gates, and I want nothing to do with this Claus & Company."

Ranklesworth let out a gusty sigh. His bushy eyebrows rose into his messy hair and, for once, his mustache actually looked like it was the right length.

"Well," he said, "I'm afraid you don't get to say no."

"Why not?" she asked. "I have never turned down a job before. In more than a century, I've done exactly what you've asked."

Even when it was stupid. Even when it was designed to make me fail. She thought that part, but didn't say any of it.

"Because this order didn't come from me." Ranklesworth's beady little eyes met hers. "It came from my boss."

"Tell him no," she said. "Or I will."

Ranklesworth closed his eyes for a moment, and she could almost read the thought balloon over his head: *Save me from uncooperative females.* Or something a bit harsher, something she didn't exactly want to see.

Ranklesworth took a deep breath, opened his eyes, and then said, "He asked for you by name. He said you are the very best person for the job."

"This job?" she asked, surprised. Ranklesworth had given her a reluctant compliment.

"Any job, really," Ranklesworth said tiredly. He clearly did not want to admit that. "You do have a higher success rate than anyone in the company."

She inclined her head toward him. Ranklesworth had never acknowledged that before.

The Ranklesworth clones were looking at him in shock. The Americans were looking at her in shock.

She wasn't sure exactly how to respond, so she didn't say anything.

"But yes, this job," Ranklesworth said. "He would say it was impossible, but he knows you've done the impossible before."

"Oh, for god's sake," she said. She *had* done the impossible. She took pride in the impossible. But she didn't want to do this. She didn't want this job at all.

It was the very first job they had ever told her to take that she was declining. And she was going to decline it forcefully, by giving Ranklesworth what he always wanted.

She took a deep breath, and said, "I'll quit before I go up there."

The clones' heads swiveled toward her. A few of the clones grinned at her, as if they had finally won a big prize. The Americans looked panicked.

Ranklesworth rolled his eyes. His lips thinned and then he shook his head, as if he couldn't believe what he had just heard.

"Much as I would love to accept your resignation," Ranklesworth said, "it's not possible here."

The clones' heads swiveled again, now looking at him in shock. The Americans frowned at him.

She did too. Ranklesworth should have jumped at the chance to get rid of her.

She braced the fingers of one hand against the cool wood of the conference table, feeling a bit breathless. They wouldn't let her quit? She had always kept that in her back pocket, just in case they stopped giving her interesting work.

That was the thing Ranklesworth never understood: he wasn't ever going to get rid of Dallas if he continued to give her impossible tasks. He would have gotten rid of her decades ago if he relegated her to a desk and treated her like the clones.

Although, this particular impossible job was getting rid of her, wasn't it? Even though, Ranklesworth said that wasn't possible.

"You've wanted to get rid of me for decades," she said.

Ranklesworth raised those bushy eyebrows, as if her comment had surprised him. It probably had. Not because he wanted to get rid of her, but because she knew about it.

"Accept my resignation, and send one of these gentlemen to the North Pole," she said.

One of the Americans actually turned his chair slightly, as if he was trying to get Ranklesworth's attention, but knew better than to interrupt.

"Can't," Ranklesworth said. "This is some kind of magical emergency, an all-hands-on-deck sort of thing. You'd be drafted even if you quit. It is, I'm told, the case of having the right person in the right job."

He sounded sincere, but she had no idea if he really was. She might have believed him if he had supported her work in the past. But he hadn't, and if she went by personal experience alone, she had to assume this was some kind of game, cleverly designed to make her the loser.

"I think I'll go to London and talk to your boss," she said. That man was the wizened little man she had met once before. He had seemed to like her, even if there were so many rules around his august personage that she half-felt like she had visited some kind of royalty.

Negotiating rules like that made her nervous, but she would do it in this instance.

"Do so," Ranklesworth said. "But bring warm clothing. They might just send you north straightaway from the London offices."

She frowned. That sounded true too. She'd actually seen it happen before. The previous Americans had gone to complain about something and never returned. They had been sent elsewhere, straight away from the London offices.

That could happen to her, even if London didn't send her to the North Pole. She might never return to Malibu, to her beach and her sky and her ocean.

That might just break her heart.

The others were quiet. The Americans were looking down, as if they were embarrassed or worried.

"Why aren't any of you fighting for this job?" she asked. She'd seen that before on the really important ones.

"Santa has a reputation," Ranklesworth said. "It's not a good one."

"Yeah, I noticed," she said.

"Not for the reasons you mentioned," Ranklesworth said. "But because he's…um…notoriously difficult for mages to work with."

"He doesn't like us much," one of the Americans said to the tabletop.

"Then why are we helping him?" Dallas asked.

"Because the magical underpinning of the universe is at stake," Ranklesworth said, as if she were the dumbest person on Earth.

That tone, she recognized. She had heard it in almost every conversation she'd had with Ranklesworth, particularly when it dealt with the way that mages and the so-called real world interacted.

She didn't ask, *What did I miss?* because that question put her in a one-down position. But she didn't exactly know how to ask what she needed to ask, so she settled on a good old American standby.

"Huh?" she asked.

Heads swiveled, except for the Americans. One continued to look down. The other put the back of his fingers against his forehead, shielding his face from everything going on at the table, the way that kids sometimes did when they were trying to become invisible.

"You really don't know this?" Ranklesworth asked. Then he shook his head, and repeated more to himself than to her, "You really don't know this."

He sighed gustily, shook his head again, and said, "Belief in magic powers magic."

Her eyes narrowed. She knew that. Of course she knew that. That was why some of the older so-called gods had less power than some of the other so-called gods. Why certain cultures thrived in certain environments, like the Faerie Kings in Las Vegas. There, the irrational belief in luck powered most of their magical devices.

Dallas had used that luck-belief once, on a job that had taken her in the bowels beneath the city, to an astonishing and crazy Faerie King casino that had literally made her head spin.

But she knew better than to remind Ranklesworth that she couldn't do her job if she didn't understand what added fuel to magic's fire.

"Millions and millions of children believe in Santa Claus," Ranklesworth told her. "For each child that ages out of the belief, another is born into the belief. The mortal culture perpetuates that belief and is complicit in making sure that children under the age of five or so all believe it."

"They don't all believe it," she said unable to keep silent. "The 'culture,' as you call it, is at best what you used to call Western culture, at worst a purely American branding episode that focuses on children raised in a Christian—"

"Really," Ranklesworth said, "I told you, no politics."

"It's not politics," she said. "It's fact—"

"I don't care," Ranklesworth said. "It's a job that we have to do."

"Then find someone else. Because I refuse." She slammed the folder on the table and walked out of the conference room, not even stopping to look at her lovely ocean.

Ranklesworth could deal with his bosses.

Because she was done.

CHAPTER 2

*I*f Dallas had had a desk to clean out, she would have cleaned it out that afternoon. But she didn't. She had an office filled with bits and pieces of former jobs, things she couldn't really take with her even if she wanted to.

All of those items, from tinny spanners to glowing wingnuts, were in her office to impress Ranklesworth and the clones. Those magical items, property of the company, were in her office rather than the vault simply to remind Ranklesworth and the clones that she could do jobs they couldn't. Her big giant F.U. to them, done as office decoration.

The rest of the office décor, from the half-comfortable chair to the end tables, belonged to the company as well, and wouldn't have been worth taking home, even if she wanted to.

Everything that she wanted at home was already at home; she kept nothing personal here except her beach shoes.

Which she picked up right now. They were some kind of rubber and mesh shoe that were designed specifically for beach use. The solid bottom protected her feet, and the mesh top allowed her to wade into the ocean if she felt like it.

She looked at the ocean through her lovely floor-to-ceiling windows. She would miss that view. Even if she bought a home along this hillside—and she could afford it, since she rarely spent her salary—it wouldn't have this exact perspective, the sense that this building jutted over the beach and might simply fall into the ocean itself.

She had loved the perspective almost more than the job. And she would miss both.

But she wasn't going to let herself be sad. Maybe it was time to move on. She really hadn't moved. She'd learned and grown a lot over the decades, but she had remained in the same place. The place itself had changed around her, and she had let that be enough.

The very thought made her nervous. Take charge of her own life? Find different work? Work for someone else? Or do something on her own for once?

She had never given any of that any thought before. And it really did break her heart to lose the work. She had loved the challenges, as well as the F.U. She loved proving Ranklesworth and the clones wrong each and every day. It had almost become an addiction.

That thought made her shiver. She didn't want to think about how the unhealthy relationships here had affected her. She didn't like thinking that she participated in them, even slightly.

She slipped on the beach shoes one last time, sending her boots home with the snap of a finger. Then she walked to the beach exit, only a few doors down from what would soon cease being her office.

She pulled the door open, and stepped outside. That transition between the cool recycled air in the building and the much warmer air outside never ceased to please her.

The ocean air smelled faintly of fish overlaid with roses from someone's ever-blooming bush nearby. She started down the familiar dirt path, curving into the overgrown bushes and shrubs that the company kept getting fined for, because the mortals thought it was a fire danger.

If they were standard bushes and shrubs, they would be a fire danger. But they had been spelled to repel fire, and their roots were extra-long, clinging to the sandy ground as protection against land- and mudslides. She walked past the windswept trees, placing her hands on their scratchy bark, like she did every day she was here, and probably would never do again.

She wasn't sad, exactly, but she was annoyed. She knew that half the company would probably misunderstand her unwillingness to do this job. They would assume she was one of those children who claimed to be deprived because Santa had never visited her.

No one would think about the fact that she had been born long before C. Clement Moore published "The Night Before Christmas," the stupid poem that some said started it all. Or perhaps Thomas Nast started it, with his caricature of the Jolly Old Fat Man published in the Important newspapers of the late nineteenth century. Or those Coke ads from the early part of the last century, with the rosy cheeked Santa offering a tiny glass bottle which, at the time, had been filled with a soft drink that also included cocaine.

She didn't care about what Santa and his minions had supposedly done to her. Since he hadn't done anything. She didn't count in his world.

She did care about how big the myth had grown, the way he exploited it, and the pain he caused.

Santa, in short, had made many lives miserable. And that upset her deeply.

If he had just been a myth, as the mortals believed, it would be one thing. Any child growing to adulthood would realize at some point or another that Santa was Mom and Dad, and if Mom and Dad were poor, then Santa wouldn't come to visit. Or if Mom and Dad didn't celebrate Christmas, Santa wouldn't come to visit.

But discovering that Santa was real? That just pissed her off to no end. Why the hell was he ignoring more than half the world? Why hadn't he solved world peace? Thousands—maybe millions—of kids asked for it every year. Why wouldn't he stop abuse and loss and all of the things kids suffered through? Why wouldn't—

A loud *pop!* sounded in front of her, and Ranklesworth stood before her. He immediately started sliding backwards down the path because his slick dress shoes weren't up to the task of keeping him upright. He flailed for a moment, then grabbed a wispy tree, and clung as his feet slipped out from underneath him.

If he had been planning a dignified arrival before her, he had failed miserably.

He cursed. Then he did something with his nose, and his shoes vanished, along with his black socks, leaving the palest feet she had ever seen in her life. He planted one pale foot on the path, winced at either the sharpness of the stones or the heat on the dirt, and then planted his other pale foot. He slowly released his hands from the tree, making sure he maintained his balance, then wiped his hands on his pant legs.

Normally, she would have made some snide comment, maybe taking him to task for never going outside, or simply reminding him that different environments required different clothing.

But she did neither. She was irritated—beyond irritated, really—that he had interrupted her last walk down to the beach.

"What do you want?" she asked, not trying to hide the irritation.

"You have to go on that job," he said.

She shook her head.

"Really," he said. "No one else can do it."

"I refuse to believe that," she said. Her ego was big, but not that big.

"The company will pay you any price you demand," he said. "As a contractor. Hell, you can charge millions if you want."

She didn't want. But the number got her attention. The company had (as far as she could tell) unlimited funds, but it was parsimonious about doling them out.

"I don't want," she said.

"How about I get you a meeting with the Jolly Old Elf himself," Ranklesworth said. "You can talk to him about your politics all day."

"I'm sure he does what he does for his own reasons," she said. "I just don't have to be a party to it."

Ranklesworth emitted one of his gusty sighs. "Look, you're upset because half the world is treated unequally—"

"More than half," she muttered.

"—even though many of them would never want him in their lives at all—"

"Beside the point," she muttered.

"—but here's the thing." Ranklesworth's face was getting red with exertion or maybe it was the effect of sunlight on his unbelievably pale skin. "If you don't go, *no one* will get anything ever again. The entire magic—"

"You said that," she said. "Magical universe. Underpinnings."

"Yes, well, maybe not as dramatic as all that," he said. "I'm sure we can come up with something."

"I'm sure," she said. "The world didn't exactly collapse when the ancient humans stopped worshipping the Greek gods."

Ranklesworth's eyes narrowed. "Nonetheless," he said pointedly, "it will cause an unpleasant disruption—"

"I got that," she said.

"—and not of adults. Of children."

"Whose parents will bring them all the toys they need," she said. "I don't need to help the privileged."

"You wouldn't be," he said. "You'd be helping those who need to believe in magic."

That caught her attention. She hadn't been thinking about magic. She'd been thinking about the commercial nature of a holiday she didn't even celebrate, a commercial nature that took over the entire American culture from the end of October through the first of the year. And she didn't have to travel much to know that in the past decade or so, certain parts of Europe were catching the same Santa fever.

Ranklesworth must have noticed her change in attitude. He dug his toes deeper in the path, legs bent. The angle he was standing at looked uncomfortable, and probably wouldn't be something he could sustain for very long.

"It's not about the stuff." He straightened his back and tried to look dignified even though one false move would send him sliding down the mountainside. "It's about the hope. The *possibility*. Santa brings a bit of magic into corners of the world that don't have hope and possibility."

"Seems like it's about stuff to me," she said.

"For some, yes." Ranklesworth glanced down the path, then grimaced, and grabbed the tree again. "And, granted, this is—as they say —a first-world problem."

She shook her head slightly in surprise. He knew that phrase?

Granted, it was one she hadn't heard for a while, but still. It showed an awareness she hadn't expected from Ranklesworth at all.

"But there are a lot of children in financially privileged households who suffer from despair and abuse and a whole host of other problems," he said. "Having that dream of magic—the very idea that somewhere in the world, something out of the ordinary occurs, and it's wonderful. That dream of possibility. That dream of hope—"

"You make it sound like a religion," she said, deliberately cutting him off. He was making her feel uncomfortable.

"You're the one who mentioned the Greek *gods*," he said. "Hope and belief and possibility come from many venues. Some call it magic. Some call it religion. Some—"

"I know this," she said drily. She did too. She didn't focus on any of it, but she knew it, in a vague, other-people-had-discussed-it kind of way.

"Right now, Santa is one of the biggest purveyors of hope in the secular Western world."

"That's just sad," she said.

"I am not in charge of what's happening," Ranklesworth said. "I am simply telling you what I know to be true. I can have someone contact you from the statistics department if you would like. Everything I've said is based firmly upon evidence."

Her heart sank. If he had numbers from the statistics department, then there really was evidence. He was a small man, an occasional bully, and excessively passive-aggressive, but he rarely lied.

"I'd like to see that evidence," she said, just to be contrary. Because she could feel herself giving in.

He slipped a bit, then arched his toes deeper into the dirt. He could have used some kind of spell to hold himself in place, but he didn't.

"Look," he said. "I do understand that you do not want to take this job. The company would be eternally grateful—"

"I don't care," she said. "I wouldn't be doing it for the company or for the damn magical underpinnings."

He raised his eyebrows at her use of the word "damn." She didn't swear on the job very often. She thought cursing showed a remarkable lack of imagination, and he knew that.

She started to tell him why she was now considering this, but stopped herself. The one thing Ranklesworth lacked was empathy. He was interested in magical power and magical devices and the way that magic worked, but not interested in the ways that magic could or couldn't be used.

She, on the other hand, had seen firsthand how despair brought people low. Despair could be deadly. And she knew, because she had seen it, that the occasional "miracle," the occasional little touch of magic, could bring a smile to a face that hadn't smiled in years.

"Why are you so certain that my failure to do this job would destroy everyone's holiday?" she asked.

Ranklesworth bent the tree even more. If he kept pulling it on it, it would eventually break.

But she wasn't going to tell him that.

He looked away from the tree and directly at her. She had never seen Ranklesworth look so serious before.

"Because the idiots waited until now to let us know there was a problem," he said quietly. "They should have notified us decades ago, but they believed they could solve it. Instead, they made things worse. And now, with only a few months to spare, they expect a miracle from us."

"Can't they just use their magic to drop presents on various households?" she asked.

He rolled his eyes. "I suppose they could, but that wouldn't fall into the myth, now would it? It is the sustaining of the myth that these machines do, along with a whole lot of everything else. Besides, I'm told that Santa and his crew poured most of their magic into devices, rather than keep that magic loose and free. And now the devices are breaking down."

It was her turn to sigh. The wind off the ocean had died down, and the air had gotten even warmer—almost hot. Normally she loved the changeability, but right now, she wanted a breeze—something, anything, to distract her.

"If you're right," she said.

"I am," he said, before she could finish.

"Then there's a chance that no matter what I do, the devices will cease working."

"I'm aware of that," he said. "I'm also aware—as is headquarters—that we have almost no one who can handle a problem of this magnitude, let alone handle it alone."

"Alone?" she asked.

"Everything at the North Pole is proprietary," he said. "They don't want outsiders there at all. The fact that they're going to open the doors to you shows the depth of their desperation."

And the reason for his.

"You already promised I would be there," she said. "That's why you're pushing so hard. You not only guaranteed that I would go, you guaranteed that I would fix the problem before Christmas, didn't you?"

His unattractively pale skin flushed an even more unattractive puce. The color alone answered her question. She didn't even have to see him nod.

"I couldn't do a job of this magnitude on my own, even if I wanted to," she said.

"They're only allowing one person into the North Pole," he said.

"I don't have enough magic to solve a problem like this," she said.

"They have magic to spare," he said.

"I thought you said it's all device-based," she said.

"The myth stuff is. But everyone at the Pole—and I do mean *everyone* —is a mage. They *all* have magic to one degree or another. You'll have a lot of resources."

"And no one experienced," she said.

"Well," he said, "that's not entirely true. They have an entire team who know how to keep all of their machinery running."

"Poorly," she said.

Ranklesworth shrugged, and that movement was all the tree could take. It slipped through his (mostly likely sweaty) fingers and bounced upward as if it had set itself free.

He lost his balance and toppled forward, hands landing in the dirt with a soft thud. His feet kept moving backwards. Runnels of dirt and sand started down the mountainside. His little stubby toes couldn't get traction, and Dallas would be damned if she was going to help him in any way.

She let him slide almost perpendicular before asking, "Do you want help?" in a tone that said she wanted nothing to do with helping him.

"No, no," he said in his most plummy accent. "Doing just fine here. More than fine, actually. Extremely fine."

He bent his knees to the path, stopping the slide, and then sat down with enough of a thud that dirt rose up around him.

"Everyone should sit in the dirt now and then," he said, as if he were trying to convince himself.

"It's sand," she said.

"It's *unpleasant*," he snapped.

Even though she didn't think it was.

"But," he continued, "there are times in life when we all need to do unpleasant things."

So, he was pretending his loss of balance was a life lesson for her. How very charming of him. How typical.

"You're going to do it, aren't you?" he asked.

She looked away. She hated that he could read her. Yes, she was thinking of doing it now.

It was the ultimate challenge. Working on magical devices that hadn't been touched by knowledgeable hands in decades. Working alone with people who probably did not want her there. Working on something with a ridiculous deadline because no one wanted to admit there was a problem.

This wasn't an impossible task. This was an impossible task on steroids. Something so hard that not even she thought she could accomplish it.

Which was why she had to try—whether she wanted to or not.

PART II

THE REAL (WELL, REAL TO EVERY CHILD WHO BELIEVES) NORTH POLE

CHAPTER 3

*M*achine Room Five smelled of hot metal and steam. The stench told Lothario Johanssen that the problem couldn't be solved with a simple turn of the wrench. He was going to have to go into the bowels of the machine for the third time that week.

He slid the sleeves of his shirt up to his biceps, not sure if the moisture on his skin was steam or sweat or both. Room Five was extremely hot, but he couldn't cool anything down, not until he knew what was wrong with the machine—this time.

He sighed, then regretted inhaling the hot air. It tasted of metal too. He leaned back just a little and did his best to take in this part of the machine. He had to crane his neck upwards to see the sides, and even then, he didn't entirely see the top.

The machine snaked its way through five warehouse-sized rooms. The top of the machine was six stories high, and each piece was littered with baubles and add-ons and jury-rigs. Room Five was the newest section—if he didn't count Room Six. Room Six housed the gigantic printer that scrolled out the naughty-and-nice list on linen paper in perfect calligraphy—when the rest of the machine was working.

It wasn't fair to call the thing a computer. It was part computer, part Analytical Engine, part Turing machine, part ENIAC machine, and mostly whimsy. His whimsy. He had created the machine in pieces over the past two centuries, infusing the parts that didn't work with his own personal magic.

He wanted to make the machine self-sufficient. He kept redesigning it, trying to make it work. The problem was that he was overworked, and his staff kept getting pulled onto other projects that apparently had a higher priority.

He hadn't really been able to add on since he managed to redesign the printer, about eighty years ago. He'd been proud of that redesign then. Now he wished he hadn't done it. Not only did Machine Room Six cause him more trouble than all the other rooms combined, but it also smelled of wet ink—which, if he used the wrong type—also made it smell of urine.

Lo had spent the last eighty years keeping the machine working, cobbling this together with that, adding parts that made some of the machine self-sufficient, wishing he could find someone else to pour their magic into this contraption, so he wasn't tied to it.

Some days, he barely had time to think. And when he did think, he thought about all the pressure on him. He had to keep this thing working so that The Big Guy could get his lists, keep track of production, monitor his delivery schedule, and maintain the magic worldwide.

The Big Guy wanted the machine to handle all the other things as well, such as employee information, supplies tracking, reindeer maintenance, and satellite/hub monitoring, but the machine simply couldn't do all of that *and* continue to print out all the details on linen in calligraphy that looked like it had been handwritten with a quill pen.

The Big Guy still said that last part was extremely important to him —and to the illusion—and he wouldn't accept a direct magical solution, which made Lo's job exceptionally difficult.

At least The Big Guy didn't want all the business information printed, so Lo cheated two or three decades ago and bought personal computers for the tech elves, the ones who could handle technology and magic without making the tech explode.

A few of them wanted tablets now, and their own mobile phones, but Lo drew the line there. He let everyone think that he thought tech should stay away from Santa's workshop, even though that was not true. He was the one who installed the Tech Toys Division after all—and, of course, he built the stupid machine. Even if he believed someone could install a working cell tower around here or figure out a way to jury-rig something that would make the mobiles and tablets work on some kind of network, he simply didn't have the time to learn all that new tech, convert systems, and maintain this damned machine.

Which was wheezing like a fat old cigar smoker who had just tried to run a mile.

That metallic-steam smell annoyed Lo. Something in this entire contraption, something *mechanical*, was about to fail.

He ran his fingers across his forehead, trying to ease the headache that was starting, which had to be from the smell, or so he was telling himself. Because if he thought it was from the heat, he would have to use the wrong kind of magic to keep himself encased in ice. And if he thought the headache was from a lack of sleep—well, then he might as well give up. Because he couldn't remember if he'd had a good night's sleep in this century, let alone this decade.

He peeled off his shirt, wiped his skin down with it, and then tossed it on the floor. He was already wearing shorts, although his feet were encased in brand new Nikes that he had magicked the moment he got them so that nothing on the machine could puncture or melt them.

He pulled his curly hair back into a short ponytail—which one of the S-Elves had told him were called man-buns now, and were only worn by hipsters, whatever they were—and grabbed his toolbox in his right hand.

Usually Lo kept toolboxes in the small workstations built into the machine, but lately he'd found that those toolboxes were missing. Either he had forgotten to replace them—which was always possible—or some of the elves were taking them for other projects. Which was also possible, but punishable by death. Or so he wished. Because nothing was punishable by death at the North Pole.

Nothing at the North Pole was punishable, except by some form of demotion. And some of the elves wanted to be demoted, because they had previously been promoted to jobs they hated. So the level of incompetence and general malfeasance in various areas of the North Pole was higher than it probably should have been, something he worried about but couldn't do anything about, given his already overloaded schedule.

He'd made the mistake of complaining once, and he would never do that again, because that got him a whole slew of surly employees for the rest of the year, until the annual revamp in January.

He had seven months until January. Six months until December. Too little time to do anything but hang on, while the machine kept growing wheezier and wheezier. When Lo did find a moment to crawl into his bed, he would doze for a few seconds before going bolt-awake, terrified that the machine wouldn't make it to December twenty-fifth.

He'd coaxed the machine through years before, and then spent the spring fixing whatever was causing the issue. But he could only coax so long. At some point, even the best machine—even the most magical machine—fell apart. Some went all at once, but a few, well, they fell apart piece by unimportant piece, until nothing worked.

This machine was falling apart piece by unimportant piece, and eventually, he wouldn't be able to will it back together again. Something was missing, something important, and he didn't know if that something was in him or if that something was some kind of technical flaw. Or maybe it was a magical flaw.

He glanced around the room. He had cleared Machine Room Five because he had this deep fear that one day he would pull the wrong lever, and the entire machine would explode.

If he got injured or (gods forbid) died in an explosion like that, he wouldn't mind (well, he would *mind*, if he survived, but he would *understand*) because the explosion would somehow be his fault. The worst thing that could happen—in his opinion—was that someone *else* could die or be injured because he made some kind of catastrophic mistake with the machine.

He grabbed one of the bottles of water attached to the far wall. The glass was cool against his fingers—the walls were built to keep everything cool, which was (he sometimes thought) the only thing that kept the machine from overheating each and every day. The maintenance elves went through the machine rooms on the daily cleaning run, and refreshed the water bottles that hugged the wall.

Once upon a time—back when the machine was young(er)—the water bottles had to be here and had to be cold so that someone could toss cold water at any part of the machine that overheated.

Lo had found another solution about a century ago, one that didn't involve glass water bottles and pails of liquid, but he decided to keep one row of water bottles at arm's reach, just so anyone working in these rooms wouldn't overheat. At least, not too badly.

He twisted off the almost-too-hot metal screw top (yet another addition made when the bottles went from repair bottles to potable water bottles), and chugged down the warm water inside. It tasted better than it should have, which meant that he might be a bit dehydrated. He set the bottle in the pallet near the door, then wiped his forearm over his forehead.

Yeah, he was sweating more than he usually did, which meant this room was hotter than it usually was, which meant he had to do something before he even went deep into the machine.

If he shut down this part of the machine, then he wouldn't be able to see what was going wrong. But if he kept it running, then it might overheat and shut down anyway.

He sighed, grabbed the pair of thick gloves he kept on a table not far from the machine, and put them on. Then he grabbed the on-off handle, which wasn't so much a handle as a long lever, damn near the size of his leg. He had to brace himself to yank the lever downward, taking most of his upper body strength just to get the thing moving.

The lever jerked downward, and something inside the machine squealed so loudly that Lo winced. To him, metal against metal always sounded like a machine crying out in pain. And this one was. The sound was high and screeching, and made that headache grow. If he thought the sound was bad, the elves working nearby had to be in serious pain. Their sense of hearing was so much greater than his could ever be.

The lever finally went all the way down, and the machine groaned. Then it wheezed again, and sighed, bits of steam rising from parts that shouldn't have steam anywhere near them. The steam plumes were heading upwards like purposeful ghosts.

Lo reached down and locked the lever in place. In theory, this section of the machine was now off. Then he removed the gloves, wiped his sweaty hands on his shorts, and watched the plumes gather into one long steam cloud near the ceiling.

Moisture dripped downward. The steam was so thick it was creating its own rain. It almost felt like the machine was crying.

Lo leaned his head against the lever's handle, just for a moment. He didn't dare tell anyone here that he thought the machine had its own moods and emotions. The crew at the North Pole would absolutely believe him, and the news would terrify them, and they would want to shut the machine down indefinitely.

The Big Guy wanted to control all the anthropomorphic magical items himself, especially the big ones. Especially the big ones that could do some damage when something went wrong.

He was the only one who could handle the sleigh (handle it *well*, anyway—although the other S-Elves, all relatives of his—could manage sleighs better than most). Except for this machine, the sleigh was the biggest magical machine in the entire place. And The Big Guy didn't need to know that sometimes this machine had a mind of its own.

Lo walked toward the machine. Flywheels were still spinning, but slowing down a little. Knobs were vibrating, and internal lights were flashing, slower with each turn of the nearest flywheel. The air still smelled hot here, but at least the machine had stopped releasing steam.

Lo ducked into the narrow passage that he had created to protect anyone who was trying to examine the machine from below. Beads of moisture covered the levers and pulleys, and a few of them glowed red.

It had gotten way too hot in this part of the machine. He had made the right decision in shutting it down.

"Hey, Lo! Got a minute?" The piercing voice belonged to Rafn, one of Lo's best assistants. Rafn actually had engineering skills. But he lacked social skills—as evidenced from that one question.

Of course, Lo didn't have a minute. He was inside the machine. He was *busy*. Why would he have a minute?

But if he snapped at Rafn, then Rafn would sulk, and right now Lo didn't need Rafn to sulk. A sulky Rafn would create more problems than he solved. Not that a sulky Rafn ever solved problems, but sometimes, snapping at people did make Lo feel better.

"Can it wait?" Lo asked, once he found his voice.

"Well," Rafn said, "not really."

There was something in his tone that Lo hadn't heard before. Something both cautious and eager at the same time.

Lo sighed, then ducked out of the passage and back into the main part of Machine Room Five. He had only been gone a minute, but the room looked worse than it had before. Water covered every surface.

Rafn was standing just inside the door, and he was the only thing in the room that wasn't wet.

"I don't want you in here," Lo said.

"Too bad," Rafn said. "Because you need to hear this."

Rafn was wearing green coveralls decorated with tiny red-and-white candy canes, the regulation uniform for Elf-gineers (which was what the engineering department called elves with engineering ability). His thick shock of candy-cane red hair was standing upright, as if he had been running his long fingers through it. Instead, the culprit was the stocking cap that all elves were supposed to wear, but were not only stupid on Elf-gineers, but dangerous as well. Rafn held the crumpled cap in his left hand.

"Need to hear what?" Lo asked.

Rafn bit his lower lip, then raised his eyebrows. His apple-red cheeks got even redder. He was clearly doing something he wasn't supposed to.

"They're bringing you an assistant," he said.

Lo let out a puff of air. There wasn't anyone in the North Pole who could properly assist him, and the Old Men in Charge knew that.

"Tell them not to bother." Lo grabbed his shirt off the floor, thinking he could wipe his face with it, but the shirt was soaked. That steam release from the machine had been worse than he thought.

"*I'm* not telling them anything," Rafn said. "I'm staying out of the way."

"Then why are you here?" Lo asked. Because being here, telling Lo that the Old Men in Charge were trying to hire him an assistant yet again, was not an example of Rafn staying out of the way.

"Um, because you should know. And they don't want you to. So I figured someone should tell you before—well, before things get worse." Rafn's green eyes were focused on Lo, not on the machine.

If anything got worse, it was the machine itself, not some assistant who would get moved laterally to another department within the week.

"I don't really care, Rafn." Lo wiped his hands on his shorts, and shoved the soaking wet shirt aside with his foot.

The air was cooling down just enough that he was getting goose-bumps on his skin. He needed to get back inside the machine and solve whatever had gone wrong this time before everything froze up—maybe literally. Since the machine usually provided the heat in this room—and it was at least ten below outside.

He had maybe three hours before the ice started encroaching inward.

"You should care," Rafn said. "The decision is made."

Lo sighed. Every twenty years or so, the Old Men in Charge hired an "expert" assistant for him. The last time, they did studies to see who would be the most compatible assistant with Lo. They went through likes and dislikes, strength of personality, skill levels, and come up with some minor S-Elf who knew nothing about engineering, but could talk a good game.

Last Lo had heard, that S-Elf was in toy management and not managing all that well.

"So, who is it?" Lo asked.

"An outsider." Rafn's voice lowered as he said the word *outsider*, almost as if the word itself was forbidden.

"Okay, that's it," Lo said. "I don't have time for this nonsense. I'm going back inside."

"Lo, I'm not making this up."

Lo peered at Rafn. "Outsiders don't come to the Pole. You know that. The outside hires all stay at various locations throughout the world. I thought you knew that too. And it's pretty obvious that whoever is my assistant will have to work at the Pole. So someone is messing with you."

"No one is messing," Rafn said. "And we've had a couple of outsiders arrive lately."

"They married into the family," Lo said, and by family, he meant everyone who worked at the Pole. Not all of them got along—just like family—but they would all defend each other to the death. Again, just like family.

Rafn bit his lower lip again, drawing just a tiny bit of blood. "This is a real outsider. Someone who specializes in magical tech."

Lo rolled his eyes. He'd met some of those people decades ago. They didn't really know much about the kind of magical tech he worked with, and then they had pissed off The Big Guy because they wanted to take apart one of the sleighs to see how it worked.

He had disabused them of that notion quickly, and sent them on their way.

"I don't have time to deal with an outsider," Lo said. "Run interference for me, would you?"

"I did already," Rafn said. "I told them that you had to focus on the machine. But they've been examining the machine—"

"When?" Lo asked. "I would have seen them."

Although that probably wasn't true. The machine was so big that they could have figured out where he was and gone into a different section. He had never set up the machine to keep others out or even to notify him when they had come in the room.

The sleigh rooms had notifications like that, and there were some around the reindeer herd as well, but Lo had never seen the need.

Now, he was irritated enough to consider implementing that policy.

"—and everybody's worried, Lo. They think the machine is on its last legs."

Lo realized that Rafn had been talking a lot longer than Lo had been listening. He'd been thinking about others looking at his machine, maybe even touching it, tampering with it.

Then he shook himself just a little. They hadn't tampered with anything. Even if they had, it wouldn't have made that much of a difference. The machine wasn't on its last legs, but it was in crisis—just like it had been for years now.

Only the crisis was growing worse, and he knew it.

Apparently everyone knew it.

"And they think an outsider can fix the machine," Lo said.

Rafn shrugged. "I don't know what they think. I just know what they did."

"An outsider," Lo said, more to himself than to Rafn. "Well, when the outsider gets here, give him the machine's specs and let him sit with those for a few days."

"The specs?" Rafn frowned. "But they're almost a hundred years old."

And they hadn't been updated. Lo hadn't had time to update anything. He actually doubted there even were specs for the printer.

"Yes, they are," Lo said.

"I'm not in charge of the outsider," Rafn said.

Lo sighed. "Find out who is, then, and let me know. I'll deal with it."

He then slipped back into the passageway under the machine. Water was dripping off every surface, but none of the metal glowed red anymore.

"Lo," Rafn said. "Lo, I can't..."

His voice faded as Lo got deeper. He didn't care what Rafn could and couldn't do. Lo really didn't care about the outsider.

The outsider would have his opinions about the machine, and if Lo handled him properly, the outsider wouldn't even touch the machine.

Lo went deeper into the machine, peering at the gears and workings, hoping today's problem was obvious. The obvious problems got solved faster.

The more complicated problems were elusive. And their solutions were never obvious.

Maybe someday, he would have time to revamp the entire machine.

Maybe someday, he would have time to draw up new specs.

Maybe someday, he would actually get a day off.

Until then, he had work to do—and he would make certain he did it well.

CHAPTER 4

*T*he North Pole really was all red and white and green, and parts of it looked like they had been assembled out of candy canes, while other parts appeared to be made of white frosting covered with glittery sprinkles. Or, as Dallas would have told anyone had there been anyone to tell, it looked like every tacky part of Christmas threw up here.

The place even smelled of chocolate and peppermint—with a trace of fresh snow mixed in for good measure.

She arrived, bundled in faux fur, wearing boots that felt like thick blankets wrapped around her feet. Her hands were encased in gloves that didn't quite keep her fingers warm. The earmuffs she wore over her ears were a mistake; she should have worn an entire hat, but she had been too vain.

How did anyone make sure their hair looked good when they had to wrap up against this kind of cold? Her nose ached, and her eyes felt both dry and icy at the same time. The scarf she had wrapped around the lower part of her face was damp on the mouth side and probably covered with tiny little icicles on the other side.

She was cursing Ranklesworth and everyone else who thought to send her here. She was also cursing herself, and her damn ego. If she hadn't thought she could best any magical machine, she wouldn't have taken on this job, no matter what Ranklesworth and the others had said. She didn't want the entire pressure of ruining Christmas on her shoulders alone.

She was standing outside the cabin they had assigned her when she arrived. A couple of elves had transported her in a miniature sleigh—not *the* sleigh, as they were quick to inform her—and they put her and her newly bought winter clothing into the cottage.

The cottage looked like it was made of gingerbread, and for all she knew, it probably was. It was brown, with (fake?) white frosting around the windows, green gumdrops pasted randomly to the sides (almost like a child had put them there), and red hard candies creating little ornaments on the sides.

The peppermint smell had been worse inside, but she had traced that to the peppermint drink someone had left for her beside a plate of cookies on the marble-topped peninsula. The entire place had given her the willies. The first floor had a 1950s kitchen with a gas stove, a Frigidaire, and a microwave the size of a footstool. The kitchen opened onto a living area with a red-and-green rug covered with a white throw rug that she hoped was made from fake fur. The couch matched the throw rug, and so did the upholstered chair and footstool. Half the place looked like it had been woven from leftover cat hair.

The only thing cozy about the entire cottage was a real wood-burning fireplace, with an actual blazing fire. She had stood near it while one of the elves took her bags upstairs to the "master" bedroom, which meant that the cottage had a second bedroom as well.

She would investigate that when she was braced. She had no idea what kind of bedroom this designer (if you wanted to call what was going on in the first floor of the cottage a design) envisioned, but she wasn't ready to find out.

Which was why she asked to see the machines first.

The elves who brought her here were disconcerted by that. Apparently, they had been instructed to cook her dinner and tuck her in for the evening. She wasn't expected to work for another day or two, after she became acclimatized (their word) to the North Pole culture.

She didn't want to be rude, so she hadn't told them that she would never acclimatize to the North Pole culture. She wanted to return to her house in Malibu, or go to the office and stare out the windows at her beloved (warm) ocean.

She had only been at the North Pole an hour or less, and she had already forgotten what it felt like to have sun on her bare shoulders, to sniff the ocean air, to feel the warm embrace of the heat baking off the sand.

She closed her eyes for just a moment, trying to resurrect that feeling, when something caressed her face. She had been in a lot of magical communities over the years, so she knew better than to start in surprise. So she opened her eyes slowly, and realized that what she had registered as a caress was really a brush of light snowflakes against her ice-cold skin.

The snowflakes looked like they'd been manufactured for a Hallmark holiday movie. They fell perfectly along the lane in front of her, and just barely interfered with her view of the cottages across the way. (She couldn't bring herself to call what was between her and those cottages a street. She doubted that lane/path/whatever had seen motorized vehicles, at least of the nonmagical type.)

The addresses for each cottage hung off a (yes, of course) red-and-white sign post that looked almost candy-cane like. And most of the cottages were faux (real?) gingerbread, although some were more ornate, like a holiday cake or one of those Christmas houses made of spun sugar that sat in the windows of some of the Los Angeles bakeries during the holiday season.

All of the cottages and houses—including hers, she presumed (but didn't turn around to look)—were outlined with Christmas bulbs, so she doubted this place was ever dark at night.

She shivered, partly because this place was so treacly, and partly because she was getting really cold. The elves had told her to wait inside for her escort (and they spoke that word without any trace of irony), but she couldn't handle the inside of that cottage for very long. She supposed she would get used to it eventually, but eventually hadn't arrived yet, and she needed to escape all of the twee.

Only to go outside into treacly.

A tall thin woman loped down the path, the giant bell on the end of her stocking cap jingling. She was wearing a green-and-white jumpsuit of some kind, with red mittens and that long stocking cap.

When she saw Dallas, her entire face made an O of alarm.

"I'm sorry," she said in a high breathy voice. "They hadn't told me you'd be outside."

"Just getting my bearings," Dallas said, because it was the only version of the truth she could manage.

"Oh, hell's bells," the woman said. "You must be freezing."

I suspect it will be a permanent state as long as I'm here, Dallas almost said. Instead, she smiled and said, "And you are...?"

"Oh, golly gee," the woman said. "I'm sorry. I'm Ingeborg. I'm in charge of showing you around, making sure you're comfortable, and seeing to it that you have all the supplies you need." Then she grinned. "You liked the peppermint schnapps, no?"

No, Dallas almost said, but didn't because the word *schnapps* surprised her. She thought it was some sweet candy drink, not some sweet candy drink with *alcohol*. Maybe she would like these people after all.

She extended her hand, wondering if it was protocol to shake with gloves on or off.

"I'm Dallas," she said as warmly as she could, with her mouth muffled by a scarf. "It's a pleasure to meet you, Ingeborg."

Ingeborg smiled, and it lit up her entire face. Her green eyes sparkled. Her candy-apple-red cheeks matched her candy-apple-red nose, but other than that she didn't seem cold at all.

She took Dallas's hand and shook, gloves on, grip firm.

"I'm supposed to help you get settled," Ingeborg said. "I figured you'd be tired from traveling, which was why I had everything going in the cottage. But you must be one of those restless types. I'd heard about that, with Californians and such, but here, we tend to move slower than you Americans do."

Her accent sounded American—although more Upper Midwest with a touch of Chicago or Michigan's U.P. (Dallas couldn't really tell the difference) than it did, say, Texas or East Coast or even that so-called generic California accent.

"Well," Dallas said, not quite sure how to take that "move slower" thing. Was it a dig? Was it an observation? Was it a warning? She really couldn't tell. "My instructions are to get the problem solved as quickly as possible. I've been told that we're very short on time."

Ingeborg shot a nervous glance over her shoulder, but Dallas couldn't tell quite what Ingeborg was looking at. The buildings receded in the distance, and Dallas thought she caught a glimpse of ice palaces instead of cottages, but she really couldn't be certain.

"I'm sure tomorrow will be fine," Ingeborg said. "They've got some meetings scheduled with various departments, to talk with you and maybe get you some assistants, and then there's a big lunch planned— we're good at lunches—and I'd like to show you our gingerbread factory—"

"Is the factory where the problem is?" Dallas asked.

"Um, no," Ingeborg said, "but we so rarely get outsiders here, and the factory is everyone's favorite place, even more so than the various toy workshops. It's—"

"I'm not here as a tourist," Dallas said.

Ingeborg looked a bit alarmed, and Dallas realized that she was speaking more forcefully than she should be. Ingeborg was in charge of taking care of her, and Ingeborg was trying to do that.

Dallas smiled reassuringly, then realized the smile wasn't going to work since almost all of it was buried by the scarf. Her crinkling eyes weren't going to give it away either, since she really hadn't felt like smiling. She hated the snow and the sweetness and she wanted to get the hell out of here as fast as possible.

But she didn't dare say that.

So she lowered her voice and said, "I'm sorry if I sound a bit abrupt, but I was told the situation was urgent. In fact, I was told that the only reason I'm here is because the situation is so urgent."

Ingeborg nodded. "It is, and I honestly don't understand what's happening. Most of us are not in the loop, as you folks say. I just need to make sure you have what you need and you know your way around.

Maybe this afternoon, before it gets too dark, I'll take you to the main part of the village? We have lovely cafés and coffee shops and an actual grocery store, if you want to cook for yourself and eat in."

Dallas felt a surprising wave of panic. She hadn't thought about money or credit cards. She had brought hers, of course, but did Santa's Village in the North Pole accept them?

Ingeborg waved a gloved hand. "And don't worry about money. We take care of our own here, and while you're here, you're one of us. You can have whatever you want whenever you want it, provided we have the item in one of our stores here. There is a ban on importing items from the outside, though, so you can't magically bring in something unapproved."

"Unapproved?" Dallas asked, not liking the sound of that.

Ingeborg shrugged. "We pride ourselves on our craftsmanship. Sometimes we can't compete, particularly in the tech realm, and often children ask for brand-specific things, which we do bring into our various warehouses, although many of the brand-specific items are stored off-site. So it's just better to get what you need here, and not worry about whether or not it's approved."

Dallas's head spun, just a little. Approved. Craftsmanship. Not approved. She had no idea what she had walked into, particularly since Ingeborg had mentioned tech.

"I'd like to see the machines," Dallas said, deciding not to parse out any other aspect of this conversation. "The sooner I know the extent of the problems that we face, the sooner I can solve them."

"It's *a* machine," Ingeborg said. "Just one."

"Well," Dallas said, thinking that might be the first problem. "I'd like to see the machine, then."

"I know," Ingeborg said. "It's just—"

"And," Dallas said, "then I'll also know what kind of assistance I need."

"Oh." Ingeborg looked very uncomfortable. "Okay. That makes sense to me."

But she didn't sound happy about it. About any of it.

Dallas suppressed a sigh. She'd dropped into countless magical businesses, dealing with their magical mechanical devices, and often found herself in the middle of some kind of office politics. Why would the North Pole be any different?

"You want to see the machine," Ingeborg said.

"Yes," Dallas said, not adding, *That's why I'm here, after all.*

Ingeborg bit her upper lip, then nodded. "Okay," she said. "Let's go."

She trooped over a small snow bank and onto a different path that Dallas hadn't seen until that very moment. The path was made of white brick and didn't have a trace of snow on it.

Dallas stepped gingerly on the white brick, afraid she was going to slide on some ice. But the brick felt solid beneath her feet—well, as solid as it could feel given the thickness of her ridiculous boots.

The path cut into a series of snowbanks which, she started to realize as she hurried along, weren't completely made of snow. The white brick went up the sides of the banks, forming snowbank-like mounds that made the banks look picture-perfect.

The path went deep into the banks, until she could no longer see any buildings, just the grayish sky above, still depositing those fluffy snowflakes onto her and the surrounding area. It took another moment for her to realize that the snowflakes were melting on the white brick, rather than sticking, which made her wonder if the white brick had some kind of heating mechanism built in.

The air didn't seem as biting cold either, because the wind had died down. Or, rather, it had been effectively blocked by the gigantic snow-banks. And then the snow ceased falling on her face and nose, and the sky disappeared.

Ingeborg had led her into some kind of tunnel, with a clear (or so it seemed) roof above, where the snow gathered.

If visitors were rare here, as Ingeborg had said, what was the purpose of masking this area? Were they hiding it from some of the employees (and should she call all of them elves?) or were they protecting the magical machines? Dallas had seen that before too. Sometimes machine magic and regular magic didn't mix, and it was best to keep them separate.

Dallas didn't ask, though, because she wasn't sure Ingeborg had the answers. And, she wasn't sure it was important to know at this early phase.

The white brick path opened up into a large common area, with white built-in tables and chairs that were scattered around. Small decorative evergreens separated the tables on one side, and pretty woven red blankets hung off quilt racks along the other side of the tables.

The blankets made Dallas realize she wasn't that cold anymore. In fact, she was sweating into her puffy coat.

She pulled down the scarf. The air smelled faintly of hot metal here, which was not a good sign—at least for the machine.

Ingeborg wound her way around the tables toward an arched doorway. What Dallas had thought was a wall of white snowbanks up ahead was actually a wall of white brick. The brick wasn't as smooth as it was on the path. The closer she got, the more she could see thin green etchings in the brick. And finally those etchings resolved themselves into beautifully drawn evergreen fronds.

They were thicker and more decorative around the lintels near a gigantic double door, which seemed to be made of wood and painted white.

"This is where the machine is?" Dallas asked, mostly because this place was making her even more nervous than the area around her cottage.

She wasn't normally claustrophobic, but she was feeling closed in here. Maybe because she had no idea where she was going and what she was going to find.

"Um," Ingeborg said. "That question is hard to answer. You'll see."

If there was an answer to any question that Dallas hated more than *You'll see*, she had yet to discover it. She bit back a sharp response, one she would have used with Ranklesworth and the clones: *I asked a damn question. I expect an answer.*

Ingeborg didn't deserve that kind of comment, not yet anyway. Apparently she wasn't authorized to say much to Dallas. Maybe, even Ingeborg wasn't supposed to take Dallas to the machine.

Most places that Dallas had parachuted into to save the day (once literally—a literal parachuting in) always set up a coordinated and sometimes misleading introduction to the problem. Dallas had learned long ago that such meetings wasted her time, and often pointed her in the wrong direction, wasting effort as well.

Ingeborg glanced at Dallas almost desperately, as if Ingeborg didn't want to take the final steps through the doors at all.

Dallas ignored the look; she really didn't care how a woman she had just met felt about anything. Dallas had a job to do, and she needed to do it, without interference—ah, hell. She needed to understand it first.

Ingeborg took a deep breath, almost a sigh, almost a heavy martyristic sigh, and placed a gloved hand flat on the wall beside the door. A panel slid back, revealing…

A coat closet. Half a dozen coats hung inside. Boots lined the ground, as did shoes with hard soles, and some athletic shoes in size order along the wall. Scarves were jumbled on a top shelf, with hats piled haphazardly near them.

"I'm sorry," Ingeborg said, "but you're going to have to leave your coat and scarf out here. The shoes are magicked so that they will be able to handle the areas near the machine. If you're going to remain near the door, you won't need them, but if you need to get close to the machine, then it's better to use our shoes."

"Are these like bowling shoes?" Dallas asked, having a particular aversion to wearing other people's shoes.

"Um, no. These would be your machine shoes," Ingeborg said. "I think they were going to give you a pair tomorrow, but it won't hurt to get at least one today."

Dallas was already cold, and she didn't really want to remove her scarf or her coat. Or take off her boots outside.

Ingeborg was wiping at what looked like another mound of snow, but which turned out to be a stubby bench near the hidden closet door.

She looked up, a frown on her face.

"I'm sorry," she said, as apologetically as she could. "But it's a rule."

Dallas suppressed a sigh. She didn't want Ingeborg to know how annoyed she was—not at Ingeborg, but at the job itself. Some of that annoyance (maybe all of that annoyance) was spilling over into Dallas's attitude about everything here.

She walked over to the closet, and peered in. The shelf of shoes was not one shoe deep, but went deep into the building. In fact, she couldn't see the back of the closet at all.

She was amazed to see a pair of white shoes in her exact size. Her feet were long and narrow, and she had long gotten used to having most of her shoes custom made or custom ordered.

She sat down on the bench, careful to keep her puffy coat beneath her butt so she wouldn't freeze her butt cheeks, and pulled off one of her boots.

The cold air actually felt good against her hot foot. She really hadn't liked those boots much at all. But it only took a moment before her foot let her know that what felt good in the moment would quickly turn into much-too-cold.

She slipped the athletic shoe on, and was happy to realize it was warm from the inside of the building, not cold because it had been in an outside closet. The shoe tingled into place and almost felt as good as her custom-made cowboy boots.

She put on the other shoe, then set the ugly boots with the other ugly boots. She shed her puffy coat after shoving the mittens in her pockets. She wrapped her somewhat soggy scarf around the hanger, and put everything in the closet, hoping it would all still be there when she left.

Then she had a weird but necessary thought:

"Can I open this closet without your help?" she asked Ingeborg.

Ingeborg started, and then nodded just a tad too eagerly. "Oh, yes, especially now that you have clothing inside. Just touch this part of the wall."

She indicated a brick with an evergreen frond that was slightly larger than the other fronds. Dallas made a mental note of it, hoping she would remember exactly where the brick was.

She was starting to shiver. The white sweater she had worn wasn't meant to deal with this kind of cold.

Ingeborg didn't seem to notice. She stepped past Dallas and pulled open one of the doors.

Instantly a waft of steam floated out, along with the faint scent of motor oil and hot metal. There was also a hint of coal, which she got more as a back-of-the-throat feeling than any kind of actual smell.

Dallas walked through the door, expecting the interior to be warmer, but not steam-room hot. Which it was. Steam puffed out of broken joists on several sections of the contraption before her.

The pipes connected to a large chimney in the center of the contraption, a chimney that went up the six-story-high ceiling, and vented out of the building itself.

Dallas remained in the doorway, trying to take in what she was looking at.

She'd seen several gigantic magical machines in her time, but they were usually identifiable. In fact, most of them had a counterpart in the so-called real world of the nonmagical. The Faery Kings focused a lot of their power in what appeared to be a gigantic roulette wheel underneath Las Vegas. The Fates, at one time, used a large spinning wheel, and all its accoutrements, but gave them up over the centuries as the very nature of their magic changed.

Sometimes Dallas had to squint to understand the machine or to see what its real-world counterpart was, but she could always see it.

Except here.

Pulleys, levers, gears, chains, chimneys, stovepipes, steam pipes, wooden railings, metal joists, doorways, windows without glass—all of it stuck together in some kind of haphazard pattern that somehow managed to work.

Or looked like it was working. The gears turned, the chains twisted along, the levers were locked into place, and the pulleys moved wheels which then moved beams which opened little doors that emitted steam.

The closest real world counterpart she had ever seen was a mousetrap—from the game *Mouse Trap*—not an actual mousetrap. And even that didn't work because that game always had some logic to it.

She couldn't see any logic here at all.

She wiped the steam off her face with the back of her hand, and noted that the steam was filled with little black flakes. The floor was wet and covered with more black flakes. Water dripped off sections of the machine, and wasn't supposed to, but no one had fixed that. Instead, they had placed buckets below the drips, as if that was some kind of solution. The water in the drip pans was rust-brown, which pointed to a whole different problem.

Dallas took a step deeper into the gigantic room, because her back was getting cold, and she didn't like the feeling of being burning hot on her front side, and nearly freezing to death on her backside.

Ingeborg stepped inside with her and moved just enough forward to be in Dallas's line of sight.

"There," Ingeborg said. "Now you've seen it. You can get the full tour tomorrow."

Dallas didn't answer her, instead walking down the left side of the machine. The materials before her were old; the wood was worn and faded and looked, in some places, like it was beginning to rot away. Deeper inside the machine, some of the wood looked new, so someone was working on this. And even deeper still, she saw a cascade of sparkling dust, which, if she had to bet, was fairy dust or pixie dust or some other kind of magic dust, maybe even holding this entire thing together.

A large stone archway separated this room from another room, and the machine continued on. It looked a little more coherent in the next room—mostly black, maybe made of iron, which would be odd, since the magical usually didn't work well with iron (although she had no trouble with it), and then the machine curved and disappeared in the distance.

If she had to compare it to anything, it would have to be a long train, although nothing that she saw was coupled together so that it could be separated, like train cars could. Maybe it was more like the images of the *Nautilus* that early artists drew to illustrate Jules Verne's work, before there were actual submarines, because no real submarine or ironclad ship or spaceship or train or anything was as long as this thing was.

Long and huge and tall and puffing out steam and magic dust and flakes of something, along with rust and grinding gears (in the distance) and maybe the hollow toot of a whistle and the background hum of something that worked continuously and not necessarily worked right.

"Oh, by Vulcan's forge," she muttered. "This thing is an impossibility."

"Well, not really," said a deep voice inside the machine. "Because if it was an impossibility, it wouldn't be here now."

That's not what I meant, she almost said, but didn't because she had no idea who had spoken. Whoever it was hadn't been the person she addressed anyway, because she was talking to herself.

What she had meant was that this was (perhaps) the original Rube Goldberg device, and unless she missed her guess, it wasn't repairable. It would need to be scrapped, and she wasn't exactly sure how to do that. Or even whom she would tell.

She glanced over her shoulder, only to discover she was alone. Or rather, she seemed to be alone. She couldn't quite see the entrance, where she assumed Ingeborg was still standing.

Ingeborg had seemed uncomfortable just to be in this area. Maybe the machine frightened her.

The machine depressed Dallas, because its magic wasn't consolidated. In a machine this big, generally, the magic threaded all the way through it, making some parts more powerful than other parts, and making the entire thing unbalanced, and difficult to deal with.

The steam seemed even thicker ahead of her. Maybe that was why the machine seemed to disappear in the distance, because it was literally disappearing in a steamy fog.

The temperature rose as she stepped into the second room. She was glad now that she had left her coat outside. She wished she could remove her sweater as well, but she hadn't thought far enough ahead to wear a thin shirt underneath it.

She would the next time she approached the machine.

She clasped her hands behind her back, and slowly walked down the side of the machine.

She had been right; it was more coherent here, as if it had been made as one unit rather than a bunch of units cobbled together. There were rivets holding parts in place, and handmade iron panels and actual dials that seemed to have some kind of function.

"We don't give tours here," the same deep voice said, sounding even more irritated. And closer as well.

"I'm not looking for a tour," she said. "I'm inspecting the machine."

"Inspecting?" the voice spit out the word as if it were a swear word. *"Inspecting?"*

"Yes." She kept her own voice calm. Apparently, she had run into one of the people in charge of the machine, even though they weren't showing themselves.

"I want to know what I'm up against," she said, still walking forward, still looking at the machine. It bulged in certain places. Some of the bulges looked like part of the design, but others appeared to be a warping from the inside, as if something were trying to get out.

"What *you're* up against?" the voice asked.

Here it was: that moment she encountered in every single job where she was called in to repair some important magical machine. The moment where she had to tell a possessive and incompetent someone that their baby was now her project.

"Yes," she said, calmly (because she had learned that calm and just a little dismissive was best). "What *I'm* up against. I've been called in to deal with the machine."

She didn't say *fix* because fixing wasn't always the right word. As in this case. Where she was probably going to have to build something from scratch.

Something banged inside the machine, sounding almost like a door closing. Her heart rate accelerated, but she made sure she didn't look startled. Sometimes, the people who were tied to their machines tried to intimidate her. They would often use some of the machine magic to push her away.

It never worked—or rather, it didn't work for long—but it did make for a few uncomfortable days.

She rounded a slight bend in the machine and saw the next archway —another room, apparently—and the machine continuing to recede into the distance.

Then a doorway opened in the machine itself, and a man stepped out. He was taller than anyone else she had seen since she arrived at the

North Pole, and he wasn't wearing green or red or white. He was wearing light tan cutoffs, and no shirt at all.

His skin was slightly bronzed and there was a smattering of hair that ran up from his navel across his broad chest. Which was wet, and made him look ridiculously photo-shoot ready, or like some clichéd desirable guy in a romance movie on a streaming channel.

He grabbed a white towel that she hadn't seen a moment ago from a peg that also seemed to appear out of the side of the machine. He wiped his face and his curly black hair (also unusual here), and turned his attention to her.

His eyes were the only green thing about him—emerald green, so bright that they seemed like they'd been illuminated from the inside. He had high cheekbones and no candy-apple red on his face at all, even though he had clearly been inside that overheating machine. His lips were thin and stretched into a frown of disapproval, which somehow did not spoil the great beauty that was his face.

It was rugged and square and lovely all at the same time, rather like the black-and-white photographs taken of mid-twentieth century movie stars. Something about him seemed both remote and mysterious.

Dallas shook herself. She wasn't usually fanciful—at least about people or elves, which he might have been, although he didn't seem to have pointed ears. He was ridiculously male, though, from the loose way he wore his shorts to the sockless feet crammed inside a pair of (she assumed) magicked Nikes.

His eyes widened just a bit when he saw her, as if he couldn't believe what he was looking at. A tall woman in an ill-fitting sweater, with an overheated face, and probably a frown similar to his.

"*You're* the person they sent?" he asked.

How many times had she heard that before, in that very same tone? For most of the twentieth century, it had been because she was female. Now it might be that, but often it was because she never looked like people expected her to. She was too tall, too loud, too—something. She couldn't quite figure it out, except that she was never the person anyone expected when they heard someone was arriving to repair (or replace) their magical machine.

"Yes, I am." Again, she spoke calmly, and kept her gaze directly on him. She didn't want him to think that he could intimidate her, nor did she want him to think that she was nice or willing to work with him or even willing to listen to him. She wasn't, not if he was going to get in her way.

"I don't need help with this machine," he said.

So his was the magic behind the machine. She would have expected someone a lot more elf-like behind any machine like this. Elves and faeries seemed to have a fondness for magical items, especially as receptacles of magic, more so than those mages who self-identified as human.

"Take it up with your boss," she said.

He stared at her, as if he were taking her measure, to see how far he could push her.

She stared back, but kept emotion out of her expression entirely. This was personal for him, but it wasn't personal for her. And it wasn't going to be, no matter how pretty or forceful he was.

"I will take it up with my 'boss,'" he said after a moment. "Stay away from my machine until I do."

That was nicely passive-aggressive. She'd only fallen for that once, more than a hundred years ago, and the man who had done it hadn't talked to his boss for weeks. She'd nagged the man and nagged the man, and finally went to the boss, who hadn't heard a thing about problems and had thought she had been working the entire time.

That particular job hadn't ended well for anyone, primarily because she never could stay on task.

"That's not acceptable," she said, and almost explained that she was on a timetable, that she needed to get busy now, that she needed to know what she was facing. Then she caught herself. Because any tidbit she gave him allowed him to argue more. And she didn't want that.

Nor did anyone else.

"What?" he asked.

"As I said, take your issues to your boss." She clasped her hands tightly behind her back, just to keep herself focused. "I'm here to do a job, which I will do."

Again, she had to bite back a *with or without you*. She didn't want to open any doors for him, and she didn't want him in the middle of what she was doing. Past experience had also taught her that letting someone with an investment in the magical machine in on her work was a disaster.

If she had been trying to make friends, she would have asked him for an explanation or a tour, but she wasn't trying to make friends.

She gave him a small dismissive nod, then continued forward with her inspection. Her walk would take her right past him, and she would do her best to ignore him.

But he was hard to ignore. She had never really met a man with such presence before. She could feel his gaze on her, and annoyingly, she wanted to meet it. She wanted to look deep into those green eyes and see what kind of man he was, if he was the kind of man she hoped he was.

No man had ever lived up to her hopes. No *person* had, really. And she really needed to stop expecting it. She was alone for a reason, and nothing was going to change that.

The thought kept her focused as she walked toward him, studying this contraption as she moved.

It was old; that much was clear. Old and cobbled together, held together by magic and spit. If this was his magic—and she was sure now that it was—she was going to need to need his help at some point.

Only she wanted to determine when that point was, not him.

So she walked past him without meeting his gaze. She resisted the urge to slow down, to touch parts of the machine just to annoy him.

She wrested her brain away from the handsome man with the attitude problem, and returned her thoughts to the machine at hand.

Or she wished she had.

Half of her brain was busy with him, and she wasn't sure how to stop that—because she had never experienced anything like it before.

CHAPTER 5

*S*he was pretty. That irritated Lo the most. She was pretty and brilliant and outspoken. She was nothing like any other woman here at the North Pole, and that irritated him too.

He wanted to go straight to The Big Guy and ask him if he was involved in sending the woman to Lo.

But Lo had never asked Santa for anything ever, not even when this Santa (who took over the job more than two hundred years ago) decided to equalize everything and have his elves and workers all get something their hearts desired for one Not-a-Christmas. (Not-a-Christmas was when the entire North Pole celebrated the holiday, usually at the start of the hard-work season, right around the middle of July.)

She was walking toward him, and he couldn't take his gaze off her. She was taller than he was—maybe six-two—in Pole-provided Nikes. (He knew they were the Pole's shoes, because they didn't melt on that floor in this heat.) Her hair was a thick reddish-brown color that he had only seen in certain kinds of wood, and her eyes matched, something he hadn't seen often at all. Her skin was darker than most around here as well, set off by a creamy white sweater that clung to her in ways he didn't want to think about.

Or maybe he did want to think about those ways.

He made himself focus.

She was here to mess with his machine. No one else had touched it in more than a hundred years. He wouldn't let her work on it either.

"You could at least introduce yourself," he said, knowing he sounded petulant, and not sure how to avoid it.

Or maybe he did know how to avoid it. He could be warm and charming if he wanted to be, if he hadn't forgotten how. He hadn't felt the need to be warm or charming in a long, long time. Other people had ceased to be important to him.

What had been important was keeping this machine working, every single moment of every single day.

For a minute, he thought she wasn't going to answer him. For an even longer minute, he thought she wasn't even going to acknowledge him.

Then she stopped, tilted her head as if considering what he said, as if what he said *required* consideration, and she sighed.

Sighed.

Like he was a burden.

Those amber eyes met his. They were filled with intelligence, which also irritated him. He didn't want her to be brilliant. He didn't want her to be competent. He didn't want her to be anywhere near his machine.

And he certainly didn't want to be attracted to her, which he was, whether he liked it or not.

"My name," she said, "is Dallas Demaris," and then she continued walking. Away from him. Like he didn't matter.

Without asking who he was.

She was playing with him, and she was winning. His irritation was growing. He could tell her to stop—which he had already done, and she hadn't listened—or he could shout out his own name—which was just plain stupid and would make him seem childish—or he could follow her, trying to see what she was going to do.

She was studying the machine like she had never seen anything like it before, which she probably hadn't. Right now, they were in the second oldest room, and the machine here was the moodiest section.

If he had time (and he never had time; he was beginning to worry he never *would* have time), he would replace this section of the machine or build a new section that did the same function. There was room at the other end of the machine, if he removed the printer. (He needed a newer, better printer anyway.)

He had already decommissioned most of the machine in Room One. That was the oldest part of the machine, and except for the magic threaded throughout the entire machine, he had rerouted most of the function of that part of the machine to Room Five.

She wouldn't know any of this. She couldn't, without him telling her. To her, the old gears and flywheels and rattling chains would look like malfunctioning, out-of-date equipment, not the casing that still housed parts of the machine.

He wasn't even sure how to tell her, even if he wanted to. Because the machine existed as much in his mind as it did here, physically. He knew what strings to pull to keep the thing functioning because he had created the strings.

She had disappeared into Room Three, where the machine ended up as parts of amalgamated metal with some actual scientific components: A bit of a Babbage machine, some manufactured gears instead of hand-made ones, an actual (tiny) combustion engine. She would wander, looking, all the way to Room Five, not understanding all the pieces that went into this, and then she would want to tear it down, or replace parts with something more technologically sound, but which wouldn't work because he wouldn't understand what she would have done, and he would need to understand it to make it integrate with everything else in the machine.

He sighed, then closed his eyes for just a moment, then opened them, because every time he closed his eyes, he tended to doze off. He had no idea that mages—mortals—anyone could get this tired and keep functioning.

And yet he was.

She was going to add to his workload, not decrease it. And when she did, she might just be the thing that tipped this entire enterprise over the edge.

"Hey!"

He didn't recognize the voice, not at first. He put a hand on one of the soggier wood braces jutting out of the machine and thought, almost reflexively, *I'm going to need to replace that.*

"Hey!" the voice repeated, and that was when he realized it was the woman, coming back.

He hadn't expected her to come back.

A frown creased the lovely area of skin between her eyebrows, and the eyes beneath them, while not sparkling, seemed to glow with that intelligence he had noted earlier.

"What's your name?" she asked.

He suppressed a sigh. Something in her tone made him wonder if she thought him just another helpful elf, not the person who actually designed the machine.

And now, he was going to have to tell her, an outsider, his name. Which wasn't going to go well.

"Lothario Johanssen," he said, because he knew if he said *Lo Johanssen*, she would misunderstand it as Lojo Hanssen, and that irritated him too. Everything about this day was irritating him, and if he was honest with himself, everything in general had irritated him in general for weeks, maybe months, maybe a year or more.

"*Lothario?*" she asked, just like everyone else did. He'd tried shortening it once to *Loth*, but that caused all kinds of jokes around here, mostly that people were loath to talk with Loth about anything to do with the machine (which was probably true).

But he hated having this discussion. He hated it because it was so damn predictable.

"I had the name long before Cervantes decided to ruin it," Lo said.

"Cervantes," she said, flatly. "I don't recall a Lothario in *Don Quixote*."

"It's there," he said through clenched teeth, even though part of him was impressed that she had actually *read Don Quixote*, which was more than he had ever done. "In one of the stories within a story."

"Hmm," she said. "Who knew?"

Lo knew. He knew the entire history of the decline of his name because he really didn't want to change it. That Cervantes had used it in "El Curioso Impertinente," and that Goethe had picked up on it, and then some eighteenth-century jerk named Nicholas Rowe who happened to be an influence on Trollope...

And Lo was digressing, mentally, when he really didn't dare, not in the middle of this discussion. And not with this woman, who was staring at him as if he had a bug on his face.

Their eyes met and he felt a jolt, stronger than the jolts he felt when he accidentally stuck his finger in one of the electrical sockets (which, so far, hadn't gotten wet, thank the Powers).

She didn't seem to feel the jolt at all. Because she still had that just-seen-a-bug look on her face.

"The actual computing power," she said, "what was it for?"

It took a moment to yank his busy brain from the history of his name to her face to a discussion of the machine. And even in that context, he wasn't sure what she was asking.

What was computer power for? For computing. For doing computational tasks quickly and efficiently, freeing up the magical and humans and everyone else to do more important things.

Like any other damn machine.

Which was probably not the answer she was going for.

He opened his mouth, trying to figure out how to answer without sounding too stupid, when she let out an exasperated sigh.

"You designed this machine, right?" she asked, a little too curtly. She was feeling impatient, and he wasn't exactly sure why.

"Yes," he said, surprised she had figured it out. Impressed, even. Because he hadn't told her he had designed the machine. She had been inspecting it, and she had realized (understood? knew?) that a certain kind of magic fueled the machine and gave it life.

All of the other repairpeople/experts/whatever you wanted to call them (and he had wanted to call them something awful each time) had never figured that out on their own.

"Then talk me through this," she said. "Who the heck thought that the North Pole, of all places, needed a computing machine, and who the heck decided that the North Pole have the dang machine as far back as...what? I'm thinking the early 1800s. Am I right?"

She was close. She was startlingly close. She could tell all of that just from eyeballing the oldest parts of the machine? He was becoming even more impressed.

"The 1780s," he said quietly.

"Ah," she said with just a hint of sarcasm. "Enlightenment and all that. But unless my history is off, there was no Santa Claus at that point, no Claus & Company, no North Pole, am I right?"

Lo let out a small sigh. How to explain the history of this complicated place? And was it really his job?

"Well," she said into his silence, "there was Father Christmas. But he wasn't a gift-giver until when...the 1890s?"

"You've read your Wikipedia," Lo said, finding his voice.

"Actually, no," she said. "I remember all kinds of trivia, and I was in London over Christmas twice in the latter half of that century, and the first time, Father Christmas was concerned with feasting and drinking. The second time, he was bringing gifts for children."

She looked at Lo sideways, as if the change in Father Christmas were his fault.

"And that's about the same time Thomas Nast started drawing Santa Claus," she said, as if there was something wrong with that.

It wasn't a coincidence. None of it was, but Lo didn't have to defend the North Pole or Claus & Company or anything that was done here to her.

"So, Santa didn't really exist back then," she said, "and Father Christmas was damn near a pagan god at the time, and no one celebrated the holiday the way that everyone who celebrates it does now, so what the heck did you design a magic machine for in the 1780s?"

So long ago. Many hours, many repairs, many jobs ago. He could barely remember those days, and yet, they seemed so close he could actually touch them. If he closed his eyes...

He shook his head, just a little.

"Joy," he said. "It was initially designed to dole out just a little bit of joy."

CHAPTER 6

*J*oy?" Dallas asked. She hadn't expected that answer at all.

She was hot and sticky, as if she was standing fully dressed in a steam room. Her hair was sticking to the back of her neck, and her sweater was plastered against her. Sweat ran down her spine like damp little fingers.

He was covered in sweat too, this Lothario person, but he didn't seem bothered by it. He was leaning against part of the machine that looked like it was made of iron, and his arms were crossed. His answers to all of her questions were short, curt, and to the point, almost making her wish that she hadn't asked them.

But, if she was going to work on this thing, she needed to know what it was initially meant for, and *joy* was not something that came to mind.

"Joy," she said.

He nodded. Twice. Then quit and looked at her again, as if she should understand that.

"You made a magical computer in the 1780s to 'dole out a little joy.' What the heck does that even mean? And why would you need a computer for it?"

"First," he said quietly. "No one knew what a computer was back then."

She made a growling sound in the back of her throat. She knew that, and she hated having it explained to her.

"So," he said, "really, this was more of a tabulation machine. The Claus family—as you know them anyway—they're in the joy business."

Her eyes narrowed. She didn't know any Claus family. She hadn't realized there *was* a Claus family. She just figured the North Pole was like Mount Olympus, filled with very powerful magical beings who had particular specialties, and who had built up their own myths around those specialties.

Maybe, just maybe, she needed to do a bit of research into Claus & Company before she went farther into this machine. But she wasn't sure how to do research while she was here, because she had no idea if they were spying on her.

"The joy business," she repeated.

"Their magic automatically confers joy," he said, as if everyone knew that. "It was confusing and a burden—"

"Sure," she muttered, not sure why the idea bothered her, although it did.

"And it needed to be corralled or people would take advantage of it." He tilted his head. "You don't know any of this."

Her face had flushed, which irritated her. She wanted to blame it on the heat, and that crawly feeling of sweat beading all over her body, but she knew, deep down, that she was simply embarrassed. She should have done some research.

She just hadn't thought she needed to.

"I was given a job," she said, her voice flat. "I'm supposed to fix a magical machine in a timeline that everyone agrees is impossible. I figured I'd find 1950s computers that got infused with magical energy. Not...this."

She waved her hand at it, and almost felt like she could see little swirls in the thick air around her fingers. The machine wasn't at all what she had expected, which she had been able to tell from the moment she saw it, but it wasn't until she hit that third room, with even more modern parts, and could see bits of the machine in the distance, including a section that had a card-punching feature, that she realized this machine wasn't making sense—at least in the box she had placed it in.

He watched her hand create its little circles, then his gaze moved to her face.

"How does a machine dole out joy?" she asked, trying to take the attention off her.

"It doesn't," he said. "The Claus family does. Even though they weren't the Claus family then. They were just a group of S-Elves—"

"S-Elves?"

He sighed. "Santa Elves. That's what we call them now, but they're a type of elf—you do know that elves have different cultures and different magicks, just like faeries do, and mages, and—"

"Yes," she snapped, although that wasn't true. She didn't know a lot about elves. She had never had to deal with elves before. She wasn't even entirely sure whether or not this Lothario man was an elf, even though she would bet he wasn't.

He eyed her for a moment, as if he wasn't quite sure what to think of her. Of course, he had done that from the moment they saw each other.

"They were just a group of S-Elves," he said, "who gave out joy. And they found that joy was addictive, and they ended up with followers, and it got what people now would call culty and creepy, and so they went into hiding, and then the S-Elves felt bad because they weren't using their magic for anything."

"It made them feel bad," she said, trying to follow what he was telling her. She wasn't sure if she needed to ask for clarification or not. Because there were many kinds of magic and some made their practitioners actually feel bad when they didn't drain off the magic somehow.

Maybe the S-Elves fell into that category or maybe they were just compassionate creatures who felt bad that they couldn't use their magic for good.

Yeah, right. Because elves and faeries and the magical always felt bad when their magic didn't work for the good of others.

"They felt bad, yes," he repeated, not answering her unspoken question at all. "They wanted a way to hand out a bit of joy to a lot of people rather than a lot of joy to a handful of people. The S-Elves figured out a system; they'd give out a bit to certain groups on various days of the year, and it worked for a while."

She frowned. She hadn't heard anything like this before.

"And then they found me." He shook his head just a little. "I was pretty different back then. Aimless, looking for something…"

He shook his head again, as if he couldn't quite remember who that person was.

"What was so special about you?" she asked.

His head jerked her way. He was clearly surprised at her question, and she was too. The words had come out blunt and dismissive, and for once, she hadn't meant them that way.

"Not much," he said after a moment. "I was on the fringes of things. Spent a lot of time with members of the Royal Society of London, the Academie des Sciences in Paris, and with a lot of the polymaths in the Americas—what was then called the Americas."

He smiled, as if at a secret joke, then shrugged. "I wasn't…I was…Not many of the magical associated with the scientists, even then."

She stared at him. Scientists and the magical were mortal enemies in many places, including what he so quaintly called "the Americas." At least he hadn't said "the Colonies," not that she would have expected him to, given his accent. He sounded like he was from "the Americas" too, albeit somewhere in the Midwest or California, somewhere that had "no accent" except "the American accent."

"So what you brought to the table was a willingness to talk to scientists?" she asked.

He shrugged again. "They tell me I have a scientific mind."

She had no idea who "they" was, and she wasn't going to ask, since she felt like they (he and she) had gotten off track already.

"So," she said, as dismissively as she could, "these S-Elves. They asked you to do what?"

"Find a way to harness and manage the joy magic," he said. "Keep track of who had received a bit this year, and who deserved a bit next year, and who might be on track to get a second dose two years from now. The machine, then, was pretty simple. It could sort names, addresses, and reasons people had received their dose of joy. It could also keep track of whether or not they appreciated that joy, and in many instances, whether or not they would pass that joy onward."

"How could they do that?" she asked, genuinely curious.

"By being nice to each other." It was his turn to use a flat tone. His gaze met hers, and she resisted the urge to take a step backwards. There was power in his eyes, power she hadn't seen a moment ago.

"Don't you think unpleasant people deserve joy?" she asked.

"Not my call," he said.

"But you just said that you kept track—"

"The S-Elves kept track," he said. "This was their machine, and their list, and I just managed it for them."

"For more than two hundred years," she said.

"Two-fifty, give or take," he said tiredly.

"It's a joy machine." The name was wrong, and could be misused in this modern world, but she didn't know what else to call the monstrosity before her. The joy part gave her a focus, and it should have given the machine a focus.

She leaned back and looked at the gigantic machine in this second room, rising all the way to the ceiling. The steam pouring off the top mostly made it into a stovepipe that exited the roof, but not all of the steam did. And that steam swirled around the chimney pipes in half a dozen colors—red, orange, blue, blackish, light green, and brown.

All of those colors had a meaning. It would just take her time to figure out what that meaning was.

"How did something designed for joy become something that rewarded greed?" she asked.

"What?" He sounded startled.

"You have little kids writing *I want this* and *I want that* and they try to be good, not so that they can give joy, but so that they can get stuff. And all the others who never get anything, they're made even more unhappy—"

"You don't understand," he said.

"You're right," she said. "I don't."

He frowned at her, as if she had already stuck a wrench in the gigantic machine and slowed it down.

"It still does dole out joy," he said. "One gift at a time."

"Wow," she said. "Either you're naïve or oblivious."

"What?" Now he did sound angry. "I'm not—"

"Naughty and nice, who deserves *presents?* Who can't do this and who can't do that, rewarding only kids whose parents have money, not paying attention to kids from other cultures. Not—"

"I never said any of that," he said. "You asked about the history of the machine, for a reason I can't fathom. I was telling you *history.*"

"Yes," she said. "Yes, you were."

That was as close as she would get to apologizing to him. She needed to keep the upper hand here, in case she had to remove him from the machine area.

"You don't say 'I'm sorry' much, do you?" he asked.

The question startled her, as if he could read her mind. "I only say it when I really am sorry," she said. "You gave me something to think about as I take a look at this machine."

"You don't need to," he said. "I can tell you what's wrong with the machine."

She studied him for a moment. There was a smudge of oil under one eye, and another alongside his chin. Whatever he was, and whatever that machine had become, it mattered to him. He clearly worked hard on it, and had for a very long time.

She had to respect that.

"I'm sure you can tell me what's wrong," she said. "I'm not ready for that discussion yet. I will tell you when I am."

His cheeks grew redder, but whether that was annoyance, anger, or embarrassment, she couldn't tell. The rest of his face remained unchanged.

"I didn't ask for anyone to come here," he said. "I've handled the machine just fine from the beginning."

Her gaze met his. Now she understood the flush. He was furious. Not at her, as much as at the hiring of her. The need for her.

She couldn't tell if his fury came because his people had gone behind his back, or because he was going to have to acknowledge that he was no longer up to the task.

Probably a little bit of both.

"Thank you for answering my questions, Mr. Johanssen," she said. "I'm sure we will talk again soon."

She managed to wrench her gaze from his. There was something compelling about him, even in his anger, something she wasn't quite sure how to deal with. Part of her wanted to talk with him, calm him down, work with him, maybe even touch his arm ever so lightly to see if his skin was as smooth as it looked like.

And that thought, that last bit about his skin, almost made her curse out loud.

She was attracted to the sumbitch. She couldn't remember the last time that had happened. And she certainly didn't remember it happening on the job before, especially a job like this one, a job that would take all of her time, and force her to treat people—maybe even him (probably him)—badly.

She turned, and headed into that third machine room, trying (and failing) to focus on the component parts. She needed to see this. She needed to see it unencumbered by anyone else's presence. She needed to see it unencumbered by *his* presence.

And she needed to think about joy. Because somehow that was the key, and she wasn't quite sure how it all fit together.

But she trusted herself to find out.

CHAPTER 7

*S*he had dismissed him. She had dismissed him with her words (*I'm sure we will talk again soon.*), with her tone (*condescending* didn't begin to describe it), with her body (she turned away from him and walked off as if he didn't matter), and with her eyes (they had seemed—cold? startled?—something he couldn't read, and something he wasn't sure he liked).

She was going to cut him away from the machine, and the Old Men in Charge were going to let her do it.

Lo was so upset he did something he hadn't done in a long time: he committed magic near the machine. He conjured a towel, and wiped the sweat off his skin, methodically, as if he were getting out of a shower.

By the time he was done, the towel was soaked, and he felt no better. He needed his shirt—he really needed a change of clothes—and he needed to calm down.

What he wanted to do was run after her and stop her from examining his machine. He wanted her to leave the building. He wanted her to leave the North Pole.

She didn't belong here—that much was clear. And she disturbed him greatly. Those eyes had held his closely, too closely, as if she could really see him, and she didn't like what she saw.

He tossed the wet towel across the room. The towel slid under a bench near the door, a bench no one had used in months, maybe years. No one sat down here. No one had time.

I've handled the machine just fine from the beginning.

He couldn't get those words out of his head. Because if one of his assistants had said the same thing to him, in the same tone, he would have heard the exact opposite of what they were saying. He would have heard them say, *Yeah, I've been screwing up, and I really don't want you to point that out.*

He sighed softly and stepped into the main part of the second room. It was cooler here, although the steam was still bad. Everything was bad. Falling apart. His own magic was stretched so thin that he was beginning to think about sleeping near the machine so that it could continue to take magic from him.

He usually didn't conjure things here, not because he was afraid of some kind of magical interaction, but because he was afraid he'd drain off some of the personal magic that the machine might need.

He ran a hand over his face, and cursed silently when he realized that his skin was still wet. Or had become wet again.

He glanced down the machine, looking for her. She was still walking it, probably seeing things from the wrong perspective, not understanding why he had added that dial or changed out that knob. She would try to remake the machine, as so many others had thought to do, and the problem was—the real problem was—

She could break it.

And he wouldn't be able to fix it at all.

Reluctantly, he headed back to Machine Room One, where he left some extra clothes. He needed to talk to the Old Men in Charge, to get them to dismiss her. He needed to impress upon them how serious their blunder was, how she wouldn't make the situation better at all; she could only make it worse.

He walked under the arch, and heard a clunk from the machine itself. One of the flywheels had worked its way loose. He even knew which one, because it always worked its way loose.

That's how well he knew the machine: he knew it down to the tiniest bolt. He knew what was wrong by sound as well as smell as well as sight. He knew this machine better than he knew himself.

He shook the thought from his head.

If he went to see the Old Men in Charge feeling as defensive as he felt right now, they would ignore him. They would treat him the way that he treated an assistant who protested too much.

Lo needed to figure out how to talk them out of this plan, and he needed to do it tonight, before that woman—Dallas? (Who named their kid after a city?)—touched the machine.

She wouldn't do so yet; she was clearly methodical and she wanted to figure the machine out for herself. That's why she asked about its origins.

And what she had said about it, becoming a greed machine, upset him more than he let on. Because greed had always been the flip side of the machine. People who received a bit of joy wanted more.

What if she was right? What if the machine had lost control of the joy? What if everything Claus & Company had worked toward had gone from a joy enterprise to a greed enterprise, and they hadn't even noticed?

He stopped in front of the closet on the wall beside the front end of the machine. That closet's lock was keyed to his handprint, something he had designed nearly a century ago. Before, the lock had been keyed to his magic, which had seemed sensible enough. Only one day, he had approached the lock depleted of magic, and the damn thing hadn't opened.

Signs of the future that he hadn't even recognized.

He put his palm against the lock and felt its whir against his palm. The machine's hum was too loud for him to hear the tumbling of the lock's mechanism. In this room, the machine sounded like the constant hum of wind. Usually he found that soothing, but today, it just got in the way of everything he wanted to do.

The locker door opened, and he leaned his head against the edge.

The sound hadn't gotten in the way. Nothing had gotten in the way, except this woman.

He made himself take a deep breath. Hot moist air filled his lungs, and almost made him cough.

Yes, there needed to be changes here, but he had no idea what those changes would be or when they could even occur.

He just knew that bringing in someone new, someone inexperienced, someone who seemed to have a grudge against the very idea of the North Pole, wouldn't help anyone.

It would only lead to disaster.

And somehow, he had to convince the Old Men in Charge of that. Tonight.

CHAPTER 8

The Old Men in Charge had their own building, well behind Santa's Village, back where most of the elves and North Pole residents never went. The so-called office buildings were back there, along with the Claus Compound, which Lo hadn't seen for so long that the last time he visited, the Compound had been called the Claus Estate (which always sounded like a redundant legal term to him).

It had been a long time since Lo had visited the Old Men in Charge too, and even longer since he had dressed up for it. He had stopped at his modest little cottage because he couldn't stand the layer of sweat that separated him from his clothing, and then after he got out of the shower, feeling somewhat human (in a good way), he had decided to go with North Pole Professional, which was unprofessional everywhere else.

Black pants (signifying that he was not elf, and not of the Claus camp), a white shirt with candy canes on the lapels and cuffs, and a green, white, and red sweater embroidered with more candy canes and decorated Christmas trees that lit up if he touched them wrong. He slipped on the white mittens (with candy canes along the back), but drew a line at the matching stocking cap. He hated wearing anything on his head. He also didn't wear the regulation black boots with the outfit either, because he'd rather be in his magicked Nikes.

He was angry with the Old Men in Charge, but he knew better than to simply storm the building. He had to show them some respect. And, given the depth of his anger, he might not be able to do that once the conversation started, so he had to show the respect with his clothing.

The Old Men in Charge had their offices in the Rock Candy Office Building on Sugar Cookie Lane. The building was one of the tallest in the North Pole, and took up what would be—in most places—a normal city block. Some mortal designer had submitted the plans and had actually come here to design the thing.

Lo had been living in the North Pole at the time, but he couldn't exactly remember how long it took to build the office building. He spent so many years inside the machine building that he rarely noticed anything else.

This evening, the Rock Candy Office Building annoyed him. It was a mishmash of styles, with a portico held up by columns made of candy canes. The curving tops of the canes doubled as light fixtures, casting a greenish light on the snow-covered sidewalk below.

He always thought that greenish light was a mistake, making the entire building look less festive and almost queasy. But he had no say in the architecture of the North Pole itself, not that he wanted any.

He walked up the three steps (white, red, and gold) leading to the portico itself. The light reflected off the clear bricks made to look like rock candy. Or maybe they were actually made of rock candy. He wouldn't put it past this place.

The end result, though, wasn't as good as the architect wanted. The building looked like a standard government building circa 1900 from anywhere in North America or Western Europe, encased in weird bricks that looked like square pieces of ice.

The double doors themselves were a little scary. If Lo didn't grab the door handle perfectly, the pointed edges of the rock candy bricks would cut through his gloves. Fortunately, the gold on the handles had been worn away at the exact right spot, and he noted, that since the last time he was here, someone (something) had chipped away at the edges of those bricks, at least near the door.

He pulled the door open. Hot air, stinking of tobacco, rushed out, enveloping him, and reminding him why he rarely came here.

The Old Men in Charge—heck, The Big Guy, and most of the S-Elves—all had a tobacco problem that dated back centuries. The pipe, The Big Guy once said, was part of Santa's identity, and he needed to maintain that identity.

But it all sounded like an excuse to Lo, an excuse to keep smoking or chewing tobacco. He wanted to hold his breath as he stepped inside, but it would do no good, because the deeper he went into the building, the harsher the smell would be.

And, as if he didn't need more of a reminder, two red-and-white standing ashtrays, designed to look like wrapped packages, stood near the door. The ashtrays were filled with cigar stubs, pipe discard, and a handful of cigarette butts. Beside the ashtrays were gold urns that were really dressed-up spittoons. Two of the Old Men in Charge preferred their "chaw" to the pipes any day.

The door eased closed behind Lo, and he blinked hard. It took him a moment to realize that lights in here had a yellow tinge, mostly caused by the tobacco smoke that coated everything, from the walls to the light fixtures.

He pulled his sweater closer as he stopped in front of the entry board.

The entry board looked like a board game tacked to the wall, with some artificial lights along the side that looked like decoration, but which were actually functional. The board allowed a visitor to state his business without talking to anyone, which saved some poor elf from spending his working days in this grungy lobby, breathing secondhand smoke.

Lo, who wasn't short, had to stand on his tiptoes to push the Emergency Hearing Button, the one that was marked EHB, instead of having the words spelled out. Most of the magical who worked here didn't even know that button existed, which was by design. Because everyone thought their issue was an emergency, and few were.

He suspected the Old Men in Charge wouldn't think his issue was an emergency either, but he would be able to convince them. The idea of losing the machine had everyone terrified.

The light on the Emergency Hearing Button blinked yellow—at least, he thought it was yellow. He couldn't really tell, given the coating of nicotine on everything. He glanced at the edge of the glove he had used to touch the EHB, and sure enough, a brownish stain coated the once-pure white fabric.

He shook his head and sighed slightly, then glanced around the entry. Doors everywhere, all of them solid and oak. He knew from experience that most of the doors led to various corridors, which housed offices and conference rooms. Claus & Company had become quite the bureaucracy while no one was looking.

The EHB turned green—or rather, a sickly greenish-brown—and double doors he had never gone through before opened wide. The area beyond them seemed dark, which made his heart beat a bit too hard.

The North Pole should not be creepy, not any part of it. And yet, this part was, just for a moment. He almost turned around and headed back into the comfort of the snow.

And then he realized that was what those doors and this tiny bit of theater was designed for. They were designed for the very moment when he had nearly turned around. Most elves, most of the magical, would have turned around, particularly if their "emergency" could wait.

His couldn't. That woman was inspecting his machine right now, and she seemed to think she knew what to do with it.

He walked through the doors, and sneezed as dust rose around him. Dust, layered with ancient tobacco. His eyes adjusted to find a court-room, with bench seats forming the aisle he walked down.

Nothing was green or gold or red or white here, like the rest of the North Pole. Here, the long bench seats were plain brown wood, without any ribbons or bows wrapped around them. The floor itself was some kind of linoleum, and he couldn't tell what the original color had been. Maybe a soft tan. Now that color was hidden under scuff marks and, yes, tobacco.

Ahead was a raised desk—too long to really be called a desk. It was the judges' bench, and clearly designed for more than one judge.

He was a bit surprised at how conventional and non-North Pole this all looked, and he was trying to remember where he had seen something like it before.

And then he remembered: He had to put in some hours seventy-some years ago (everyone did) to watch an upcoming film called *Miracle on 34th Street* to make sure it did no harm to Santa's image. Everyone got index cards with a yes/no option (*Was this film favorable to Santa?*) along with a space for comments.

He couldn't even remember what he thought of the film, but he remembered the black-and-white courtroom scene, where one of the lawyers dumped all the unanswered letters to Santa from the post office onto the judge's bench. And that moment, that incident in that film, made Lo feel shame.

He had forced the organization to hunt out those unanswered letters, and did his best to have their contents programmed into the machine. Which had led to another of the machine's overhauls, because that was simply too much information arriving so late in the holiday season. Initially, the Pole couldn't act on that information, and had to rely on parents.

Maybe that was what caused this Dallas woman to think that only rich children got their wishes from Santa.

Her comments had been perplexing. Almost as perplexing as her presence.

Lights came up in the well of the courtroom, adding that silly sickly yellowish light to everything. Dust motes floated around like little bugs, trying to find a place to settle.

Lo had no idea where to settle either. He wanted to see the Old Men in Charge, but not as a supplicant. As an equal.

A door in the back opened, and a wizened man with a yellowish beard entered. He was wearing a blue velvet robe decorated with moons and stars. The robe was as faded as he was. The white hair on the top of his head was thinning, revealing a pinkish scalp. It looked like the hair from the top of his head had migrated to his eyebrows, the inside of his ears, and his nostrils.

Just before sitting down, he looked at Lo, and Lo started. That was Damien. The last time Lo had seen Damien, Damien had been one of the younger Old Men in Charge. Not that he had been young. But he hadn't been wizened and bent and wispy.

"Good Sir," Lo said, inclining his head just a little in respect.

Damien clambered into one of the large padded chairs behind the judge's bench, then leaned back and pulled a pipe from the pocket of his robe. He patted his other pockets, looking for something, which turned out to be tobacco.

Lo sighed inwardly. He was around difficult smells all the time—the machine gave off more smells than the reindeer after a bad meal—but the pipe tobacco favored by most everyone in the Pole was truly foul.

Sure enough, Damien finished tamping his tobacco into the bowl of his pipe, and the lit it, puffing as he did so. The sickly sweet smell of vanilla mixed with cherries with an underlying scent of burnt rubber made Lo's eyes water.

Damien did not look at him. Instead, Damien puffed for a moment, released one smoke ring and then removed the pipe from his thinner-than-remembered lips.

"I suppose you're here about the girl," Damien said.

"Um," Lo said, not really wanting to correct one of the Old Men, but needing clarification just in case, "I doubt Miss Demaris would be considered a girl."

"She's female, ain't she?" Damien asked, with an emphasis on the *ain't*. He had been a big fan of American westerns eighty years ago or so, and had adopted a lot of the mannerisms of the old weathered tough guys in those films and books, who sat on porches and commented on everything around them.

"Um," Lo had no idea how to deal with this. He thought he would see all of the Old Men, not just Damien.

Damien leaned forward. "You want to answer me, Mr. Johanssen?"

Last name with honorific. That was new. And different. But then, Lo had never pushed the EHB before.

"I came because a woman named Dallas Demaris is, as we speak, inspecting the machine," Lo said. "She claims she was brought here to deal with it."

He didn't want to say *fix it* because he had the sense there was more to her visit than merely fixing the machine.

"Yeah." Damien leaned back. "The girl."

Maybe by Damien's standards, that beautiful and brilliant woman was a girl. Lo had no idea how old she was, but he figured she was close to his age. Which made her centuries younger than Damien.

"She's why you're here," Damien said. "Isn't she?"

"Only peripherally, Good Sir," Lo said. Then he decided to take a risk. He clasped his hands behind his back, and stood as tall as he could. "I would like to wait until the others arrive, if that's all right by you, Good Sir."

"Well, it's not," Damien said, "because clearly you don't know procedure. The EHB gets misused enough that we have developed a system. One of us hears the petition, and then we decide if it's worth bothering the others. Lucky you, you got me. Yes, me, newly awakened from a major nap."

In other words, tired and cranky and not happy to be in that chair. Got it. Lo didn't nod, because he felt that might be inappropriate, and the last thing he wanted to do at the moment was antagonize Damien, since Damien was his only hope of slowing this disaster down.

"All right, Good Sir," Lo said, "I—"

"And dispense with the 'Good Sir' nonsense," Damien said, "and I'll dispense with the 'Mr. Johanssen' nonsense. We aren't on any kind of record, and we've known each other since 1800 or thereabouts. So let's get to it."

Lo swallowed involuntarily. He felt like a newly minted mage instead of the man in charge of one of the most important magical machines in the world.

"All right then, thank you," he said, avoiding Damien's name, because…well, just because. Lo needed to focus on his petition, not on the verbal politics.

Damien raised his bushy white eyebrows.

"The girl," Damien said as a reminder. "You're here about the girl."

They were going to repeat the entire conversation so far, only without the formal language if Lo didn't find a way out of the loop somehow.

"She says she's here about the machine," Lo said. "And I didn't request any help. She—"

"You never request help," Damien said. "You have needed help since 1950 or so, real concrete help, and you haven't asked for it. You —"

"I listened to all of you and hired help in 1900," Lo said. "The machine broke—broke completely—because of what that idiot did. Fortunately we were running on a small scale at that point. L. Frank Baum hadn't written his exposés—"

"They weren't exposés," Damien muttered. "They were plants, thanks to the Image Specialists."

"Whatever." Lo waved a hand dismissively. He tried to avoid the Image Specialists and Image Headquarters as much as possible. In fact, he doubted he had been anywhere near that building and everyone who worked there in at least sixty years. "My point is—"

"Your point is that you had one incompetent and now you won't get the help you need." Damien pulled the pipe out of his mouth, tapped the bowl on the bench, and grabbed his lighter. He paused with the pipe in one hand and the lighter in the other. "You are being dangerously stubborn."

Lo's heart sank. He wasn't going to get any assistance from Damien. Lo had no idea how to get the other Old Men in Charge into the room.

"Dangerously?" Lo asked, even though he probably shouldn't have.

"Dangerously." Damien waved his pipe at Lo. "That machine is on its last legs."

"It's not that bad," Lo said, wondering if he lied.

"It is that bad," Damien said. "We are getting complaints everywhere."

"Everywhere?" Lo asked. "How can anyone complain about the machine? No one works with it except..."

He stopped himself. The Naughty and Nice list got updated and printed every week and taken to The Big Guy. The S-Elves reviewed all the data the machine produced, and sent the orders for toys, along with the address changes, to the various departments so that they could do their work.

No one touched the machine except him, but the entire North Pole worked with the data the machine produced in one way or another.

Damien raised those bushy eyebrows even higher.

"You sent for that woman, didn't you?" Lo asked. By *you*, he didn't mean Damien personally. He meant the Old Men in Charge.

"We have been attempting to find you assistance for some time," Damien said, a bit too formally for Lo's tastes. "We have even asked you to come here and discuss the issues with us, but you have declined."

"I haven't declined," Lo said, wondering if he actually had declined. He'd been so busy and so tired, he wasn't sure what he had done and what he hadn't.

"Recently, you have sent Rafn with messages," Damien said. "We have repeatedly told Rafn that we want to speak with you. You refuse, and by doing so, you have put him in an uncomfortable position."

"I didn't mean to," Lo said, and he truly didn't. He hadn't given it much thought. He knew Rafn had come into whatever machine room Lo had been working in and delivered messages from the Old Men in Charge, or exhorted Lo to talk to someone about the machine, or even to bring in more help, and Lo had always told Rafn that there wasn't enough time to talk with anyone, that Lo had something more important to do.

"So you brought in this woman to get me to come to you?" Lo asked.

"*I* didn't, no." Damien put the pipe in his mouth. Then he stuck the lighter in the pipe's bowl and puffed a few times, trying to get the foul thing to light again.

"But you all did, right?" Lo asked.

Damien puffed, and smoke finally rose out of the pipe. He set the lighter down, then pulled the pipe from his mouth.

"We have had inspections of that machine," he said.

"Who inspected it?" Lo asked. "When? No one told me."

Besides, how could it have been inspected when he was there all the time? Although he wasn't in every room at every moment.

"And really," Damien said, as if Lo hadn't spoken at all, "it doesn't take a genius to see that the machine is failing. You do realize that the smoke rising out of the chimneys is yellow, right?"

You do realize that the smoke coating everything in this building is yellow, right? Lo nearly snarled, but caught himself as the thought went across his mind, before the words actually came out of his mouth.

"The machine needs work, I grant you that," Lo said.

"You do, do you?" Damien asked, putting the pipe between his teeth. He groped for the lighter yet again.

"But this is the wrong time. We are starting into the busy season. If anything goes wrong—"

"We are in a world of hurt," Damien said. "We understand that. And, still, we don't think it can wait."

"Maybe you should listen to the only person who understands the machine," Lo snapped. "It has to wait. If you're set on bringing someone in, I'll find the best candidate in January—"

"We have already researched the best candidate. She is with the machine now." Damien gripped the lighter as if it were a talisman.

"You don't know what the machine needs," Lo said.

"It needs someone with experience in modern magical machinery," Damien said.

"No," Lo said. "The machine is unique. It needs guidance from someone who will work with me, because I'm the only one who knows how it works."

"And if something happens to you?" Damien asked gently.

"Nothing will happen to me," Lo said.

"Said everyone," Damien muttered, "all of whom eventually had something happen to them."

Lo felt his cheeks heat for the second time that day.

"The machine will eventually break down," Damien said. "And considering the vastness of the tasks it faces, it will probably break down as we tax it. Which means it will break down when we need it the most."

Lo couldn't really argue with that. He'd been worried about it, but unsure what to do about it.

"So," Damien said, setting his pipe and his lighter down. He leaned forward and made sure he held Lo's gaze. "You will work with the girl, and you will not complain. You will listen to her and treat her well..."

When haven't I treated people well? Lo nearly said, but didn't, because he realized, right at that moment, that he was getting an edict from on high, even though only one of the Old Men In Charge was in the room.

They had been waiting for him, all of them, planning to give him this speech for a long time. And he was missing the speech because he was getting angry at their behavior, rather than listening to what Damien had to say.

Lo made himself focus—again.

"...or," Damien was saying, "you will be removed from the machine."

"What?" All idea of cooperation vanished with that last part of the sentence. "You can't remove me from the machine. I'm—"

"The only one who knows how it works." Damien sighed. "We know."

"No," Lo said. "The magic the machine runs on. It's mine."

Damien looked at him as if he had grown a third head. "You didn't think, in two hundred years, that you should have *told* someone that."

Damien's voice was actually shaking. And it took Lo a moment to realize that Damien was furious.

"I thought it was self-evident," Lo said. "The sleigh runs on The Big Guy's magic—"

"Not anymore," Damien said. "We've changed Santas in the past two hundred years. *Twice.* Three times if you count that idiot Wenceslas, who was not the—"

"Good king upon whom the carol was based, I know," Lo said, wanting Damien to get to the point.

"The magic in the sleigh," Damien said slowly, "is S-Elf magic, refined and rejiggered so that it works with any S-Elf, and some others besides. It's *not* One Man Magic. No one does One Man Magic anymore. It's not even called One Man Magic anymore, or so they tell me."

"What do they call it?" Lo asked, trying to derail the tirade.

"*I don't know!*" Damien actually bounced in his chair. "I can never keep track of what anyone calls anything anymore, and everyone yells at me for it. I just know that we don't call it One Man Magic anymore, and who cares what it's called anyway?"

Lo actually took a step back. He had never seen Damien so perturbed. Or maybe the actual word was *angry*. Lo had never seen Damien angry.

"All I know," Damien said, "is what you should know. What *we've* all known for decades now. Maybe even longer, because I lose track of time."

He picked up his pipe and set it down again, so hard that Lo thought the pipe would break.

"One Man Magic," Damien said, "is not wise, it's not right, and it's been banned at the Pole for more than eighty years."

Banned? Lo frowned. Banned? They had actually banned something here?

And then he remembered all the things that had been banned—like outsiders. Like that woman inspecting the machine.

How much had he missed because he hadn't been paying attention?

"No one told me it was banned," Lo said, and then decided that sounded mealymouthed. Defensive.

He'd been defensive all day.

"Would it have made a difference if they had?" Damien asked, his tone curt, his temper barely in check.

And curse him for being so perceptive. To change the One Man Magic (or whatever the hell it was called) would take a whole new machine.

Damien waved the pipe at him. "Don't answer me. I'm angry enough. I don't want to hear more excuses."

Lo hadn't been making excuses. He hadn't. He had been telling the truth. He knew the Old Men in Charge wouldn't believe anything he said, and he knew—

"You will work with the girl," Damien said, enunciating each word clearly. "You—"

"You said that," Lo said, not wanting to hear the admonitions again, even though he probably missed half of them. "I can't guarantee that the machine will make it through whatever she's going to want to do to it."

"Can you guarantee the machine will make it through anyway?" Damien asked, so curtly that Lo wasn't sure Damien even expected an answer.

"Guarantee?" Lo asked.

Damien's eyes narrowed so much that they were hidden beneath his bushy eyebrows. "Guarantee," he said.

"I've never been able to guarantee—"

"I was around, young man, when you promised us a machine was the answer to all of our problems." Damien waggled his pipe at Lo. "And I *guarantee* that you told us you could *guarantee* that a machine would do everything we needed and more. We *trusted* you."

"That was centuries ago," Lo said.

"And we have to trust you more now, because of circumstance," Damien said. "So don't lie to me and say you never guaranteed anything, because you did. You clearly did. And now you can't guarantee anything."

Lo's heart was pounding hard, as if he was trapped in the middle of the machine when it was releasing too much steam and he couldn't find the source.

"I'm older now," he said. "A little wiser. I don't guarantee—"

"Don't humor me," Damien said. "Don't talk down to me. Don't make excuses. The truth is that you can't guarantee we will have a working machine next week, let alone next month, let alone in the all-important Christmas season."

Lo felt the blood drain from his face. The gigantic courtroom had actually gotten colder—or at least it felt that way.

Damien must have noticed Lo's reaction because Damien's expression softened.

"I know you've been working yourself nearly to death, Lothario," Damien said. "I know you haven't had a day off since the previous century. I know you're doing your best. But it's gotten beyond you, and you refuse to admit it."

Lo crossed his arms, more as self-protection than because he was angry. Even though he was. This was the thanks he got for all the work he had done? Being told everything was beyond him?

"You will work with the girl," Damien said, "and—"

"You've said that," Lo said. "You've said it twice now. I get it. I've already said I would work with her."

"But what you're missing, young man," Damien said, "is that she's in charge."

"She's an outsider," Lo said. "She can't be in charge."

"Normally, no," Damien said. "But you've used your seniority as an excuse to get rid of others in the past. And you don't have that opportunity this time. She works for us. And if she says she can't work with you, then you will be reassigned."

"Reassigned?" Lo asked. "Where would you reassign me?"

"With luck, nowhere," Damien said. "We don't want to reassign you. But it's up to you."

Lo stared at him, and Damien stared back without fidgeting. It was clear that Damien was speaking for all of the Old Men in Charge, so going to them for a different ruling wasn't possible. Nor was going to The Big Guy. This incarnation of Santa didn't like to be bothered with North Pole business, even when it involved his all-important winter sleigh ride.

"I could quit," Lo said, realizing he was bordering on childish.

"Yes," Damien said. "You could."

A chill ran down Lo's spine. Did they want him to quit? In the past, when he'd said something like that, the Old Men in Charge would beg him not to quit.

Had it gotten that bad, and Lo hadn't even noticed? What else had he missed?

"But you won't," Damien said. "You will work with the girl—"

"Oh for the sake of all that's magic, yes, I know," Lo said.

"And you will make the machine work for this winter's season. Or you will come up with another solution. Whatever it takes." Damien hadn't moved his eyes at all. Lo wasn't even sure Damien had blinked. "Is that clear?"

Lo let out a slow breath. They had backed him against a wall. He was going to have to risk the machine. He didn't want to, but he had no choice.

"Yes," he said reluctantly. "That's clear."

"Good," Damien said. "Now, go fix that girl dinner. She's pretty and she's probably feeling a bit lost around here. Most outsiders do when they first arrive."

"If you want her to stay, you don't want me to cook for her," Lo said, finding the very idea of spending free time with that woman repugnant. He needed to focus on the machine.

Damien chuckled. "Well, then," he said, "do what you need to do. And report back to me—without using the EHB—in exactly one week. I'll have Rafn remind you of the date."

"Thanks," Lo said, even though he didn't mean it. He didn't mean any of it. He wanted it to be yesterday, before he'd heard of the woman, before this edict had hit him, before he had known that his life was going to change.

But he didn't have that kind of magic. He couldn't go backwards and fix what had come before.

No matter how much he wanted to.

CHAPTER 9

*D*allas stood in front of the last big section of the machine in Room Four, and tried to reconcile what she saw with what that (handsome) Lothario person had told her.

The machine was designed to dispense joy.

And yet this machine, in this room, looked completely joyless. Unlike the machine parts in the previous three rooms, this machine—at least the section that went from the middle of the room into Room Five —was tall, rectangular, and uniform. It had tapes that revolved around the middle, what looked like a stereo speaker at eyeball level, and a flat whitish-gray surface that was covered with knobs and dials and lights that flickered in a pattern.

She had seen machines like this one before, in both the Greater World and in the magical realm. In the Greater Room, machines like this filled office complexes in the 1950s and 1960s, substituting size for raw computational power. Now, most Greater World residents wore more computing power on their wrists than the old "computers" that filled rooms (and sometimes warehouses).

For a while, magical machines mimicked those Greater World machines, but had other functions, mostly using magic to keep communities like this one in what seemed like electric lights and heat (but was actually magical approximations of the same).

This room had a dry electrical smell, so this part of the machine was powered by something other than steam, or this Lothario person had found a way to move the steam power into this room without moving the actual steam itself.

The steam had done its damage, though. Her hair was wilted against her head, and the white sweater clung to her like wet toilet paper. She was ever so slightly chilled, which told her that this room was degrees cooler than the other rooms were.

In the Greater World, machines like this needed some form of air conditioning to keep them from overheating. Either this machine didn't have that problem, or there was no heat in this room at all, and the chill from outdoors kept the machine cool enough.

She put her hands on her hips and studied the dials and the blinking lights, seeing the patterns, and wondering at them.

And at the sense of hopelessness that accompanied them.

Maybe that hopelessness was coming from her. Maybe the exhaustion and exasperation she was feeling had translated itself into her work.

She couldn't always tell when that was the case, so she decided to head back to Room One. The best thing to do would be to go outside and enter Room One without any emotions lingering from this room, but she didn't see an exit—or at least a clearly marked one.

Not to mention that she wasn't dressed for the out-of-doors.

Then she let out a long breath. She'd been feeling very uncomfortable in these rooms, which was probably part of the magic, designed to drive away anyone who wasn't associated with the machine.

She walked away from it to the far wall, where the door should be. The wall was undecorated, and it had no windows at all. Had she gone downhill? Deep inside the building? She hadn't been paying attention to elevation, so she didn't know.

She took one more step forward, as she tried to figure out the layout of this part of the building, when a door appeared in the wall before her.

So the magic hid the door until it was needed. Seemed like a waste of magical energy to her, or maybe it was just sloppiness. Maybe the door was hidden on the outside as well.

She was about to walk through that door when she realized she didn't dare. Ingeborg had let Dallas into this building. Dallas didn't have any kind of pass, magical or otherwise, that would get her inside.

She could end up locked out and lost in the snow. And considering how wet her sweater still was and how warm she had been, that could be a bad thing.

She sighed heavily. She hated mages who were full of themselves. They made it difficult for anyone to work with them, or to repair what they had done wrong.

And, truth be told, to even see what had gone wrong, because the problem was usually buried deep inside all of the personal magic that was threaded through the machine itself.

She walked back alongside the machine, noting that along the way, it had lost whimsy and charm. Walking the way she came made it clear that add-ons and doodads were lacking as she got closer to the "modern" part of the machine. Deep inside Room Three, the machine had pathways and pipes and a few parts that looked like they'd been made of little triangular hats.

But nothing like that existed in Room Four, not even on the older part of the machine closest to the door.

She frowned, the thoughts of the doodads and the personal magic, inspiring a feeling that she couldn't quite identify. But it felt like a hunch.

To act on that hunch, she needed to go all the way to the end of the machine, which she hadn't seen yet.

She pivoted, and headed toward the end of the machine, walking past the cleaner lines and the cooler temperatures, the blinking and ever so faint beeping, and the whirring of those reels of tape, going backwards, then forwards, and then stopped, staring at the entrance into Room Five.

The entrance was unimaginative as well. The connections between the first three rooms were arches. The first was a stone arch that resembled brick blocks of snow. The second was a stable arch that looked like it had been covered with a sparkly wash. And the third was an arch that almost could have been carved out of marble.

The machine never really went through the openings between the rooms. The openings were there for the living creatures to go through. Really, the machine appeared to be in one large room, with divider walls added to help delineate the space (and maybe to hold up the ceiling at certain points.

She couldn't even tell if the rooms were part of additions that had been built as needed or if the building itself was incredibly gigantic, with parts of it unused, like a warehouse, maybe, or some kind of storage facility.

She didn't rule any of that out, but she couldn't tell by eyeballing it, either.

She would need the history of the entire machine at some point, and the history of the building that surrounded it.

But she had planned to ask for that tomorrow when she met with the people that Ranklesworth had told her were called "The Old Men in Charge." When she had bristled, he had laughed.

The Pole isn't known for its progressive ideas, he said, as if it had delighted him that she would be going—on her own—to such a place.

Nothing about this place was right for her.

But it did intrigue her.

Although that doorway between the fourth and fifth rooms really caught her attention—and not in a good way.

This doorway was rectangular, with sharp edges, and some blond wood trim. It looked like a standard doorway from a badly built house in a 1970s Greater World suburb, not like the arches that had come before.

The doorway didn't even look solid to her. It looked like it had been made of flimsy material that was already starting to crumble.

She stepped through the doorway into Room Five, and was startled to see that the machine only covered about one-tenth of the floor. And what was here was more piping than it was machine. It was as if this section of the machine wasn't really machine at all, but bits and pieces ready to be assembled into whatever the machine could be.

There was one rather large contraption at the end. It appeared to be an accordion attached to a bellows, with a pipe organ on one side, and parts of a Jeep on another. She looked for tires, but didn't see any.

Instead, there were openings in various parts of the machine. Flat openings with rollers. She squinted, saw some little jets above the openings, and smelled—ink? Old-fashioned ink, the kind made with hawthorn bark and wine.

Behind a section of the machine was linen, folded in squares, but still attached.

She crouched and touched the edge of the folds, and realized that what was in her hand wasn't linen at all, but parchment. Thick parchment, the kind that didn't rip when it was pulled.

As this part of the machine seemed to want to do.

"It's the printer."

That was Lothario's voice, and it made her jump. She hadn't heard him enter the room.

His tone was dry, almost self-deprecating.

"The *printer?*" She couldn't keep the incredulousness from her voice. With parchment and *ink?* "You do realize that you can buy a printer for $20 on eBay, right?"

She turned toward him as she spoke, and in that whirl of movement, she realized that a man who made a machine like this had probably never heard of eBay.

"eBay," she said, hoping her tone had moderated some, "is…"

"I know what eBay is." He didn't even sound insulted. He sounded tired. And he looked different.

Gone was the man who wore cutoffs and athletic shoes and whose bronze skin glistened. This man wore a red, white, and green cardigan decorated with enough candy canes and Christmas ornaments to get second prize in an ugly sweater context. He wore a white shirt beneath it, and black pants.

The only thing that made him look like the man she had seen before (besides that chiseled jaw and those amazing cheekbones) were the Nikes on his feet. Except these were black to match the pants.

He held mittens in his right hand and a stocking cap in his left.

At least the sweater wasn't pilled. Both it and the pants looked like they hadn't been worn much at all.

There were so many things she could say. She could comment on his clothing, but then changed her mind. Because he looked as uncomfortable in those clothes as a human being could. And he didn't look like he'd been sweating, like she did. Calling attention to appearance at the moment would probably put her in a one down position.

She could also taunt him about the machine itself, but she didn't want to open that discussion. Not yet, anyway. She needed a bit more time and study.

Still, she couldn't stop herself from mentioning the printer.

"What do you need a printer for?" she asked, working to keep her tone neutral. Because this was, in some ways, a last straw for her. Nothing in these rooms made sense, not in any organized way.

To her surprise, Lo smiled tiredly. She had expected defensiveness instead.

"The Big Guy wants his lists on parchment."

She blinked, trying to parse the sentence. It took a minute. The Big Guy. Santa? And lists. Did Lo mean the infamous Naughty and Nice lists?

"Why doesn't someone just write them out?" she asked.

Lo's tired smile seemed deeper, even more exhausted than it had a moment ago. "They're too long. It'd take five elves three weeks."

"Even with magic?" she asked.

"We're all about handcrafting here," he said.

She frowned at him.

He shrugged. "Elves can't use magic to compile the naughty and nice lists."

"But you can use a machine for it," she said.

"A *handcrafted* machine," he said.

She glanced at the machine, looking as far down its length as she could, with the knobs and buttons and pipes sticking out, the steam rolling across Room Three shrouding it in a kind of fog, and she half-smiled.

Yeah, that was handcrafted, all right.

"Seems like a distinction without a difference," she said. "The machine uses magic."

"The machine focuses the magic," he said, and he wasn't talking down to her. He was just stating a fact. "The work around the magic is done by hand."

She didn't completely understand. The elves couldn't sit down and use their magic to compile a list on parchment? They had to handwrite it? That was one option, and the other was to use this contraption? Which also used magic?

She was shaking her head before she even realized she had started doing so.

"Magic use is restricted here," he said. Then his smile brightened. Or rather, those emerald eyes did, just a bit. "I'm sure I have a copy of that list around here somewhere."

"What list?" she asked. She really didn't want to see the Naughty and Nice list. She suspected it was a big part of the problem, not part of any solution.

"Magic usage rules here in the Pole," he said. "The dos and don'ts."

She had never been any place that had restrictions on magic. If the magic existed, then the practitioners could use it any way they wanted to—and if they chose to use it for ill, the other mages would deal with them.

"How come no one told me about this?" she asked.

He shrugged. "We don't get a lot of outsiders here. Maybe no one thought of it."

"Or maybe they'll tell me at the official meeting in the morning," she said, more to herself than to him.

"Maybe." He stared at her. Those green eyes were mesmerizing.

She expected him to tell her now to go, not to bother, to leave him alone. But he wasn't. His entire mood seemed to have shifted, and she wasn't sure why.

She trusted that mood shift a lot less than the anger.

"Why are you offering to help me now?" she asked. "You were opposed to me an hour ago."

Or maybe it was longer ago. She had lost track of time in here.

"I'm still opposed to you," he said. Then moved his head sideways, as if he were mentally correcting himself. "Or rather, I'm opposed to the job you're supposed to do."

He paused, almost as if saying the next word—which she was convinced was *but*—would commit him to something he didn't want.

Finally, she said it for him.

"But?" she asked.

"They tell me..." He stopped again, tilted his head, looked at something beyond her, and then closed his eyes. He was clearly considering what to say next.

Then his eyebrows went up, and he shrugged. His eyes opened, his gaze capturing hers again.

"They tell me that the future of the machine is in your hands," he said.

"My hands?" She sounded surprised—hell, she was surprised—not that she controlled the machine. She expected that. In fact, she had demanded it. She needed total control over the project, if she was going to work on it, particularly something with this kind of time limit.

"Don't play naïve with me," he said, and for the first time since he entered this room, his voice had a bit of a charge. "You knew that when you got here."

"Yes," she said. "But you didn't. I didn't..." *expect you to acquiesce so quickly.* She kept those last words to herself.

He let out a small sigh. "I have no further recourse," he said. "It's work with you or leave."

"Leave?" She hadn't expected that. Did they kick people out of the North Pole? Was that in one of the rules?

"Well," he said. "That was mostly my interpretation. Because I wouldn't be able to go anywhere near the machine anymore, even if you did keep it."

"I never said I would get rid of it," she said. Because she hadn't discussed with him what she was going to do. It seemed like getting rid of the machine would be the easiest option. Especially now that she knew of this threat.

He was watching her, trying to see how she was taking this conversation.

"But you believe that's the easiest option," he said.

"It doesn't take much magic to modify computers these days. Whatever your computational needs, we can meet them with existing technology." She sounded almost like a tech convert, and she knew it. But he had to know what the options are.

"You're not thinking this through," he said.

She bristled. "What am I not thinking through?" she asked coldly.

"We have a tech area here," he said.

"I know," she said. "I'm looking at it." And to call this tech wasn't really fair. It was…something else. A true melding of machine and magic and *handcrafting*. Or whatever else he wanted to call it.

"No," he said. "We have an area that's part of the workshop. Tech Toys. Only elves and the magical with your abilities—and mine—can even go near the Tech Toys division."

He seemed humble when he said "and mine," not like he was trying to make himself her equal, but as if he was stating a fact, just like he had done when this conversation started.

"How else do you think that kids get the latest tech gadgets from Santa?" he asked.

"Um…their parents?" she said.

"All the Tech Toys?" He shook his head. "That's not realistic. We have our supplies of tech gadgets. They come into the workshop, get modified, and then sent out."

"Modified?" she said.

"Joy, remember?" His expression seemed a bit sad. Was he disappointed she had forgotten that?

She hadn't really. She just didn't apply the joy magic to outside toys, at least not in her head.

"What about joy?" she asked.

He blinked at her, as if he couldn't conceive of the question. He opened his mouth, then closed it and nodded, as if he had just had a conversation with himself.

"There's a lot that goes into joy," he said. "Even with the toys that we don't craft, we make sure that they're exactly what the child wants. The Santa toy is the special toy, the one that gives as much joy to the child as possible."

She resisted the urge to cross her arms. She didn't believe that. Kids nowadays got what they wanted, and then discarded it just as fast. *Things* didn't give anyone joy. Never really had, and never really would.

But she wasn't going to argue that with him, not right now, anyway.

"So," he was saying, "the lists become important. Not just what a child wants, but what they need. What most people don't think about is that joy is as essential as breathing."

Her eyes narrowed. She felt like she was getting the company line right now, not actually having a conversation.

"Some children need more joy than others," he was saying, "and sometimes that was with the surprise gift. That's why so many kids get what they've asked for and then they get what they *haven't* asked for, but that particular item will give them joy over time."

It was taking a concerted effort to keep from rolling her eyes.

"You were telling me about Tech Toys," she said, keeping her tone as neutral as possible.

"Yes," he said. "That's my point. If we ignored modern technology here, we wouldn't fulfill our mission. Some kids need a tech toy because it will add delight to their life—"

"Joy," she muttered, feeling like she was correcting him.

"—and others will get a tech toy because that will open the door to their future, giving them a lifetime of enjoyment."

"You think that presents do that?" she asked.

He stopped, tilted his head, and frowned at her. "We're going to have that argument again, aren't we?"

She didn't answer him.

"If you're going to question our mission, then maybe you're not the person for the job," he said. "Unfortunately, I can't say that to the Old Men in Charge. You'll have to say it."

He was actually offering her a way out of this assignment. And, now that she was here, she really didn't want it.

She didn't have time to examine that reaction, so she ignored it. For the moment anyway.

"I'm the only person with enough experience in magic and machines to have a hope of solving your problem," she said. "So, please, keep telling me about Tech Toys."

That last sentence sounded sarcastic, and she didn't mean it that way.

He leaned back on his heels and crossed his arms.

"All right." His tone was different, colder, less open. So was his face. His expression was wary, as if he no longer wanted any part of this conversation.

"We have to be able to give modern technology to kids," he said, "or we fail at our mission. And we can't just hire mortals to deal with the Tech Toys, because they have to be infused with magic."

"You're giving magical machines to children?" She couldn't be more shocked. That was incredibly dangerous.

"No," he said. "We add a bit of joyful magic to every gift we give. It has to be the perfect gift, even if that feeling of perfection lasts for only a moment. Or even if the kid feels disappointment at what he receives. Over time, he will figure out that this one gift will be life changing."

"He," she said. There was so much wrong with the thinking here, and that one little word was part of it. He. Half the children they worked with had to be girls. That word did not include them.

But Lo seemed to miss what she said or, more likely, missed the significance of it.

"Our mission is to give joy. Just a little bit. Every gift has to do that." His gaze hadn't left hers. "So, we know how the tech works. We even have people who can work with that tech. But that's not the point. We don't want laptop computers and the latest tablet or a smart phone. We don't need wearables or anything else. While we give away those contraptions, we don't use them here. And replacing this machine with one of those won't work here. Those devices won't work for what we do."

She had dealt with companies that suffered from that same misunderstanding before. They couldn't separate their magical machines and the harnessing of the magic, from mundane tasks that needed no magic.

The problem was finding someone with whom she could discuss that transition. And it didn't seem like Lo was that someone.

Although Dallas was buoyed by the idea that there was an entire division here at the North Pole filled with people who could combine their magic with tech, without making the tech explode.

Still, she couldn't let Lo out of this argument, not that easily. He had to know what she was thinking. He didn't have to like it, but he did have to understand it.

"It seems like those devices will work just fine and have computing power left over," she said. "You just need lists. Spreadsheets. Computers have been making spreadsheets from the beginning. The earliest desktops could handle spreadsheets, and with more finesse than this contraption."

The word *contraption* slipped out, probably because she was annoyed.

His lips thinned, as if he was holding back words.

"If you think all we need is something that compiles lists, then I've failed at explaining our mission to you," he said.

"The only thing that seems to be missing from your mission is that idea of handcrafted work. You'd be using tech that wasn't handcrafted. And I'm sure someone could change the rules to make that work." She even had an idea who she might talk to about that. There was clearly a chain of command around here, and she would go up it if she had to.

His jaw was working from side to side as if he was grinding his teeth.

"In fact," she said, "those devices would be like so much other tech that you have here, things that mortals invented that make life easier for all of us in the twenty-first century."

"You haven't been around here long enough to see that we don't use those devices," he said. "We don't have automobiles. We don't let planes land anywhere nearby."

"But you have ovens and refrigerators," she said. "Or, at least, the cabin that I'm staying in does. It also has a toaster and a microwave. I'm sure I could use magic or my fireplace to boil water, but I'm happy to have other choices."

He glared at her. He was finally beginning to understand her point, and he didn't like it.

Maybe because it made all the work he was doing on this...*contraption*...irrelevant.

"It's not that simple," he said. "You can't just bring in some modern devices and expect them to be up to the task. Or expect that we can work with them."

"You've already shown me that you have an entire group of people—or maybe elves—who can work with the devices." Her sweater was drying against her skin, making her very uncomfortable. And since the steam was in the other room, she was also starting to get chilled. "And I don't know the history, but I'm sure it took time for the people who live here to accept refrigerators and ovens and—"

"You don't know the history," he snapped. "There were decades of fighting, and even now, we don't have the kind of electrical grid that the mortals have elsewhere."

She was going to ask where they got their power, but she decided not to. That would be a question for the Old Men in Charge, in the morning.

"Besides, let's assume you do bring in the devices," Lo said. "Let's assume that you can get staff to work with them without causing technical difficulties. We still have issues. You see, the lists aren't just—lists."

He flapped his hands ever so slightly, as if he couldn't figure out how to describe what he meant.

"Lists are the manifestation of what we do," he said. "Back in the day, we did it without lists at all. There was just—oh, never mind."

He let out a small sigh, then leaned over the so-called printer.

"Look," he said, "let me get you the *list* of magical rules, and maybe you'll see."

"See what?" she asked.

"Why we do what we do," he said.

"I know why you do what you do," she said. "You just explained it to me."

She hated it when people repeated themselves in an argument, especially one they were losing.

"No," he said. "You don't know all of it. This list will answer of your questions. You need those questions answered before you see the Old Men in Charge anyway."

He sounded tired, as if he couldn't quite face what was ahead of both of them. She wasn't exactly sure why.

But she knew she wasn't going to be able to dissuade him from showing her that list. So she remained silent. Besides, there might be an upside to getting that list. She might be able to see the printer in action.

Maybe that would teach her something.

It would be nice to see how the entire machine worked.

He waited to see if she was going to argue with him some more. But she remained silent. So, after a moment, he put the mittens under his arm, then looked around, as if he were searching for a pile of paper. Then he shook his head slightly, and walked over to the machine.

"Here," he said. "You want to see this anyway, right? Let's just print you a list."

He sounded like anyone would around computer equipment. *Here, let me open a file, push a button, and print a list.*

But she had a hunch it wouldn't be that simple with this contraption.

He handed her the mittens and the stocking cap. They were chilled even though he had been inside for at least fifteen minutes.

He then leaned over the Jeep part of the so-called printer, found three buttons that made a screen fold upwards, the way that some windshields folded upwards on off-road vehicles.

The screen had a long list of possible printable items, all of which were written in a computer font she recognized from the 1980s. It was an unfortunate orange, and a overlarge blinking cursor was on the side of them.

He hit something in the middle of the list. The screen blacked out for a half a second, and then the listed item started blinking, just like the cursor.

Something inside the machine, not far from Dallas, began to heave. It sounded like a malfunctioning bellows, whistling and blowing at the same time. The machine vibrated, and in the other room, a jet of steam streamed across the main floor behind Lo. Had anyone been standing near it, they would have gotten burned.

Lo glanced over his shoulder, sighed, and shook his head. She could almost see him making a mental note about the steam release.

But she didn't say anything. Instead, she watched the machine shudder. The whistling/blowing sound grew almost unbearable, and then something rattled.

She peered to the side, saw the folded parchment get pulled into the machine itself, going underneath the flat part like cloth in a clothing press. The air smelled of hawthorn and vinegar, the smell growing so strong that her eyes started to water.

After another minute of this, the edge of the parchment came out one of the openings, sliding around a spindle that she hadn't noticed a moment ago. The spindle turned, as hot air blew on the parchment, apparently drying and sealing the ink.

Then a bit of red something or other fell onto the middle of the parchment, and a metal arm she hadn't seen before unfolded itself, and pressed a round end onto the drop.

After she saw that, she realized what the red was. Wax. And the arm held a seal that looked like crossed candy canes.

She was going to be real sick of seeing candy canes before she left here.

Another arm pushed the spindle off its cradle, and it bounced into a wicker basket near the pile of parchment.

The machine stopped moving. It wheezed once more, less like a bellows and more like someone who had exerted too much energy and moaned as they quit.

Her mouth was open, and she wasn't exactly sure when she had done that. She forced it to close, because at the moment, she was too stunned at what she had seen to say anything.

But Lo saw this sort of thing all the time. And he wasn't watching her—or at least, he wasn't watching her now.

He bent at the waist, grabbed the spindle, and rose, extending it to her with a flourish.

"Milady," he said, with the exact right amount of sarcasm. He knew that the machine had surprised her.

She took the spindle. It was warm to the touch, but the wax had hardened around the parchment. What she had thought were candy canes weren't. They were initials. LJ.

His initials, done in a font that made them resemble candy canes. She almost asked if he could change the initials to hers or anyone's, but didn't. She wasn't ready to get into the details of the machine. Not yet.

Although she was intrigued, and a little bemused by what she had seen.

And her mood had lifted.

Dammit.

She was feeling something akin to joy.

She raised her gaze to his. He smiled at her, as if he knew what she was feeling. She wasn't going to give him the satisfaction of saying it, though, or even mentioning that joy.

She actually had to work at keeping a smile off her face. She didn't want him to know that this little interaction—this little *gift*—had jolted her with some magical joy.

Nor did she want him to know that she had needed it.

She held the end of the spindle in her left hand, and used the forefinger of her right to slide underneath the wax, releasing it from the parchment. That was an old move, one she hadn't done in more than a hundred years.

It felt odd and familiar at the same time, and—dammit—gave her even more joy. The simple things.

The parchment loosened its tight hold on the spindle, and she slid the parchment off, then grabbed the edge and opened the parchment.

It unrolled and fell on the floor, extending all the way to Lo's magicked Nikes, with a part of the parchment still rolled up. There was writing on every bit of the parchment, a long list that appeared to be in brown ink—except where it was highlighted in red or green or marked with shiny gold stars.

The first part, the part she held in her hands, looked like the opening page to a long handwritten novel.

It read, in what appeared to be beautifully done calligraphy, written by an expert hand:

Rules For The Magical Residing In The North Pole

The list that followed was not numbered. Instead, it had a tiny little dot before each item. Sometimes the dot appeared to be a dot of ink, and sometimes it looked like a piece of mint candy. Every once in awhile, a gold star shimmered in place of the dot or the candy image.

The fonts—if they could be called that—varied in size, as if the list was written by different hands.

She slipped the parchment through her fingers, moving downward, enjoying the feel of the material and the faint scents of candlewax and warm ink. Everything about this list was pleasurable, except the actual words themselves.

* *The Magical shall comport themselves with dignity at all times.*

* **The Magical shall ask permission before performing any kind of magic on the non-magical.**

* *The Magical shall not use magic for personal gain.*

Some of the rules, at least the ones she could see at a glance, seemed like common sense. Others seemed unclear upon a second read. What, for example, did "personal gain" mean? If she used her magic in service of her job, was that personal gain?

She didn't ask Lo to clarify though. He wasn't the one she answered to, after all. Besides, she was still feeling the effect of that joy magic.

She couldn't tell where her own emotions began and where the joy ended. She had no idea if the pleasure she felt in touching the parchment, smelling the faint odor of wax and ink, was actually hers, because she missed the sensuous nature of old-fashioned communications, or if that was simply the magic having an impact on her.

She knew that she had never consciously longed for parchment communications, but she also knew that there were pleasurable aspects to physical objects that simply did not exist on computers, such as the smell and feel of old books, or the tactile experience of browsing a clothing store. So she wasn't ruling out that the pleasure she felt—after that initial rush of joy—was entirely her own.

Still, now that she had had a moment to experience the parchment and the list, she couldn't stop herself from commenting.

"The Big Guy needs a little jolt of joy magic every now and then, does he?" she asked. "Or was that little *zing* deliberately manipulative, so that someone viewing the list wouldn't be immediately put off by it?"

Lo grinned. For the first time, the expression on his face matched the sparkle in his eyes, and made him stunningly handsome. Breathtakingly handsome.

She made herself breathe in deeply (although not obviously). She didn't know what was causing this attraction—maybe it was just the residual magic in the machine area or maybe she had just been alone too long—but she wasn't going to let any of it get in the way of doing her job.

Lo didn't seem to notice her internal dialogue at all. He said, "You should scroll farther down the list. Somewhere in the middle it says, *Everything created in the North Pole and given away shall contain a measure of joy.*"

"This was a gift?" she asked, a bit confused.

"I gave it to you," he said.

And he had bowed as he had done so. With a flourish.

Knowing that gesture would have activated the joy magic. Or maybe that gesture infused the spindle with joy magic.

She wasn't sure, and she was disoriented enough to feel a bit out of her depth.

She didn't work with that kind of magic, after all. She worked with barriers and edges—keeping magic from overloading machines or other kinds of tech, or pulling magic from the same kinds of tech.

"You mean, if I were to rip off a piece of this parchment, write on it, and give it to you, you'd experience joy magic?" she asked.

"Not quite," he said. "You would have to infuse that torn piece of parchment with joy magic."

"I don't do that," she said.

"Right now, no," he said. "But you need to learn. Because not doing so violates one of the magical rules."

"And what's the penalty for violation?" she asked.

His grin faded. "Well, it might not mean much to you. Too many infractions mean you will have to leave the Pole."

He was right: that didn't mean much to her at all. Part of her would be happy to leave. A smaller part than a day or so ago, but a part.

Although all of this magic had her worrying that she was being manipulated in ways she didn't entirely like or understand. The people here had given her a place to stay and packed that place with food. Would she feel joyful as she ate, even if she had been in a bad mood before that?

Or were the shelter and food simply part of the contract that the Pole had with her office? Did anything under that contract count as a gift?

Did the shoes she was wearing? Ingeborg hadn't technically given them to Dallas, had she? All Ingeborg had done was open the closet, and told Dallas to take a pair of shoes, or she wouldn't be able to go near the machine.

Still, those shoes had felt (still felt, truth be told) astonishingly good against her feet.

Lo was watching her, as if he expected her to say something else. She had no idea what to say. She thought she had known what to do, before he had come in here and confused things.

She would need time to think about her next steps. And maybe she needed to visit Tech Toys, just to see what was going on there.

She let go of the edge of the parchment, and it wound itself around the spindle again. The wax sealed it, even though the wax wasn't hot.

She tapped the spindle against her free hand. "I clearly have a lot of reading to do," she said with a smile. She wasn't sure if that smile was sincere or not.

The idea that everything here could toy with her emotions deeply unsettled her.

Somehow, she hadn't expected the North Pole to pose an emotional threat to her.

"You could just press the parchment against your forehead," he said. "You will absorb the rules."

She was familiar with that magical spell, and she found it particularly onerous. She had done it once, during a magical practicum, and hated the result. Ideas that hadn't felt like hers spilled out of her mouth. Memories that weren't hers lurked on the edges of the information she had learned.

That was as insidious, if not more insidious, than the joy magic itself.

"If I do that, do I absorb the joy too?" she asked, and as the words left her lips, she realized she sounded almost bitter.

His eyebrows went up. "I was just trying to make things easier for you," he said.

"I'm not here for easy," she said, slapping the spindle hard against the palm of her hand. The slap echoed in the room, almost as if she had slapped the side of the machine.

"Noted," he said.

"Good." Her smile had faded long before she noticed it was gone. Somehow she had challenged him, and they both felt it.

Her hand closed around the rules. The joy had faded. Now she felt annoyance. Between learning the contraption (she wasn't even sure it should be called a machine) and learning the rules, she was going to have a tough first week.

The fact that the person she would either spend the most time with or spend the most time fighting was not only handsome, but also her type, annoyed her even more.

She didn't need distractions.

She needed to work.

And somehow, she was going to find a way to do just that.

PART III

THE MISSION

CHAPTER 10

*M*idnight found Dallas snuggled on the soft couch underneath a hand-knitted afghan of gold, red, and white. She had actually chosen that afghan because it was one of the few with no images at all, from candy canes to Santa faces (complete with white tufted "whiskers"). She was already tired of all the Christmas imagery, and she hadn't even been here twenty-four hours yet.

She had taken a shower when she returned, because she was covered with dried sweat from the steam near the contraption, and because she smelled faintly of cinnamon, motor oil, and vinegar.

Turned out (after the shower) that the smell of cinnamon wasn't her; it was one of the underlying smells in the entire cottage, along with vanilla and nutmeg. The motor oil, vinegar, and sweat all belonged to her.

She wore one of her own sweatshirts and sweatpants, even though someone had left a comfy robe on the bed. She tried not to use much of anything in the cottage until she researched joy magic, particularly as it was used at the North Pole.

Fortunately, she had brought three ereaders and two dedicated laptops, as well as half a dozen of her own wi-fi hotspots. She had initially thought she didn't want to use the North Pole's wi-fi, only to discover there was none.

Just like there was no nearby cell tower, and, if her eyes could be believed, no electrical grid either. The entire place ran on magical energy, which she might have found cool, if she hadn't found out about the joy infusion thing.

The ereaders and laptops were her research tools. She also brought a few magical tomes with her, but she didn't use those as much and, truth be told, she was a bit leery of using any magical item in the North Pole at all at the moment.

She needed to learn the magical history of this place, and she was getting frustrated. Because there was no history to be found.

The place was either a black box (as one critic put it) or one of the best PR manipulators in the entire magical universe.

She wasn't sure if it mattered as to which one it was. The effect was the same; she couldn't find the information she wanted.

But she did learn a bit about emotional manipulation of the magical kind. There were different kinds, with two predominating. First, there was actual manipulation: trying to get someone to do something contrary to their own nature or desires. That was evil magic, black magic as it was called in some places (she hated the term), and was often the gateway to truly nasty stuff.

And then there was a second kind of emotional manipulation magic. It was considered nurturing.

She wasn't sure how she felt about any kind of manipulation being considered nurturing, but then again, most magic was manipulation or it was about deceiving the senses or it was treating the mortals as something different than the magical, all things that made her feel a bit odd if she thought about it.

She tried not to think about it by not being around mortals as much as most of the magical.

Anyway, the nurturing kind of emotional magical manipulation, as far as she could tell, did the best it could to alleviate suffering of one kind or another, by handing out (in small doses) "good" emotions, like joy, hope, and affection. Of course, all of those could be manipulated into something bad as well, and the spell books she was consulting (all on her ereader) reminded her that intent was as important as result.

As if she could figure out the intent of an entire village of magical beings.

Maybe they just wanted their living space to be happier and more comfortable than most. Or maybe they manipulated outsiders all the time.

Whatever it was, she decided she wanted no part of it. So she spent most of the evening cobbling together a shield spell that would last longer than a few hours.

At least with that spell coating her (and turning her fingers into something akin to magical Teflon, since most spells arose from the touch of a hand on something), she could be certain that the feelings she had were her own.

Unless, of course, the damn spell wore off. Or, of course, unless she encountered a magic more powerful than her shield spell. Which might happen here, considering that the S-Elves had been practicing their brand of magic for centuries, and she had just learned that shield spell.

She had used one of the laptops to check her employment contract with her company, and another to check the company's standard agreement, which she sure as hell hoped they had used to hire her out to the North Pole.

That agreement also protected her from manipulative magic, and should the company discover that she had been subjected to magic that sought to alter her behavior, they could terminate the contract immediately, and seek other remedies.

It took a bit of digging but, indeed, her company had used their standard agreement as part of the North Pole contract. The North Pole addition was all about confidentiality and nondisclosure.

Anything she learned about Santa or the way the North Pole worked or the workshop or Claus & Company had to remain secret. Any breach of confidentiality would lead to dire consequences.

Those consequences were not enumerated in the contract, which made her even more nervous than she had been earlier.

But other things in the full contract actually eased her mind. The contract provided for her room and board. It took her a while to find that clause, but it relieved her, because it meant nothing in this cottage, including the food, was considered a gift.

She needed that reassurance before she ate anything else. She was going to be cautious, though, about accepting gifts from anyone here, for any reason.

Which lead her to those damn magical rules. She had put the spindle near the door, meaning to return it in the morning. If she got the rules from the Old Men in Charge, that would be part of her contract, not a gift from someone who might be currying her favor.

Anything Lothario gave her would be outside of the contract. Anything that the Old Men in Charge gave her would be part of the contract.

She needed to get some stipulations of her own as well, that the tools she might need to do her job would not be considered gifts, but simply items of her employment.

She made a list of all the items she thought she might need, and then decided to make a list of all the people (and types of people) that she might need to help her. She wanted as few inhabitants of the North Pole in her little world as possible.

The last thing she wanted or needed was to be constantly subjected to manipulative magic—of any kind.

The best option she had was to declare the machine dead, tell the Old Men in Charge to scrap it, and then send in a team—who would be kept isolated—to build an actual computer network, using mundane mortal machines, that would keep the North Pole running.

Oh, Lothario wouldn't like that.

She leaned her head back on the soft couch cushion. She had no idea why she was thinking of that man so much. She shouldn't have been. Had he used some other kind of manipulative magic on her? She certainly hoped not, because she would have to work with him.

She rolled her head to the side and stared at the magic rules spindle. She had deliberately left it in a basket near the door. At some point, she would have to read those rules: she needed to know how this place worked on a deep level.

But she didn't want to touch the spindle that Lo had given her, particularly since he had admitted that it had joy magic. She didn't know how far that manipulative magic emanated, but she wanted it as far from her as possible.

She sighed. This place was unnerving her. She waved a hand, and the basket rose. Then she moved her fingers ever so slightly so that the door opened.

Cold air and a sprinkle of snowflakes floated inside the cottage. The air made some of the cinnamon scent dissipate. The cold actually smelled good.

She made herself focus, and eased the basket around the door. Then she sent the basket, and the spindle, outside, embedding them both in the nearest snowbank. She put a little guardian spell on them, so that they wouldn't be dislodged by wind or buried under the night's snowfall.

Then she turned slightly on the couch, facing the door. More snowflakes floated inside, looking like little white winks of magic that she had often seen on children's television.

She rubbed her hands over the air, as if she were cleaning a window with her palms, and scrubbed the area around the front door, as well as anywhere the wind had gone, of magic that had come from that spindle.

It had taken a bit of thought to come up with the right spell, because she didn't want to scrub anything of Lo's magic, considering his magic permeated the North Pole. Nor did she want to scrub out all of the joy magic, because, again, it permeated the Pole.

She didn't want to break the systems here. She just wanted to keep her emotions (and her thoughts) her own.

After a few minutes of scrubbing, she brought her hands down. With a flick of the fingers, she pulled the door closed.

The cold air lingered, almost comfortingly, and then the wood in the fireplace popped, startling her. She glanced at that wood, wondering, for a second, if it was the source of the smell.

But it wasn't. The wood smelled faintly of pine, which she greatly preferred to the cinnamon.

If she was going to have to live here, she was going to have to take control of her environment.

So she waggled her fingers a little and brought up the wood smoke smell, forcing the cinnamon—no matter what caused it—into the background.

Then she let out a small breath. At least the place was livable now. And she needed sleep.

She had a big meeting in the morning, and she had to be ready.

Because a battle was about to begin.

CHAPTER 11

For the second time in less than twenty-four hours, Lo showed up at the Rock Candy Office Building, dressed properly and deeply annoyed. He had been summoned by the Old Men in Charge, not to take part in the meeting, but to do a presentation on the machine, as if Dallas hadn't seen it at all.

The meeting wasn't going to be held in that dusty old courtroom, but in one of the conference rooms on the second floor. Lo arrived early, took the worn marble steps two at a time, and found himself alone in the wide corridor leading to the largest conference rooms.

The room the Old Men in Charge had chosen for this meeting was at the end of the hallway—an L-shaped conference room that, if Lo remembered correctly, had great views of the entire Santa Valley. He tried the door, only to find it locked.

He was the first to arrive.

Of course he was. Because he was the only one who was actually on a real clock. He needed to be with his machine. It had blown a gasket—literally—at 4 a.m., and he'd been deep in the bowels of Machine Room Two until about fifty minutes ago. Then he'd had to put his work on hold to take yet another shower, get dressed in his only other dressy outfit—black pants (again), white shirt (this time with tiny wreaths on the cuffs and collar instead of candy canes), the same sweater (because he wasn't ruining another in the tobacco stench of the Rock Candy Office Building), and—because he was feeling defiant—no gloves, no stocking cap, no white boots. Just his usual magicked Nikes.

This floor was no better than the downstairs. The light fixtures were just as yellow as they were on the floor below (maybe more so), the air reeked of cigars, and every surface was coated with a slight brownish film. He didn't want to sit down, so he paced as he waited.

Then he heard footsteps on the stairs. Not the slow deliberate footsteps of the Old Men in Charge, but resounding clomps that sounded both heavy and light at the same time.

Lo walked to the edge of the stairs, thought about leaning on the square balustrade, and changed his mind when he saw the top, which should have been a whitish marble, was streaked with brown and yellow, just like everything else in this place.

If he wasn't leaning, he would look tense and disgruntled, so he moved to the other side of the corridor, particularly since his half-second glimpse revealed brownish-red hair and just a hint of a jawline that had entranced him during those few hours of sleep he had gotten the night before.

He crossed his arms and perched between two tall candy cane ashtrays that smelled more like sour pipe tobacco than any kind of peppermint. He pretended to lean against the wall, because, for some reason, he wanted to look cool and collected in front of this woman, instead of as deeply panicked as he actually felt.

She revealed herself one step at a time. First, the top of that beautiful head, her hair shining almost copper in the strange light. Then her wide brown eyes and flawless dark skin, strong nose, even stronger cheekbones, and lips that were set in a straight line.

Thank everything magical. Because if those lips had been pursed, he would have been entertaining other thoughts about them (not that he wasn't—but those thoughts would have been easier to banish, which he was trying to do—even when he was thinking about the thoughts as he was doing right now).

Her lovely neck rose out of a white cowl that looked almost like a scarf over the black suit jacket draped comfortably around her shoulders. She wore perfectly pressed black pants and beneath it all, black cowboy boots with some kind of leather tool work that seemed both expensive and fragile at the same time.

Over one arm, she carried a thick white wool coat, and beneath that, some kind of satchel of a type Lo had never seen before. In the other hand, she held the magical spindle that he had given her the night before, wrapped in some kind of cloth he had never seen before.

When she saw him—and she did halfway up that second flight of stairs—her lips thinned even more.

She clearly did not approve of him or his presence or, most likely, the way he was looking at her.

"I didn't think you were on the team that hired me," she said.

"I'm not," he said.

"Then what are you doing here?" She made it sound like she was in charge of the entire North Pole, and he was the one who had transgressed.

"I am supposed to do a presentation for you on the machine," he said.

"That won't be necessary," she said. "You can go back to fixing the latest emergency."

So dismissive. And it was beginning to piss him off. If she had known just how much work he had put into that machine…

She probably did know, and she probably was trying to goad him. That she could goad him meant there was not just attraction but misdirected passion, that was going to leak out around him, like steam leaked out of the machine.

His cheeks heated at the image, which wasn't as good as he had thought it would be. Or maybe they heated because he was annoyed at her. Or because he was repressing his thoughts about her—or trying to repress his thoughts about her—or, rather, failing miserably to repress his thoughts about her.

He took a deep breath, and tried to shove the internal dialogue away. The last thing he needed was to be attracted to the person who wanted to destroy his life's work.

"I am not going to ignore a summons just because you said I could."

He had been going for a flat tone, but he ended up sounding both stuck-up and annoyed.

She raised her eyebrows, and took the last step. As she did, she extended the hand with the spindle.

"This is yours," she said.

"I meant for you to keep it," he said.

"I'm not accepting gifts here at the Pole," she said.

He stared at her for a moment. Her gaze was level, and seemed as dispassionate as her voice. But there was something beneath it, something charged.

She hadn't liked the joy magic.

He took the spindle, not sure what to do with it. She walked past him, then stopped at the candy cane ashtrays.

"This place is filthy," she said.

"Yes." Lo rocked forward on the balls of his feet, mostly so he wouldn't go back farther and brush against that wall. "I wouldn't say that too loudly, though."

"How hard is it to clean something?" she asked.

"Oh, there are cleaners here," Lo said. "They just happen to smoke as well."

She rolled her eyes and walked past him, swinging that satchel like a weapon. As she walked, her boots clomped, making her sound heavier than she actually was.

"I wouldn't set your coat down anywhere," he said, calling after her like a lout. He resisted the urge to slap the spindle against his palm.

She ignored him as she looked at each door, clearly searching for the conference room. She would find it at the end of the hall, but Lo wasn't going to point that out.

Instead, he watched her, letting all his mixed emotions wash over him.

If he had met her in other circumstances, he would have bought her a drink—not that there were many drink choices here. What passed for bars were attached to family-style restaurants, and usually served coffee or chocolate drinks, or something with too much rum or various toddies, all of which were too sweet for him.

Or he would have offered to cook for her, if he could remember how to cook. He used to have specialties, but they went by the wayside, just like everything else in his life.

He would definitely have flirted with her, just because he found her so attractive. He would have said something witty—if he had remembered how—and he would have bantered with her, keeping her near him just with the power of conversation. And maybe, they would have laughed and exchanged those looks, the kind people exchanged when they found each other interesting.

She finally found the conference room, and tried the door. It was locked. She lifted her hand, looked at it as if it were coated with something awful (and it probably was, from that doorknob), and almost wiped her palm on her pants. At the last minute she stopped herself, shaking her hand like she was trying to air-dry it.

She was probably using some kind of spell on it.

Then he frowned and tilted his head. She looked different today. It wasn't just the clothing or the way she walked. Something about her seemed—starker, crisper, almost reflective.

He squinted, trying to see any magic that was floating around her. She sparkled. Not like someone throwing sparkling lights at a Christmas tree, but like she had some kind of protective barrier around her.

He would have sworn she hadn't had that the night before. He couldn't remember if he looked, though.

Protective barrier. He pushed away from the wall with the heel of his shoe. Usually someone did that when they were feeling threatened.

How could anyone feel threatened here at the North Pole?

He walked toward her. She was standing in front of the door at the end of the corridor, coat still draped over her arms. Even from here, he could sense her reluctance to sit down.

She watched him walk, and her chin went up ever so slightly.

Had she put up that protective barrier because of him? Had he unnerved her somehow?

He remembered that shock in her eyes when she realized the magical rules were infused with joy magic. Had she felt something then?

Did she have something against joy?

Her head tilted ever so slightly as she watched him come down the corridor.

He wasn't imagining it; she was a lot more reserved than she had been the day before.

He hoped it was the circumstance—she was about to go into a meeting, after all.

As he had that thought, the door behind her opened. Dallas turned at the sound. Damien leaned out of the conference room, his beard looking even more yellow in the lights from the corridor.

"We're ready for you, Miss Demaris," Damien said.

Dallas visibly bristled, probably at the "miss." Lo smiled, knowing she couldn't see him. If she was going to let language upset her, she wouldn't last long with the Old Men in Charge. They were anachronistic for the North Pole; Lo had no idea what the modern world—the world outside of this snowy paradise—would think of them.

He hurried down the corridor. Dallas looked over her shoulder at him, those lips tightening into a frown of disapproval.

But Lo couldn't tell if that disapproval was for him or for the Old Men in Charge or for Damien's "miss."

Lo reached the end of the corridor, just as Dallas walked past Damien.

Damien's gaze met Lo's. Damien's blue eyes looked as bright and sharp as blue eyes could, almost like crystal wells of sun-dappled water.

"We don't need you yet, Lothario," Damien said. "Just wait here."

And then he slammed the door so loudly that dust fell off the walls. The stench of tobacco rose with the dust. Lo stood outside the conference room, hands clenched around that spindle, the parchment bending under the force of his grip.

He took a deep breath, so that he wouldn't pull that door open and join them.

He needed to play this cool. And he needed to be smart.

Although, in this instance, he had no idea what smart was. He had no idea how to save the machine, maintain the lists, and make sure that

Christmas went off without a hitch, all while dealing with a clearly powerful outsider.

One he was attracted to.

Then he raised his chin, just like Dallas had done a moment earlier. He had been worried about her reaction to him, those magical protections she had coated herself with.

But he hadn't given any thought to the fact that she might have magically manipulated him. Maybe the attraction wasn't real. Maybe she had performed some spell or infused something or other (her perfume?) with some kind of manipulative magic.

Although, he had lived here for a very long time, and he knew what manipulative magic felt like. It always felt a bit coercive.

Except for that tiny burst of joy magic that came from gifts. That felt like a hint of sugar and cinnamon on the tongue, just enough to give pleasure, but not enough to make a person sick.

Had she given him a tiny burst of manipulative magic, just enough to feel that first second of attraction, but not enough to actually change how he felt about her?

And if she had, had she done it with others as well, or had she just targeted him, knowing that he would be her nemesis on the machine itself?

She would have to be quite the schemer to set something like that up, and she hadn't struck him as that person, at all.

He turned toward the door. If he let himself in...he ruined any credibility he had with the Old Men in Charge. If he stayed out and in the dark, he would have no idea what they planned for his machine.

If he listened in, he could say he was just monitoring when he was going to enter. No one would believe that, but he wasn't sure anyone would blame him for that either.

Of the three choices he had just come up with, listening in was the best.

Although, if he had been consulting with someone, he knew that the best option—the smartest option—was to wait until they summoned him.

Wait patiently.

While the machine chugged away unattended.

And other people plotted a future they didn't entirely understand.

With a sigh of resignation, Lo whipped his right hand in a circle, creating a clear crystal glass. Some mages would have been able to listen by creating a tiny opening in the wood. But he had been working so long with machines to funnel his magic, using an item like a glass crystal seemed more natural.

It was also less likely to be discovered.

He used the side of his fist to clear one little section of wall, grimacing at the oily feel of the layered tobacco. Then he stuck the glass against that section, and created a tiny little headphone. The headphone, also made of glass, cupped the outside of his right ear like a tattoo.

At first, he could hear voices, but no words. Then he raised his right hand and turned the glass, like he would turn the dial on an ancient radio. The voices became recognizable.

One more turn, and he heard words.

"...you are the best..."

Lo couldn't tell who the voice belonged to. The sound wasn't quite that fine and he had to strain to hear the words exactly.

"...they tell us..."

He concentrated, but still couldn't quite focus.

"...not used to outsiders..."

He let out a small sigh. They were still in the preliminary speechifying that went with every meeting held by the Old Men in Charge. They loved to hear themselves pontificate.

Lo used his already filthy hand to wipe off a bench pushed against the wall, and sat gingerly on the edge of the seat.

It would be a long morning. And he doubted it would be a good one —for him or for the North Pole.

CHAPTER 12

*D*allas hated these kinds of meetings. They were the worst part of every single job she had ever taken. Either she had to prove herself or she had to listen to speechifying or she had to correct know-it-alls about what they faced.

She had a hunch she would have to do all three here, and she didn't want to do any of it.

The old man who had opened the door for her—and he was *old*—was bent and too thin. He wore a wizarding outfit that could have come out of a bad Harry Potter movie rip-off, all purple and black with gold stars and moons. The old man's white hair was thinning on the top of his head, revealing a scalp that was oddly pink.

He waved a crabbed hand toward a long conference table, and told her to sit anywhere.

As if she could have. All of the chairs were taken by old men of various shapes and sizes. Only one chair remained open, and it was against the wall.

She wasn't going to sit there. In circumstances like this, she had learned it was better to stand, just like she did at the office at home.

The conference room itself looked like it had been remodeled in the 1950s. Its walls were paneled with cheap brown wood that matched the conference table, and the pilled carpet beneath her feet. If the one remaining chair was any indication, the chairs matched as well. Only they had vinyl backs and seats, also in that same sad brown color.

If anything, though, the air was just as foul in here as it was in the corridor. Even though there were windows that overlooked...well, something...they were smeared, probably with the same tobacco stains that coated everything else in this place.

The windows hadn't been opened since the Jurassic Period, and the vents probably hadn't been cleaned since then either—although, it was possible that what Lo had told her was true: the cleaners in this building (magical or otherwise) also smoked, so they didn't notice the problem at all.

The old man who sat at the head of the table noticed the look she had given the remaining chair, and probably noted her slight grimace of distaste. He was one of the few men in the room who still had a straight back and perfectly aligned shoulders. His silver hair was swept back, and he wore a grayish-silver suit that glistened, even in the yellowish light.

"Miss Demaris, would you like my seat?" His accent reminded her of the accents of countless 1930s American movie star—not quite East Coast, not quite British, not quite European—but something clipped and snobbish that suggested he was a lot richer and a lot more posh than she could ever be.

She smiled at him and added just a bit extra Texas to her speech. "Thank you, Good Sir, but I'm doing just fine standing."

She kept her wool coat draped over her arms, although setting it down would probably not be the problem she anticipated. She was going to have to clean the thing anyway, given the amount of tobacco she was encountering everywhere in this building.

And the tobacco stench was foul, a mixture of pipe and cigar smoke, with an underlayer of low tar cigarettes.

The smell made her slightly queasy, and gave her a bit of a headache between her eyes. But she wasn't going to let that have any effect on her or what she needed to do here.

They were looking at her expectantly, as if they didn't know what to do with a person in their midst who wasn't old, wasn't male, and wasn't part of their little cabal. The fact that she didn't want to sit down seemed to confuse them as well.

But she didn't dare think they were old and harmless. They looked frail—each and every one of them in his own way—but that look was some kind of mask. Not a magical one—they were showing her their real appearances—but some kind of natural cover.

It wasn't until she looked in their eyes that she saw how active, alert, and intelligent they were. And how powerful.

She messed with these men at her own peril.

"It's a bit uncomfortable, having you tower over us," muttered the only obese man in the room.

He sat in the very middle of the far side of the table, curved back to the window. He was too fat to look like any image of Santa Claus. Not that he would have anyway, since he was also bald, with no facial hair whatsoever.

She didn't respond to his complaining, because that would put her on the defensive. Instead, she looked at the man at the head of the table, keenly aware that he had not introduced himself or anyone else.

Power plays. It was all about power plays. The worst part of these rescue jobs.

Then she heard a kind of clang to her left. A tiny magical portal appeared against the wall near the door.

Lo had set up some kind of listening device, making a magical machine so that he could listen in.

She didn't look at it, and neither did anyone else in the room. She had no idea if they were even aware it existed. But she wasn't going to underestimate any of these men. Individually, they had more magic—and more years of practicing magic—than she did, and combined...well, she didn't even want to think about it.

"Your bosses tell us you are the best," said the dapper man at the head of the table.

She waited, not confirming or denying what her so-called bosses said. Nor did she explain that they weren't bosses in the traditional sense of the word.

"They tell us," the dapper man continued, "that you can repair our machine, and it definitely needs repair."

He let that sentence hang so that she could jump in if she wanted to. She did not want to. She wanted this conversation over so that she could do her job.

"We have our man outside," the dapper man said. "He can tell you the history of the machine, and give you a tour."

"Do you mean Lothario Johanssen?" she asked, figuring right now that they were all playing. These men knew that she had already seen the machine, and they knew she had met Lo. She would play. A little. "If so, we met last night. I asked Ingeborg if I could see the machine right away."

A couple of the men—younger looking (if she could judge)—glanced at each other. But everyone else kept staring at her.

"Mr. Johanssen was there, and talked to me about the machine, giving me some of the history." She made sure she had a smile planted on her face. "He tells me that the magical machine is designed to give out little bits of joy."

She didn't ask if that was correct. Instead, she just stopped speaking, so that they could correct her if need be.

The dapper man raised his eyebrows just a little, as if to say, *Go on.*

"What I was told before I got here," she said, deciding to give them just a bit, "is that if this machine is not repaired or replaced very quickly, Christmas as curated by Claus & Company will not happen this year."

She had worked hard to pick the right words, because she didn't want to say that Christmas was canceled.

"Curate?" the obese man snapped. "*Curated?* Are you a non-believer?"

She didn't look at him. She kept her gaze on the dapper man.

He shrugged ever so slightly and said, "There is a question on the table."

So he wanted her to answer the political question. *Non-believer* indeed. She hated the word, almost as much as she hated all that it implied.

She did have an answer planned, although not for that question specifically. She hadn't expected the *believer* part of it. That suggested a fanaticism she wanted no part of.

So she spoke slowly. "I was born before Claus & Company got involved in the holiday."

The men all watched her, as if that did not answer their question. It probably didn't, not in the way they wanted.

She was going to have be clearer, even though she didn't want to be.

She looked directly at the obese man, whose face was as red as his Santa shirt.

"To answer your point," she said directly to him, "I don't ascribe to beliefs of any kind. I do my work, which is combining technology with magic in the most efficient way possible, and I go where the company sends me. They have sent me here. They gave me a deadline. I need to understand if what they told me about the job is correct or if I have misunderstood."

The men looked at her as if she had grown a third head. Maybe to them, she had, because her accent had vanished, and she was letting them see her as she really was.

She also was telling them that she wasn't going to play any games, not now, and not ever. They had to accept her for who she was, or she was going to leave.

If she had to, she would make that clear as well.

She hoped it wouldn't come to that.

She continued, "I also need to understand exactly what the machine's function is, and how it fits into the company you've all built. I have my own assumptions—"

"Assumptions?" asked the only dark-skinned man in the room. He had apple-red cheeks, though, that looked like they'd been painted on his round face. She recognized his visage as one that had come into prominence in the 1970s, when mass media (in the United States, at least) finally realized that Santa needed to represent more than one race.

"Yes," she said. "Assumptions. The machine seems deeply out of date, and not up to the task you've assigned it. I'd like to be charitable, and believe that the machine's failings are what has caused the failings at Claus & Company."

The face of every single man in the room flushed. More than one grimaced at her. She could feel the collective magic rise, as if someone (maybe all of them) wanted to release some kind of spell that could hurt her.

She wondered if anyone had ever challenged them about Claus & Company, the holiday, or the way they ran things.

Maybe not, given how the people she had met at the North Pole acted.

The men glared at her. She kept her own expression neutral.

"Failings?" the dapper man finally asked. He expanded the word ever so slightly, emphasis on the *fail* part, and not the *ing* part. He almost lost the plural as he spoke.

Something in the way he said it sounded both offended and accusatory, as if she were the one who had failings, not these men, and certainly not Claus & Company.

"Yes," she said. "Failings. There are a lot of them."

Eyes narrowed, mouths thinned. The tension in the room grew. She almost looked at the crystal device that Lo had attached to the room, just to see how he was reacting as well, but she didn't.

She had her hands full with these men.

"We were assured that you knew what you were doing," the obese man said, as if criticizing Claus & Company meant that she didn't know her job.

She looked at him, making her expression hard and mean. But she didn't answer him. Instead, she deliberately, and slowly, moved her gaze back to the dapper man.

"I need to know if those failings are intentional," she said, "or just the fault of an out-of-date system, an overworked machine, and a closed community."

"You're judging us," the dapper man said.

"Oh, probably," she said. "But that's irrelevant."

Two of the younger men started, as if they couldn't believe any of those words had come out of her mouth.

"The only things that are relevant," she said, "are the things that will enable me to do my job. Which means I have to know the function of the machine, the goals of Claus & Company for this machine or a future machine, and whether or not what I see as problems are built into the system or an inadvertent by-product of the system."

She wasn't going to list the failings, not until pushed.

"We have no failings," the obese man snapped.

"Bjarne," said the man who let Dallas into the room. His tone was sharp, an actual rebuke.

The obese man—Bjarne—glared at the man who let her into the room.

That man said, "Forgive us, Ms. Demaris. We are not used to criticism."

No kidding, she almost said, but somehow managed not to.

"We have been rude all along. We haven't even introduced ourselves," he said. "I'm Damien."

"It's a pleasure to meet you, Good Sir," she said, pointedly not giving him permission to call her Dallas. She wasn't going to put herself in a one-down position.

"You have mentioned failings twice now," Damien said. "Whether or not we like to hear the word, we should probably hear you out before we get too defensive. As you said, some of these 'failings' might actually be intentional."

She barely prevented her mouth from making a wry smile. Somehow, he had made himself her ally, and yet managed to question her judgment at the very same time.

"Yeah," she said, not because she agreed with him, but because she needed a moment to assemble her thoughts. She wasn't sure she wanted to be polite, but she also had one small chance here to make a difference, and alienating these men even more might be a bad thing.

Or not.

She really couldn't tell.

"When I was given this assignment," she said, "I told everyone that I was not the right person for the job. I do not *believe,* as you said, Mr. Bjarne."

She had no idea if he was a *mister,* but she figured pretending to be polite couldn't hurt.

His eyes narrowed even more. She was getting the sense that his dislike actually bordered on hatred now that she had made her confession about belief.

"I was told," she said, "that what I believed did not matter, that the machine was the important thing, and that only someone with my skill set could deal with the problems you face as quickly as you needed those problems solved."

"I can't believe there isn't someone else with her skill set," Bjarne said to the round-faced man to his right, loud enough for her to hear.

"In your shoes," she said, "I wouldn't have been able to believe it either. But it's rare to have any mages with technical abilities, and most of the ones who do were born in the late twentieth century. They're adept at working with modern chip technology, cell phones and tablets and laptop computers. I doubt any of the younger mages have even seen anything like your machine."

"So your bosses think you're the best," Bjarne said to her directly. "We already know that."

She made herself breathe out evenly so she didn't snap back at him. "You are welcome to have any of those younger mages attempt to work on your machine. I was not happy to come here—"

"The failings, Ms. Demaris," the dapper man said, and again, he put the emphasis on *fail*, as if it were all her fault.

She gave him a half-smile, then nodded in acknowledgement. Time to give the speech she had planned.

"I am deeply disturbed by your system," she said. "It enables greed in the children it does serve, and hurts the children that it doesn't serve. I also do not like the way that children from different cultures get ignored by Claus & Company. I told my..." She had to pause so she didn't add "so-called" to the next part of the sentence. "...bosses that, and they didn't care about what I thought. They believe—based on what you all told them—that you want your machine issues resolved, and to do that, you need me."

Bjarne's jaw set. Damien held up a placating hand in Bjarne's direction, and then turned toward her, clearly waiting to see if she had more to say.

"The machine itself does very little of what a modern computer does," she said. "I have more computing power in my phone than that machine has. But, Mr. Johanssen tells me, the machine inculcates everything with joy, and that no mortal-made machine could ever do. So, let me ask again, what is it that you need your machine to do? Once I know the answer to that question, I can help you or give you advice that might change the direction of your company, or recommend a replacement for me."

Bjarne looked away from her. Several of the younger men looked down. A slight frown appeared in the dapper man's forehead.

Damien eased his hand down. Apparently, he was no longer afraid anyone else would speak out of turn.

"You do realize you are questioning our entire business model," he said quietly.

"No," she said, "I don't realize that. I am asking what that machine does. Your business model is...your business."

Sometimes she wasn't as articulate as she wanted to be. She almost rolled her eyes at herself.

"I need to know exactly what job you've hired me for," she said.

"Fix the machine," Bjarne growled.

"We are not *failing* anything," the man to Bjarne's right said, so defensively that she had a hunch he already knew about the failures she had mentioned and decided not to deal with them.

"All right," she said. "You want the machine to continue to make *naughty and nice* lists, to print them out for...The Big Guy...." She hated that phrase. "And to coordinate what information you have. You also want just a bit of joy in everything the machine does."

"For the record," the dapper man said, "the machine does not give out bits of joy. The gifts themselves have just a bit of joy placed in them."

"How can you begrudge giving joy?" one of the younger men asked her. "How can you act like we're doing something wrong?"

Because you are, she wanted to say. But, clearly, maintaining the business model they'd had since the nineteenth century was the point, not adding in the changes that she believed necessary.

Her heart sank, just a little. She had hoped that this discussion would go differently. But of course it wouldn't.

Because it never did. Whenever she went into a business that was hidebound, it remained hidebound. She would repair whatever machine they needed repaired, and flee, rather than working with the company to improve their delivery systems or their record-keeping or fine-tune their magic—whatever they used the machines for.

She didn't even answer that younger man. Instead, she looked at Damien, then at the dapper man.

"By the end of day," she said, "I would like a paper list of the functions that you need the machine to perform. I will make certain that it can perform those functions for you. If I believe that it can't, I will make recommendations, based on your list, for some kind of improvement."

"And you can get all of that done before the Season ramps up?" one of the younger men asked. There was no animosity in his tone, thank heavens.

"I hope so," she said. "I will do my best. I will probably have to cobble together something so that the machine will function through this holiday season, and then we make whatever improvements you need by *next* holiday season."

The men just stared at her, as if they were waiting for something more.

Finally, the dapper man said, "No replacements? No changes?"

"I don't know," she said. "I only looked at the machine yesterday. I didn't study it in depth."

They continued to stare at her. She wanted to cross her arms. She wanted to tell them that they were on their own. She wanted to shake each and every one of them, and move them out of their hidebound world, and into the twenty-first century.

But she waited.

Finally, Damien said, "Well, then, we should bring in Lothario...?"

"I'd rather talk with him one on one," she said, now that she knew what was going on. He would clearly remain the person in charge of the machine, which was what he wanted anyway.

And she would have to work with him.

"One thing I do need, however," she said, "is a list of the magical rules for behavior here in the North Pole. I don't want to inadvertently insult anyone."

She hoped they heard that as it was intended, meaning she didn't want to insult them either. (Except maybe a little.)

"You shall find a magical rules list in your cottage when you return," the dapper man said, "along with the list you requested from us. From you, we shall need a timetable."

"I'll have that for you by the end of the week," she said, "once I know what I'm facing."

And with that, she resisted the urge to sigh. Because what she was facing was helping people prop up a system she did not believe in. Usually that wasn't a problem for her, but here it was. She could see some of the active harm.

And she had no idea what to do about it.

CHAPTER 13

*L*o stopped in the middle of the corridor, his heart aching. He almost couldn't concentrate on the tiny voices flowing into the glass headphone he had placed around his ear.

As he listened in on the meeting he was not invited into, but should have been, he couldn't really distinguish the voices of the Old Men in Charge. They were tiny and tinny, coming through the magical glass he had adhered to the wall, but that wasn't why, exactly.

The Old Men just sounded the same. They had spent so much time together over so many centuries, that their speech patterns mimicked each other. The headphone he had made wasn't that sophisticated either; it altered timbre, raising deep voices, and lowering higher ones.

Lo could hear Dallas's voice, though, and not just because she was the only female in the room. She had that mixed American accent, which she occasionally leaned on to sound a lot more Texas than it normally did, and she spoke a lot more forcefully than the Old Men in Charge did.

And she didn't whine.

They did.

Lo had never realized that before.

He had stood up when one of the old men said that Lo should be brought into the room, and then, when nothing came of that, Lo started to pace, partly to keep himself from opening that door, and letting himself in.

He wanted to go in, desperately, particularly as the conversation started to go south. She was talking to the Old Men in Charge about their failings. No one did that. No one questioned them.

But she was.

And then she said, *It enables greed in the children it does serve, and hurts the children that it doesn't serve. I also do not like the way that children from different cultures get ignored by Claus & Company.*

Even through the tinny headphone, he could hear the passion in her voice, the anger, the sheer fury.

It was that passion, that fury, that caught him, and made him remember that she had said something similar when he was trying to tell her the history of the machine the night before.

She had used the word *greed* then too, and had said something about the naughty and nice list only rewarding kids whose parents had money.

He had written it off last night, thinking she had been one of those kids who had never gotten what she wanted for Christmas—because, he had always been told, some kids never knew what they wanted, and were doomed to be disappointed.

But she had answered someone's belief question—Bjarne, because Bjarne always asked about belief. He had been in charge of belief, back in the day, and had actually toyed with using Claus & Company to start a religion until someone—probably the previous Big Guy—had talked Bjarne out of it.

This morning, though, she had said she was too old to be involved in any gifting. Her comments had a ring of truth—or at least truth for her.

Rewarding greed, ignoring other cultures, not up to the task.

Lo had stopped walking because he couldn't walk and listen and think at the same time.

The argument was going on around him, almost as if it had crawled inside him, but his brain was still pondering her words.

What if she was right? She was risking losing this job to express those opinions.

He wiped a hand over his face. She didn't seem like someone who cared about things like jobs or alienating others. She was one of those people who didn't seem to care what anyone thought.

He let out a small laugh. He had been that kind of person once. Back when he first built the machine. Back when he believed he could help Claus & Company, before it became the juggernaut that it now was.

He hadn't been paying a lot of attention to the way this business was being run. He mostly ignored the S-Elves. He hated the questions of loyalty and belief and maintaining image, but they usually didn't concern him.

He had been so busy that he hadn't really noticed how constricted the North Pole had become either.

When was the last time he'd had a real conversation with anyone? When was the last time he expressed an opinion without feeling like someone was looking over his shoulder?

Of course, most of his opinions had been about the machine, and he knew that the machine was barely hanging on, so he felt very judged. But about little things. When was the last time he had had a good conversation about little things, without feeling—?

The conference room door opened, and he whirled.

Dallas exited, her coat still hanging over her arm, her expression cool and calm, which didn't entirely look natural on her. The door slammed shut behind her.

Then her eyebrows went up, and a touch of a smile appeared on her face. She reached out with her right hand, and turned the hand so that it faced the wall, fingers bent like she was about to catch a baseball.

That little movement, that little bit of magic, dislodged his crystal glass from the wall.

The glass slid into her hand, landing upright, as if she were going to drink out of it.

Only the edges of the glass were yellowish, and some brown streaks were running down the side.

"I'm amazed you could hear anything, given the crud on these walls," she said.

Lo wasn't quite sure how to respond. His emotions were all over the place—admiration for the way that she caught him listening in, annoyance that she had caught him, disgust at the stuff on that glass, and just a hint of embarrassment for his eavesdropping.

He used the thumb and forefinger of his right hand to dislodge the headphone from the area behind his ear.

She walked toward him, extending the glass. "I suppose you're angry that they didn't call you in. I didn't see a need. I also know that you're busy with that machine, so don't let me keep you."

She was taking over, in every way.

"Walk me back to the machine," he said.

She shook her head. "You know how to find it on your own," she said, extending the glass at him even more. The sarcasm in her tone was...lovely. He actually found it appealing, which annoyed him as well.

He took the glass. Its surface was slimy. "I thought you were going to work on the machine."

She swept her hand down the front of her body, careful not to get any of the dirt from the glass on herself.

"These are not work clothes," she said.

He nodded. He wasn't in work clothes either.

"I'd like to talk to you," he said.

Her eyes narrowed. He had initially thought them some kind of brown, but, he realized, they were the color of rich wine. Startling and intelligent and oh-so-clear sighted.

"I don't want to fight with you." She didn't sound tired. She sounded...fed up? He didn't know her well enough to be sure. But she moved her head ever so slightly toward the conference room door, so that he got the context.

She was done talking. She wanted to get to work.

"I wasn't planning on fighting." He gave that conference room an even more pointed look. "You've said some things that I need clarified."

Those eyebrows went up farther, and her gaze grew sharper. She seemed intrigued.

Or maybe he merely hoped she was intrigued.

"Let me take you to lunch," he said.

"There's a place to take someone to lunch?" she asked.

"There are several, actually," he said.

"I don't want a gift," she said, and in that, he heard a certain wariness. She really didn't like the joy magic. He was finding that fascinating.

"I'd say that we'd buy our own lunches, but that's not possible," he said.

"Well, I'm certainly willing to buy mine," she said.

"That's not what I mean," he said. "The food is provided here. Even in the cafés and restaurants. All five of them."

She frowned ever so slightly.

"And don't worry," he said, flipping the spindle from one hand to the other. "Eating in a café is not considered a gift either."

"I'm not worried," she said. "My food is part of my contract."

He nodded.

"But I'm going to decline," she said. "I need to get to work."

He almost moved in front of her, to block her way, but he knew that would be an extremely unpopular maneuver.

"I need to get to work as well," he said. "This is probably the longest I've been away from the machine in years, at least while I'm awake."

"So," she said, and stepped slightly sideways so that she could walk past him. "I'll see you after I change clothes."

"Wait." He held up the hand with the glass, then closed that hand into a fist, making the glass disappear.

She watched it vanish, her expression impassive again. Did she see that as some kind of threat? He hadn't meant it that way.

"Before we get back to work," he said, "before we—you—make any decisions about the machine, I'd really like to talk."

"I don't need to have my position clarified any more than I already have," she said. "I understand my job. I've simply got to do it."

"Then tell me what you understand," he said, "because I don't know what they expect of you."

She looked at his now-empty hand. "You should know. You listened."

"Yeah." He felt frustration growing. "Look, please. Half an hour. We'll meet at the food truck, and walk to the machine."

Her head snapped back just enough to make her obvious surprise visible. "There's a food truck here?"

"Yeah." He smiled. "And it's pretty good, too. Let me give you directions."

She let out a small laugh, then shook her head. "This place constantly surprises me."

It stopped surprising me years ago, he almost said, but didn't. Because if he said that, he would have to add, *But you're surprising me. A lot.*

And he was finding the surprise—intriguing. And worrisome. And just a bit scary.

Just like her.

CHAPTER 14

The food truck was parked just off the main drag, as Lo had called it, although to Dallas, the wide street that housed most of the businesses in the North Pole wasn't a "drag" at all. It was a picture-perfect street from some holiday movie, wide and barely shoveled, with snowbanks tastefully marking off the paths that lead to nearby businesses.

She had gone home and changed into some old jeans, fur-lined boots, and three layers of shirts—a cable-knit sweater over a long-sleeved T-shirt over a tank top. She figured she would need all of them when she worked on the machine.

Over all of that, she had put on her parka, and she was glad of it now. It looked like she'd be out in the snow and the cold for quite a while.

The businesses on the main drag all had Christmas lights (of course) and looked like they'd been shipped in from an alpine movie set from the 1930s. Lots of fake Scandinavian designs (or maybe they were real Scandinavian designs; how was she to know?), lots of toile work, lots of rococo edges. Everything was a chocolate brown with green and white and red decorations.

The doors to the buildings (arched doorways, really) had lovely windows and usually had a wreath at eye level. On either side of the door were windows as well, displaying whatever the store sold, if it was a store, or something related to the business, if it wasn't a store.

She wasn't sure if any of them were stores, not really, because it didn't seem like anyone got paid here. She would have to investigate all of this later. If she had time.

The food cart itself looked like part of a snowbank. It took a moment for her eyes to find the outlines of the cart, which was as lovely and pristine a white as the snow itself.

As she got closer, she realized the cart wasn't a food cart like the ones in California. It wasn't a truck or a gas-powered vehicle with a full restaurant inside.

This cart was actually built like a peddler's cart, with a front that had a bench for the cart's driver. The front of the cart was tipped slightly into the snow, bracing it upright. The shafts and trace were still attached, but buried in the snow, apparently so that the horse or horses or reindeer or whatever pulled this thing when it wasn't serving food, could retire somewhere warmer until they were needed.

Near the cart, the scent of pork frying with onions and garlic filled the cold air. As she got closer, she also smelled baking bread. Closer still, and the scent of peppermint mingled with chocolate, and finally her stomach gave in.

It growled.

She was hungrier than she thought.

She rounded the last snowbank, only to see a small line—four people —waiting for food. Most of them were standing comfortably on the path, but one was a small elf, wearing green everywhere, and a stocking cap with a bell on the end, just as if he (she?) had jumped down off a shelf.

The elf was shifting from foot to foot, clearly cold, and he (definitely a he, now that she saw half his face) had his hands shoved under his armpits in a vain attempt to stay warm. He was next in line.

Dallas got at the end of the line, wondering how she was going to explain that her meals were paid for by Claus & Company. Three people worked inside the cart, all of them wearing hairnets and blue aprons over blue and white clothing.

The lack of red, green, and gold actually made Dallas's eyes relax. She'd been growing tired of the color scheme here.

The elf climbed up on an ice block Dallas hadn't even seen until he used it to make his order. He spoke rapidly, seeming to know what he wanted.

That made her look at the menu. She had no idea what half the food was. Latkes, spaetzle, gubbröra, leberkäse—the list went on and on, and had no pictures at all.

She wished she was carrying her phone, so that she could look it all up, and see what was truly being offered here. And what, underneath it all, was giving off that slightly fishy smell.

"You look lost," a deep male voice said in her ear.

She started. It was unusual for anyone to sneak up on her, let alone get this close. She turned, expecting to see the man standing so close that she'd have to push him back.

Instead, she was looking at Lo's face, which was nowhere near her head. He was the proper distance behind her, and he smiled at her surprise.

"It's a bit of an amplification chamber here with the snow columns," he said softly. "So if you don't want to be overheard, save your comments for later."

She appreciated the warning. She might have started back into their discussion on the machine.

She waved a mittened hand at the cart. "I have no idea what any of this is," she said.

"Ah, not a regular visitor to Northern Europe," he said.

She had been. She had done a lot of work on magical machines in various parts of Scandinavia, Sweden, Norway, and Germany. But she had never ordered food. She had just eaten whatever her hosts had given her, and then had gone back to work.

She had no idea how to explain that or even if she should.

"Tell me what you're in the mood for? Pork? Beef? Chicken? Fish? I'm afraid no one really does vegetarian here, and vegan is laughable. Dairy is in everything." He wasn't smiling as he said that last. Apparently the dairy thing was a problem for some, and he was being sensitive.

"Fish? Where do they get fish around here?" she asked, deciding not to talk about the other cuisines. She liked dairy, especially cheese. She usually lived on cheese and bread whenever she was in Europe. "I thought this part of the pole was landlocked."

"Pickled," he said. "The fish is all pickled. And believe me, it's an acquired taste."

She shuddered. She'd had lutefisk and other kinds of pickled fish, and she was not a fan.

"And be careful," he said. "Any kind of egg dish, like an egg salad, usually has anchovies."

Her shudder grew worse.

"So, if you trust me, I'll order for you," he said. "Let me ask again: Beef? Pork—?"

"You pick," she said. "As long as it's not pickled, I'll be all right."

"Then we'll go with the staple." He stepped in front of her, and smiled at the red-cheeked young man taking orders. The young man even had a hairnet on his wispy blond beard. "Meatballs."

Dallas opened her mouth to protest, but then closed it. She had said Lo could pick, so she let him.

The young man said something to Lo, and they both laughed. Then one of the women leaned out of the back, and commented on the fact that Lo was actually getting lunch. Apparently that was a rare thing.

"Make it good," he said. "This will be our guest's first trip to this cart."

"Ah, yeah," said the woman, smiling at Dallas. "We'll make sure it's not your last, then."

Dallas smiled politely, and wondered how they could guarantee it. They were chattering in the back, with just a bit of laughter.

She was watching Lo closely. He didn't pay for anything, so he wasn't giving her a gift.

He beckoned her to come closer, which she did, nearly hitting the toe of her right boot on that ice block.

The woman handed Dallas a cloth bag filled with boxed food that steamed. Then the woman handed her a thermos.

Dallas thanked her, and moved out of the way, so that others could get close.

Lo followed, carrying just as much food.

"What is all of this?" she asked, lifting the bag.

"You'll see," he said. "It's best if we eat it here."

"Outside?" she asked.

"Otherwise, the machine area will reek of food for most of the day," he said.

She was going to freeze to death, and no one would care. These people thought it normal to eat outside in snow. She barely liked standing in snow for ten minutes.

Lo lead her to an open area filled with tables that were made of polished wood, with etchings on top. Matching benches stood on either side. Farther away, there were tables made of polished ice. The benches near those tables, also made of ice, had little divots, clearly made by warm butts.

Most of the ice tables were filled. The wooden tables were not.

Lo sat down at the edge of one of the tables, and pulled the boxes out of his bag. The air smelled of onion and butter, and Dallas's stomach growled again.

Dallas hovered for a moment. She had never eaten outside in the cold. It felt weird to do so.

Lo continued to pull out food, as well as serving utensils. Dallas watched, wondering how long it would take to walk back to her place and eat there.

Probably long enough for the food to grow cold.

She sighed and sat down, tucking her parka underneath her bottom so that her butt wouldn't get cold—immediately, anyway.

Lo pushed two of the boxes toward her. One box was large, plate-sized. The other was much smaller, and had "dessert" written along the top.

He waved at her thermos. "I assumed coffee. If that's not right, go back and get what you need."

She was going to end up mainlining coffee for the next few weeks, maybe even the next few months, if that meeting this morning was any indication. She was going to have to repair the machine, so that it would remain the same inefficient thing that it had always been.

She peeled off her mittens and shoved them in her pockets. The cold hit her bare skin, cramping her fingers. Lo didn't even seem to notice, but then, he lived here.

She lived in a place that hadn't seen snow in decades, and she liked it like that.

Still, she decided not to complain (out loud, anyway), and tugged the larger box open. Inside, perfectly round meatballs rested on a bed of macaroni, covered in a light cream sauce. On the right side, some red berry things were shoved against the food, and on the left, some green vegetables that looked vaguely like brussels sprouts.

The steam hit her, smelling of ground pork and onions, making her mouth water.

She picked up a fork and waved it over the berries. "What are these?" she asked.

Lo looked up at her. "Lingonberries."

"And they are?" She sounded fussy. She was feeling fussy.

He shrugged. "Berries...? I don't know. They go well with the meal. Try one."

She decided to try the meatballs first. They were soft and delicious, made with some pepper and allspice mixed in with the meat. The cream sauce was rich and filling all by itself.

She finally tried the lingonberries, only to discover that they were tart and sour with just a hint of sweetness, which somehow enhanced the flavors of the entire meal.

She let out a small contented sigh, and then worried if the enjoyment she was having of the meal came from the food itself or because someone had given it to her.

"You can't be suspicious of everything here," Lo said, gently.

She looked up at him. She had the sense he understood exactly what she was going through.

"Sometimes a meal is delicious in its own right," he said. "That doesn't mean someone put a dollop of joy in it."

"But you said everything here was filled with joy," she said.

"We try," he said. "That doesn't mean we're trying to manipulate you."

She wanted to argue that. Because, really, everything that had a joy not her own was manipulating her.

"Think about it," he said. "You know how magic works. Eventually you become immune to certain spells. No one here knew you were coming or where you were going to eat. So the joy that's in the food is legitimate joy, not behavior-changing manipulation. No one here is going to feel different because they ate the meal."

There was some logic to that. Dallas nodded at him, and continued to eat before the food got too cold. The meal was delicious, even though it had to be crammed with calories. She hadn't eaten anything this rich in years.

She was going to have to quit long before she finished the box in front of her. And the dessert was going to have to wait until later.

Lo was eating slowly. He set his fork to the side, and glanced around.

No one was sitting near them, which seemed to make him relax a little.

"I wanted to ask you what you meant by the children being left behind," he said. "We pride ourselves on making sure every child who wants one gets a visit from Santa."

She shook her head. She had known this conversation was coming. She simply hadn't expected to have it with Lo.

"I take it there's no echo chamber here?" she asked.

His mouth was a thin line. "That's right."

She let out a small sigh, then pushed the second half of her food into a pile, and folded the box closed. She put the dessert box on top of it.

"I didn't mean to make you stop eating," Lo said.

"If I eat any more," she said, "I'll be too full to do anything this afternoon."

She was already approaching that state. She grabbed the thermos, twisted off the top, and set down the plastic cup. The coffee was rich and dark and aromatic. Not fancy, just good strong coffee.

Which she needed.

Lo watched her every move. He was clearly going to wait until she answered the question directly.

"How long has it been since you left the North Pole?" she asked.

He leaned back just a little, frowned, and then shrugged. "The machine has been all con…" His voice trailed off. "Um, I have no idea. A long time."

"How long?" she asked. She knew she was pushing, but she wanted him to be clear on this.

He was shaking his head. "Not in this century," he said.

"And before that?" she asked.

He opened his hands. "I did some field work at some of the bigger computer centers, talked to a few computer scientists at MIT and Caltech, as well as—"

"How long?" she asked, not willing to let him ramble. She had a guess, and she wanted him to confirm it.

"I don't know," he said quietly. "Mid-century, maybe?"

That's what she would have guessed, based on some of the computer tech that he had incorporated into his machine.

"A less enlightened time," she said as charitably as she could.

His frown deepened. "What does that mean?" he asked, sounding offended. Apparently, she hadn't been charitable enough.

She grabbed her mittens. Her hands were cold, and her mittens were warm from being inside her pockets.

She was going to have to give the delicate little speech she had planned for the Old Men in Charge, the speech they had short-circuited with their defensiveness.

It looked like Lo might be just as defensive.

"There were about 2.5 billion people on the Earth in 1950," she said, "and mass media wasn't like it is now."

"Meaning…?" he asked.

She raised a finger, silently asking him to wait. He looked at that finger as if it had offended him too, so she slipped on the mittens. She would end this conversation quickly if he got even more defensive.

"Now, there are 7.5 billion people, more or less, and they're all connected. Or they can be, if they want to."

The look on his face told her that he knew that, and she was insulting him by being this clear. But she was going to build her argument.

"The commercialization of Christmas," she said, "had some strange impacts on non-Christians, the non-religious, and other religions that celebrate holidays at the same time of year. More and more of them added gifts into the mix."

"Yeah," he said curtly. "But Santa doesn't belong to a religion. He is his own entity."

"And this morning, I just got asked if I was a believer," she said.

Lo closed his eyes, then nodded, and opened them. "I'm not going to apologize for the Old Men in Charge."

"I'm not asking you to," she said. "But the world has moved beyond your little operation here. Let's take other cultures out of this, cultures that don't accept capitalism or celebrate holidays that began as pagan holidays or Christian holidays. Let's just look at children who want some attention during the holiday."

She didn't say gifts. She wasn't really thinking of gifts.

Lo sighed and folded up his box. He set it back in the cloth bag. "Kids don't always get what they ask for, and some ask for something for someone else—"

"And there are so many children who would like one toy or maybe even a nice shirt," she said. "They don't get a present at all. Their parents can't afford one, if they even having living parents, and the holiday passes them by. These kids go to bed hungry and some are homeless—"

"We don't have that kind of magic here," Lo said. "We try to get the word out. We have a charitable arm to handle some of that. Otherwise, much as we would love to create world peace and get rid of poverty, that's not our magic. It's one bit of joy—"

"Which these kids don't get," she said.

"Complainers—" he started, and then saw something on her face. Whatever that something was (probably the anger that was welling inside her) stopped him from continuing along that line. "How do you know that kids aren't being reached?"

"If you did the job you think you're doing," she said, "how come there are thousands of giving trees all over America, not to mention other countries that make Christmas a national holiday?"

"Giving trees?"

She fished her phone out of her pocket, and opened the photos. She didn't want to use magic for this, because she didn't want to be accused of altering the image for her own political purposes.

She had taken pictures the previous Christmas, like she always did, photographing the giving trees with their little pieces of paper, marked *Girl Age 7* or *Boy Age 3*. She wanted to make sure no one added more paper, because at the end of the holiday season, at the very last minute, she fulfilled the remaining gifts on at least one tree. She couldn't afford to do all of them, but she could do one, usually the one with the most left.

She slid the phone over to Lo, who stared at it like it was going to burn him.

"What am I supposed to see?" he asked.

"These trees are everywhere," she said. "The paper ornaments become gift tags."

She tapped the screen and made the image grow so he could read the ornaments for himself.

His face flushed. "What is this?"

"They're called giving trees. Usually homeless shelters or impoverished schools or religious institutions have them so that kids who would normally go without on Christmas will get at least one gift. It's an impersonal gift—I mean, how am I supposed to know what 'Girl Age 5' wants? Does she already know how to read, does she like books? Should I buy her a pink stuffed animal or a pink sweater or maybe she hates pink and only takes what's given because that's all that's available."

He was staring at the images as if he had never seen anything like this before. "How many of these trees did you say?"

"I have no idea," she said. "They're everywhere. They show up in November. You have to give by mid-December. And then there are the Toys for Tots drives, and the sponsored giveaways, usually from some local media company, or firehouses or police departments. And even that doesn't reach all of the children who need something. Just one gift. Just one little piece of hope during the holiday."

Lo raised his head and turned away ever so slightly, but not before she saw that his eyes were lined with tears.

"Niko," he said more to himself than to her.

"What?" Dallas asked.

"Niko." Lo wiped a thumb underneath his lower eyelid, first one, then the other. "He's The Big Guy's third son. They had a falling out. Niko said that we weren't doing the job, that our charity was failing, and everyone thought he was bitter because he wasn't really in line for the Big Sleigh—"

She assumed the Big Sleigh was a euphemistic way to refer to the job of Santa.

"—and Niko vowed to do what he could. But he kept demanding that Claus & Company do more, and eventually, there was some kind of rift, something big." Lo shook his head a little. "He runs some charity in the Greater World now."

She hadn't expected anything like that. A rift? In Claus & Company? Among the S-Elves? Among Santa's direct relatives?

From everything she had ever heard, life was perfect here. How could there be a rift?

Well, then, clearly, not everything was perfect here.

"He runs a charity?" she repeated, thinking maybe she had misheard. "I assume it's tied to Claus & Company."

Lo shrugged and ran a hand over his face, his thumb and forefinger lingering over his eyes.

"A charity," she repeated for the second time. "With all of the resources available here."

"Yeah." Lo hadn't moved his fingers away from his eyes. Then he did, and smiled at her, but his eyes were sad. "You're telling me that Niko was right."

It was her turn to shake her head. She didn't want to be involved in any family feud.

"I don't know anything about Niko," she said. "I just know that your system fails more children than it helps."

Lo bowed his head. "I don't know how that can be. We work so hard…"

She didn't interrupt him, just let him sit with the information.

Slowly, he raised his head. "But the children we do help, the ones we're in touch with, they're doing all right, aren't they?"

"I have no idea," she said. "I don't have much contact with children year-round."

"Yet you see the children who get nothing," he said. It didn't sound accusatory, more questioning.

"Everyone does," she said. "If they only look."

He leaned back as if she had slapped him. He had taken that as a criticism. She hadn't meant it that way. She raised a hand, as if to hold off his reaction.

"I didn't mean—"

"It doesn't matter," he said. "I've been so busy keeping the machine alive that I stopped doing the most important thing."

She frowned. "What's that?"

"Making sure that it serves its purpose," he said.

"I thought its purpose was to handle the lists," she said.

"Among other things," he said. Then he smiled, sadly, wistfully. His gaze hadn't met hers in a long time. "You know, when I offered to build the machine, I saw a need for it. I knew how the company was working, and I knew what direction it wanted to go in. I also knew what was going on in at least parts of the world."

She sipped on her coffee. It had already cooled. It was cold out here, but she had stopped noticing, which surprised her.

"I knew that as medicine improved, the relationship of adults with their children grew closer. Children weren't as vulnerable, so they could be spoiled more." His sad smile grew just a little. "That's when we learned, or maybe when I learned, the limits to our magic. We couldn't save lives, and we couldn't stop sicknesses. We didn't have that kind of magic. We couldn't change culture and we didn't know about germs, just like everyone else. We just knew that cultures with a history of cleanliness had fewer incidences of disease and death. But we didn't know how to share that information, and believe me, I worked on it."

Then he shook his head again, as if getting rid of that thought. He sighed, that sad smile plastered on his face as if drawn there permanently.

"We did what we could, and the machine made doing what we could faster and better, and I got sucked into keeping the machine going...." He stopped, bent his head again, and ran his hands through his hair.

She couldn't take it any longer. She hadn't meant to make him so very sad. She had expected anger, denial, even a demand that she leave.

But not sadness.

She extended her hand across that cold tabletop, and touched his elbow. He brought his head up, his hair tousled. His sad smile was gone.

"If what you're saying is true," he said, "they're not going to want to fix this."

They, she assumed, meant the Old Men in Charge.

"They've been around so long, they think they know everything. They haven't listened to anyone for a very long time."

She wanted to say, *What I told you is true*, but she knew better than to do that. She'd watched others change long-held opinions, and those people had gone through stages.

First, they didn't believe. Then they heard. And then, they doubted, just a little. Sometimes, they sought out proof. Sometimes, the denial came back. And sometimes, they made changes.

He was in the third stage. Whether or not he'd make changes remained to be seen.

"What do you suggest we do?" she asked.

He gathered the last of their lunch into the cloth bag.

"You take the thermoses," he said, "and I'll take the leftovers and desserts and put them in the break room that's near the machine."

"I thought you said that if we ate near the machine, the smells would linger."

"I did," he said, "because the break room is no place to eat. But it does have a refrigerator and a microwave. We can heat up food if we want to. I usually use the refrigerator to store my meals, and then take them home. If I remember."

He smiled wryly, but the smile didn't reach his eyes.

She had really saddened him. That surprised her.

"You go ahead to the machine," he said. "I'll catch up with you."

That surprised her as well. She had figured he would want to supervise her, now more than ever.

"All right," she said. "I'll see you there."

She stood and dusted off the back of her parka. It was cold, but she wasn't. She was a lot more comfortable than she expected to be.

"Do you know how to find the right building?" he asked.

She nodded.

"I'll join you shortly," he said.

He clearly needed time alone. She didn't blame him. She had given him a lot to think about and, to his credit, he was thinking about it.

She poured the rest of her coffee into the thermos and put the cup on the top. Then she took the thermos he held out to her. She smiled at him—and she had a hunch her smile was just a little sad too—and then she headed back the way she had come. She had no idea if this was the most efficient way to get to the machine building, but she was going to go the way she knew.

She felt shaky and unsettled, not at all the way she had expected to feel after telling someone here at Claus & Company about their failures. She had expected to feel adrenaline, some righteous indignation, a bit of fury.

But not sadness. And a feeling that she might have just started something that she couldn't control. As well as something that might create change—and not necessarily for the better.

CHAPTER 15

*L*o couldn't move. Not yet, anyway. His limbs felt heavy. The full extent of his exhaustion hit him, and not just because he had stopped moving at full speed.

He had a sickening feeling that all of the work he'd been doing had been for naught.

The skies had turned a powdery gray. Snow was coming. The air had a crisp, damp edge that told him that the snow would be plentiful, and serious, a storm rather than flurries.

He should get up, but he should have done that a few minutes ago, when Dallas wandered off in the wrong direction. She was going back the way she came, not heading directly toward the machine.

She probably didn't know the abundance of trails that meandered through Santa's Village. They weren't well signposted because there was no need for that. Everyone who lived here had lived here a long time. Or they were born here.

Which made her comments all the more plausible.

The North Pole had become even more insular than it had been designed to be. It was always a secretive place, partly to add an air of mystery. But those who didn't want to live here left to work at the various outposts around the world.

Lo had no idea if they had sent word back about giving trees and children left behind. He wasn't sure they had noticed.

Most of the elves and mages who worked at the various outposts had specific tasks, like checking chimneys and double-checking the lists to see if children had moved in the intervening year. Claus & Company tried, in its last-century way, to make sure every child was covered. But they thought of moving as a threat, not gaps in the system.

Lo could see how the focus could get lost. Most of the elves and mages weren't trained to look for trends. They were supposed to do a specific job, and they did that job, usually with aplomb.

He let out a small sigh, his—fifteenth, maybe?—since Dallas had told him about the giving trees.

He glanced toward her, but she was long gone.

She did have an agenda. She wanted to replace the machine, and the best way to do that was to get him out of the way. But the Old Men in Charge would prevent her from creating a new machine, and she seemed to know that.

However, if she had Lo on her side, everything would change.

He stood, his knees cracking just a bit. He couldn't remember the last time he had sat still that long.

He didn't know her. He didn't know what she wanted and what, really, her company wanted either. He had no idea if she was doing their bidding or acting on her own impulses.

He also didn't know if the company she worked for did better (made a profit? Were they trying to profit?) if they replaced magical machinery with something of their own. He knew some organizations that always liked to use their own magic and their own equipment, sometimes to the detriment of the people they were trying to help.

Lo picked up the cloth bag, then set it down again. He couldn't resolve this by guessing. He actually needed information.

He glanced around. The other tables were empty, except for one of the ice tables closest to the food truck. There, some young elves sat and ate and giggled, clearly having a great time.

Lo couldn't hear them, so he knew they couldn't hear him either.

So, he sat back down. Then he moved the cloth bag to the food truck side of the table, so that no one could see what he was doing, even if they looked.

He whirled a finger in a small circle, and created an opening in the cold, clear air. He sent a little magical push through that opening, searching for Niko North.

For a long minute, nothing happened. Then the opening grew. It was bright yellow, with touches of blue, and it took a moment for Lo's eyes to process what he was seeing.

A sunny day at the edge of some very large blue lake. Only there was no beach. Something white, maybe concrete, and the sounds of laughter and conversation filled the air.

Then Niko North's face filled the opening. He looked the same—square jaw, angular nose, and pale blond hair that needed just a bit of a trim.

But, Lo hadn't realized until this moment, just how much Niko looked like the other S-Elves, particularly in the Santa line. They all had that angular face—at least when they were young and relatively thin. Niko wasn't relatively thin. He was thin, which was unusual among S-Elves.

His pale blond eyebrows had gone up, wrinkling his ridiculously smooth forehead.

"Lothario Johanssen? Is that really you? Where are you?"

Had it been so long that Niko had forgotten what the main part of Santa's Village looked like?

"Santa Central," Lo said.

Niko let out an audible sigh. "I should have known, but I had hoped that you were elsewhere."

"With all this snow?" Lo asked.

"It is winter in some places other than the Pole," Niko said, but he sounded a bit sad about it. Lo wasn't quite sure why.

"I have a question for you," Lo said.

Niko gave him a sad smile. "All business, right up front. I guess that's no surprise."

That caught Lo up short. Apparently, he had just been rude and he hadn't realized it. He also had no idea why his being rude was no surprise. Had he been rude to people a lot? Or maybe this wasn't about Lo. So he said as politely and with as courteous a tone as he could manage, "I'm sorry. Did I miss a memo?"

"How about 'How are you, Niko? How's married life treating you? Do you like living in the Greater World—?'"

"You're married?" Lo felt as if he were suddenly riding down an avalanche. The S-Elves always had elaborate weddings, with ice sculptures and piles of gifts and music and fancy clothing and drinking. Actual drinking, which almost never happened here at the Pole.

Had Lo been so busy he had somehow missed Niko's?

"For two years now," Niko said. "You didn't know?"

"No, I didn't," Lo said. "Last I remember, you were working with the charitable arm and you tried to implement things that the Old Men in Charge weren't that fond of."

Niko let out a breath of air, as if he were trying to calm himself with his breath. "You...never got the invitation to the wedding?"

Lo's cheeks heated. He hadn't paid attention to a lot of niceties over the past decade or two. "I don't know," he said. "I've been deep in the machine."

Niko smiled. "Which is normal."

"Not like this," Lo said. "The machine...oh, it's a long story, Niko."

Niko nodded. He was clearly moving, because the scenery behind him had blurred. The blue lake met a bluer sky, and Lo could see sailboats on it. The sun made the water twinkle.

When had Lo last experienced summer? Hot summer? Sitting-on-the-beach summer? He couldn't remember.

The perspective shifted again, as Niko clearly sat down. The smooth metal of some kind of pole—a telephone pole? Weren't they made of wood? A streetlight, then? A sign pole?—was visible behind him, as well as some kids bobbing in and out of Lo's sight, as they were apparently riding skateboards.

He had no idea where Niko was or what he was doing or how any of this was happening. He couldn't quite remember where Niko was supposed to be—Chicago? St. Louis? Detroit? Somewhere Midwest. But the area around Nike didn't look urban. Except for the metal pole, and the concrete, and the kids on skateboards.

"You said you had a business question." Niko's voice had gentled.

"I do, yes." Lo glanced around. The elves who had been sitting at the table near the food cart were gone now. Lo was alone at the tables, and for good reason. A chill wind had come up. He was actually getting cold, which almost never happened to him.

Niko was watching him, waiting patiently. Lo had interrupted Niko doing something or other. Lo should probably hurry up so that Niko could get back to it.

"You're working with the charitable arm, right?" Lo asked.

"I have nothing to do with Claus & Company any longer," Niko said.

Lo frowned. He'd heard that Niko was a problem from time to time, and Niko's vocal displeasure at the way that Claus & Company handled the poverty and religious issues from the Greater World had upset the Old Men in Charge, but to have nothing to do with Claus & Company?

That was unheard of.

"You're an S-Elf," Lo said. "You're in the running for Santa should something—"

"No," Niko said. "I'm not. My family and I don't speak at all anymore, Lo."

Well, then Lo *had* missed a memo. The rumors were that Niko had become unreasonable over some charity thing and that he had opted to stay in the Greater World, but the extent of this rift—that they didn't even celebrate occasions together…Lo hadn't heard about it at all.

"You didn't have the wedding here, then, did you?" Lo asked, and felt stupid the moment the question had come out of his mouth. If Niko had had the wedding here, Lo would have heard about it, and probably remembered it, considering the guilt he would have felt for missing it.

"And no one from there showed up either." Niko's square jaw was set as if he was clenching his teeth.

Lo had stumbled into an emotional thicket he didn't know how to extricate himself from.

"I'm sorry, Niko," he said. "I had no idea."

Niko smiled without humor. "Clearly. Your question?"

"Um, well, I'm going to have to phrase it differently," Lo said. His mind was racing. He had assumed that Niko was still with the family business, and had insights on how the business worked inside the Greater World.

But Niko wasn't, and that made Lo uncomfortable.

Niko sighed, and glanced at someone Lo couldn't see. He could hear laughter in the background—those skateboarders—but he couldn't hear anyone else nearby.

"You...um...live in the Greater World now," Lo said, and instantly wished he could retract the words. Yes, of course Niko lived in the Greater World. That was clear. "Have you ever seen giving trees at Christmas time?"

"Giving trees?" Niko thankfully didn't point out that Lo had been stating the obvious before that. "You mean those trees with cards on them that people can take to provide gifts to needy children?"

Lo suppressed a curse, and it took a bit of effort. He couldn't remember the last time he had repressed an actual foul-mouthed curse. Sometimes he uttered light curses, usually about the machine. But something foul—he hadn't done that in a long time.

It showed just how angry he was. Because Niko's response verified what Dallas had said. Those trees existed.

"Yeah," Lo said quietly. "I mean those. Have you seen any?"

"They're impossible to miss," Niko said. "They're everywhere. And they don't get the job done. Used to be, people would clear the trees long before Thanksgiving, but in the past decade, things have gotten worse. The difference between rich and poor, at least in the developed countries, has grown, and the need for even the basics have grown. You have no idea how many children live in poverty, Lo. And worse, how many are homeless. You—"

"I thought we were doing something about these things," Lo said, not sure he wanted to hear the entire litany of woe, particularly if it matched what Dallas had told him. "You know. The charitable arm."

"Oh, we tried to do something in the 1990s," Niko said. "The charitable arm actually did things. One of my uncles started a program that launched some of the charitable toy drives, which met some of the need at holiday time. And when I was still part of Claus & Company, there was a poverty wing of the organization and a religious wing, trying to get gifts to kids with no fixed address and to kids who practiced religions other than some form of Christianity. But the outreach, particularly in the religious wing, was incredibly insensitive, and—"

"Insensitive?" Lo asked. "How can gift-giving be insensitive?"

"Not every culture thinks children should be given a gift in a ritual setting, Lothario." Niko's voice was softer, his tone gentle, even though his words were not.

Lo nodded. He sort of understood that. Kinda. But those really weren't the words that had caught him. The words that had caught him were in the middle of the first part of Niko's rant. *No fixed address.* Lo hadn't thought of that. Homeless to him meant that they had no home, and he knew—he *knew* because he had programmed the machine—that every single official shelter received gifts for its inhabitants.

"I was told, just today," Lo said, "that we're missing thousands of children from our lists every year. And worse, we're insulting some families. And worse than that, we're inspiring greed by focusing on gifts rather than...I don't know. I don't completely understand that argument. But we're not doing as much good as we think we are."

"That's fascinating," Niko said. "Someone at the North Pole told you that?"

"An outsider, but yeah, here. Not an hour ago."

Niko's eyebrows went up again. Half of his mouth quirked up in a smile. "Wow. Speaking truth to power."

"You're saying that's correct?" Lo asked.

"I don't know about the greed," Niko said. "But yes, the rest of it? Absolutely. Any child living below the poverty line or even slightly above it doesn't really get to celebrate the kind of Christmas that my family champions."

"But we're set up to bring toys to kids like that," Lo said, aware that he sounded defensive.

"Once upon a time, maybe," Niko said. "But the need is great, and the problems are vast, and a system set up in the 1940s and 1950s is just not equal to the task of handling twenty-first-century problems."

"Is that why you left?" Lo asked.

"I—we—" Niko stopped himself and sighed. "I tried to set up a bigger charity inside of Claus & Company. They deemed it a failure before it started, and moved on."

There was something in his tone—anger?

Was this the source of all the rumors? Niko's charitable arm?

"I never heard about this," Lo said. "Which isn't a surprise, given what I do. But I would have thought that they would bring you back here if the charitable arm wasn't working the way they wanted it to."

"Well, they tried to bring me back," Niko said. Yep, that was definitely anger in his voice. "*After* they shut down the charity. They were going to send me for behavioral therapy, to remind me what you all do there."

You all. Like he was no longer a part of Claus & Company. Or the family. Or any part of it.

"They were going to send me to work in the Toy Workshop and work my way back into everyone's 'good graces.'" Niko's eyes were flashing. "I was trying to help children, and Claus & Company wasn't willing to do what it takes. All that image and marketing focus has hurt the company, Lothario."

Lo hadn't thought of it that way. He'd been thinking about image and marketing as it pertained to the interactions *inside* the Pole. The marketing people were obsessed with Santa's image. One of them had gotten the bright idea to photograph the machine and use it in marketing, but Lo had stopped them—mostly because he didn't want anyone to see how cobbled-together the machine was.

He hadn't realized that marketing and image management were a problem outside of the Pole as well.

He needed to think about this, all of it, and he couldn't do it here, on the bench, in the growing cold.

But he didn't want to be rude. Again. So he said, "If you're not working for Claus & Company, then what are you doing?"

Niko gave him a slight smile. "I started my own charity. It's much smaller than something I could have built with Claus & Company's resources, but the charity is growing, and we're making a difference here in Chicagoland."

"Chicago?" Lo asked. "You're only focused on Chicago?"

"We can't afford to go larger," Niko said. "Not yet. As I said, the need is too great."

"And yours is a Christmas charity?"

"No." Niko glanced again to his side, as if someone else were monitoring the conversation. "We're trying to provide assistance year-round. Not just gifts. But food and shelter and clothing. Mental health services. Domestic abuse prevention. Anger management. Substance abuse programs—"

"That's not what Claus & Company does," Lo blurted. This place was about gifts, and gifts only.

"Oh, believe me, I know that," Niko said. "Hence the rift. I wanted to change the mission. No one does that, and stays with Claus & Company. Not even an actual Claus."

Lo ran a hand over his face. His eyes had filled again. He had worked his butt off, and for what, exactly? Not what he had so proudly pontificated to Dallas. Joy for everyone?

"So," Lo said, because he couldn't keep quiet. "That dollop of joy we were raised to revere. That's...what? So last century?"

Niko's face had grown very serious, and Lo thought he saw compassion in Niko's eyes.

"Joy is important," Niko said. "Now more than ever. That dollop of joy matters, Lothario. Don't let me or anyone else tell you differently. That bit of joy sometimes gets people through horrendous days. And that's worthwhile."

It was a pep talk of sorts, but Lo didn't want a pep talk. He wanted reality.

"But, if what you're saying is true, we're not even doing that." Lo said.

"You're doing more than you think," Niko said. "It's not always the presents. It's the escapism in the holiday movies on television and the stories that people share with their friends. The season itself provides some joy."

"We're not creating those things," Lo said.

"Oh, you've done some of it," Niko said.

"Not me," Lo said.

"Well, no, not directly," Niko said, "but Claus & Company has spon-sored a few things."

"A few." Lo felt miserable. He hadn't wanted any of this news.

"More than that, though," Niko said, "Claus & Company has inspired a lot of holiday joy. The image and marketing wing has really dialed up the holiday in the last two decades. That's both good and bad, but mostly good."

"It's good?" Lo wasn't sure he understood. He thought Niko had just told him that image and marketing was bad.

"Mythmaking can help. Stories help," Niko said. "It took me a long time to accept that one of the best things I do every year is play Santa at local events."

"You 'play' Santa?" Lo asked.

Niko gave him the first real smile of the conversation. "Yes, and I enjoy it more than I probably should."

"Well," Lo said, "I don't work for image and marketing, and I'm certainly not going to play Santa somewhere. I'm supposed to keep the machine going, because without it, I'm told, the entire enterprise will fall apart."

He sucked in a mouthful of cold air, half wanting Niko to stop him from continuing. But Niko didn't say anything; Niko just listened.

"I've spent decades, Niko, keeping the machine going. And now, you and—" Lo almost said Dallas's name, then stopped himself. He didn't want Niko to know about her, for reasons Lo hadn't really explored yet. He substituted, "—and this outsider tell me that what we're doing has no meaning. We're supposed to keep the lists, so every child who wants one gets at least one toy. We're failing at that."

Niko stared at him for a long moment, and then said, "Yes. Yes, you are."

Lo let out a shaky breath. "And you're telling me your family knows this?"

Niko shrugged, then shook his head. "I told them. But I don't think they believed me, Lothario. They blame me for being a malcontent and a screwup. I don't think they want to hear it."

Lo nodded. He had heard the malcontent arguments, the screwup comments. He had heard that Niko had left because he preferred the Greater World.

Lies? Or was that word too harsh? Had Claus & Company finally started believing its own hype? Thinking it did everything right when in truth it struggled with its very mission?

"I'm sorry to be so blunt," Niko said into the silence.

Lo didn't remember Niko being the kind of man who apologized like that. The Claus family rarely apologized for anything. Maybe things had changed.

"I'm the one who should apologize," Lo said. "I interrupted your day."

"It's all right." Niko's smile had faded into something polite. "I haven't talked about home for a long time."

"Do you miss it?" Lo asked before he could stop himself.

Niko shrugged. "Parts. Friends, mostly. I don't miss the politics. I don't miss fighting for everything I believe in."

Lo nodded. He was just beginning to understand what Niko was talking about. Until now, Lo had dealt with all of the politics by ignoring it.

And then the Old Men in Charge hired Dallas and, if Lo didn't do things the way someone wanted him to, would take his machine away from him.

He was no longer sure if that would be a bad thing.

"If you're going to make some changes," Niko was saying, "you probably shouldn't mention my name. I haven't been there in years, but my departure was not on the best terms."

Lo nodded. "I understand," he said. "I'll keep you out of it."

Niko nodded, and looked away as if something besides the skateboarders caught his attention.

"Thank you, Niko," Lo said. "You didn't have to talk to me, and you certainly didn't have to be honest with me. I appreciate it."

Niko's gaze returned to Lo. Niko gave him a small smile.

"Any time, old friend," Niko said, and, with one large hand, he squeezed the portal between them closed.

Lo found himself staring at gray clouds where Niko and the sunshine had been. Snow was beginning to fall, and a wind had come up. The food cart was shuttered. He was alone out here, and a storm was brewing.

More than one, maybe. He didn't like thinking that Dallas had been right. More than right, if Niko could be believed.

Which begged the question: If she was right, what could Lo do about it?

He had no idea. But he had a hunch—a very strong hunch—that Dallas did.

CHAPTER 16

*D*allas stood at the very end of the machine, near the so-called printer, hands on her hips. Sweat trickled down the right side of her face. She had taken off the sweater and the T-shirt somewhere along her tour. Now, even the tank top felt like too much. And her jeans were sticking to her backside in an unpleasant, clammy way.

She really had no idea how she was going to make this contraption functional. The Old Men in Charge wanted it to keep doing what it was doing, only more efficiently, and she supposed that was possible. But she wasn't sure how. And she wasn't sure what she could contribute besides an extra pair of hands to help Lo keep the machine running.

He was the one who knew how to coax it to run even when it shouldn't. And he had made all of the disparate pieces work together even though, logically, they shouldn't have worked at all.

That was the problem, ultimately. There was no logic here. Somehow, Lo had constructed this contraption with a wing and a prayer. A dollop of magic here, a bit of common sense there, and the machine worked.

She was actually afraid to tamper with it, for fear that she would break it. And if he were taken off the project entirely, she was afraid the machine would stop working.

She was afraid it would go on strike or mourn.

She wondered if anyone else in the North Pole had figured out that this machine was sentient. It had become an actual creature, which was what happened to some magical items when they were used continually by the same person. It was as if they were part canine, and wanted ever so much to please their creators. They were less machines and more companion.

It would break the machine to lose Lo. She wondered if it would break Lo to lose the machine.

She let out a small sigh. What might happen didn't matter. The Old Men in Charge had made it clear: they wanted to keep the machine running. And Lo had made that clear as well, before she had realized the extent of the problem.

She just wasn't sure what she could do here.

She wiped the sweat off the side of her face with the back of her hand, and then burped. She'd been burping onions and allspice ever since she overate at lunch. Her sweat probably smelled of garlic, not that there was anyone here to notice.

"Thinking about tearing it down?"

Lo's voice startled her, and surprisingly—to her, at least—her first thought was of the garlic she ate and the fact that her tank and her jeans showed just how sweaty she was.

She turned toward him, feeling wilted, and probably looking it as well.

He looked different than he had at lunch. Sadder, if that was possible. Exhausted, which she hadn't noticed before. Smaller, in an odd way, as if their conversation had diminished him.

Maybe the day before, she would have told him one of those jokes that hid the truth: *I'm not allowed to tear it down, remember?* She would have said that with a smile to lessen the impact of her words.

But she didn't have the heart, not after seeing his face. Maybe not even before.

"I was trying to figure out how, exactly, it works," she said.

"I don't think it matters." He clasped his hands behind his back, as if he didn't know what to do with them.

She didn't quite understand what he meant. Of course it mattered, and he knew it. The Old Men in Charge wanted the machine to keep functioning. Everyone made it clear that the machine was the key to a smooth holiday season.

How the machine worked was the key to keeping it alive. Or functioning, at least.

"I was wondering if you would do me a favor," he said.

She braced herself. She couldn't make a lot of promises about the machine. She wasn't really in the position to do any favors around the machine at all.

"What do you need?" she asked.

"I need an escort," he said.

Her cheeks heated. She was probably misunderstanding him. She *hoped* she was misunderstanding him. But she wasn't certain. In some ways, the North Pole was stuck in 1950s Western culture. Gender norms seemed prevalent, and ideas were stuck in a nonexistent past. She wasn't sure, though, if 1950s Western culture used the word "escort." She wasn't sure if that word was even allowed in this very strange place.

"What?" she asked, trying to keep the word neutral, but failing. She had hoped that her question wouldn't have a sharp edge to it, but the edge was there despite her best efforts.

He frowned, clearly not understanding the inadvertent curtness in her tone. Then he blinked, shook his head slightly, and rolled his eyes.

"You're determined to think the worst of me, aren't you?" he asked.

"No," she said a little too quickly. There might have been some truth in that question. More truth than she wanted to admit.

"I need an escort—a *guide*," he emphasized the last word, as if she was stupid. Maybe she had been. "To help me navigate the Greater World."

She was torn between apologizing, telling him that she had a job here, and asking him what he wanted with the Greater World.

He didn't wait for her verbal response.

"I want you to show me these kids you've been talking about. The ones who we've missed." He raised his chin as he said that last, almost as if he could add to his own defiance, just by making that movement.

"I don't know them by name," she said.

"That's not what I meant. The shelters, the homes. I'd like to see those trees too, but this isn't the season."

She let out a small sigh. "I'm not the person to take you on a trip like that."

"You're the one who brought it up," he said. "You're the one who is righteously angry about it. You're the one who got me to—"

He cut off as if he didn't want to say any more, as if he had almost gone too far as it was.

"Got you to what?" she asked.

He shook his head, then stopped that too. And sighed.

"I contacted a friend. He lives in the Greater World. He confirmed what you said."

"So have him be your escort," she said. "I have a job to do."

Lo nodded. Then looked down. He looked like the young boy he must have been, someone without a lot of support or courage, someone who had expected to be yelled at.

"I thought of that," he said. "I just thought…"

…that he could prove her wrong, probably. That he could show her that he knew better. That's what these corporate types were often like, particularly when their beliefs were challenged.

He raised his head slightly. There was no guile in his expression at all. Just that deep sadness mixed with exhaustion.

"I…um…didn't want to go alone," he said.

She almost blurted, *But you'd have your friend.* But saying those words felt as wrong as challenging him on the machine itself.

There were so many other responses she could have made: *What are you afraid you'll see? Do you need other eyes to help report back to the Old Men in Charge? Do you need me there to prove you're right and I'm wrong? Or vice versa?*

Instead, she surprised herself by saying, "How long do you plan to be gone?"

"Not long," he said. "I can't leave the machine alone for long."

That was true. She could offer to handle the machine, but she wasn't sure if that would be a hollow offer. If he was gone for a long time, she was certain the machine would deteriorate or maybe even fail altogether, and no amount of coddling it would help it recover.

"Shouldn't someone stay here, take care of the machine?" she asked.

"Probably," he said. "But I'm hoping I can spare a few hours."

Hours. For some reason she had been thinking days. She could spare a few hours too.

"All right," she said. "I can accompany you. Where do you plan to go?"

She expected him to say Los Angeles. Maybe even hoped he would say Los Angeles, so she could return home, if only for one night.

"Chicago," he said.

Chicago. She hated Chicago. She'd had a lot bad experiences in Chicago. She'd encountered corporate cultures in Chicago that made Claus & Company's seem enlightened.

"You don't like Chicago," he said, apparently reading her expression.

"It's as good as anywhere," she said, even though that wasn't true. It wasn't as good as most places, at least to her.

But it would prove her point.

Right smack in the middle of America, where people like him probably expected everything to be Just Fine.

And where things were not Just Fine—and maybe never had been.

"When do you want to go?" she asked.

"Now is good," he said.

She almost protested. The sweat. The tank top. The jeans. Then she remembered: it was July in Chicago. She would fit right in.

She just had to grab her shirt for the air-conditioning—if they found any.

"All right," she said. "Let's go."

PART IV

CHI-TOWN'S SAD AND SEAMY UNDERBELLY

CHAPTER 17

*T*hey arrived, per Niko's instructions, at an unimposing building in an old neighborhood that Lo wasn't sure he'd seen before. They ended up in some back alley, near a dumpster that reeked of rotting food. The brick walls on either side of that dumpster retained heat, and there was no air movement.

It felt like he and Dallas had landed in a malfunctioning steam bath, rather than outside in Chicago's hot summer.

It was the hot summer that made Lo decide against standard North Pole travel. Everyone at the Pole had access to a sleigh, and many used the sleighs, particularly to arrive at some place outside of the Pole during that place's winter.

But he would have had to do some research to get the sleigh into the right neighborhood where it wouldn't be noticed. He could have used his own transport magic, but he hadn't done that in more decades than he could think of, so he asked Dallas to help.

That surprised her: she hadn't expected the request. He had to explain the sleighs, which made her smile. Apparently no one had brought her to the Pole in a sleigh, which had surprised him: he thought everyone traveled to the Pole by sleigh.

But not Dallas.

She looked like she belonged in this hot place, with her blue tank top, matching jeans, and the spelled athletic shoes she'd worn in the machine room. A shirt dangled from her right hand, as if she expected the weather to suddenly cool down.

He didn't look like he belonged, even though he was also wearing jeans. His work shirt was red and green and white, perfect colors for the Pole, but out of season here.

He wiped a hand over his forehead, and half-smiled to himself. It wasn't like they were in a malfunctioning steam room. This oppressive heat felt familiar: it was the same as the machine room on a good day.

"I take it this is *not* your friend's business." Dallas looked at the old red brick around her, as if searching for a door.

"It's probably around front." Lo didn't want to tell her that Niko was known for missing details. Even though, given what Niko had told him earlier that day, what Niko was "known for" might not be accurate.

Dallas nodded, and headed down the cracked concrete of the alley. Lo followed, stepping gingerly over the cracks, also trying to avoid a greenish-gray slime that was flowing toward the dumpster like a tiny river. The stench seemed worse the longer he was here.

He had forgotten this part of hot summers—how quickly something could move from fresh to stink. And he had forgotten—if he had ever known—how rancid garbage could smell in this kind of heat.

The heat was making him tired. Or maybe the sadness from all he had learned that day was tiring him. Or maybe just being away from the machine sapped his energy.

He shoved that thought out of his mind. He needed to focus on what Niko and Dallas had been telling him. He needed to see what the crisis was, for himself.

If he saw it, then he might be able to augment the machine to help in some way or another.

Although that thought also defeated him. Because the machine was built to add a dollop of joy to things, not to solve world hunger.

And he knew, if he said that sentence aloud, he would be accused of being insensitive.

Maybe he was.

Or maybe the tiredness made it hard for him to deal with anything effectively.

Dallas and Lo emerged on a tree-lined side street. Three- and four-story brick buildings stood cheek by jowl with some square mid-twentieth-century "modern" buildings. On a Y intersection just up the street, Lo saw a particularly ugly one-stop-shopping store (couldn't call them drugstores anymore; he knew that much), and behind the buildings across the street, high rises rose. Some were glass and concrete, but others were also brick, showing the age of this part of Chicago.

"Old Town," Dallas said. "It could have been so much worse."

"What?" he asked.

"The neighborhood. It's called Old Town," she said.

"How do you know that?" he asked.

"I've worked in Chicago more than once. The super-rich neighborhoods are filled with mostly awful people who feel entitled, and the poor neighborhoods have mostly nice people who suffer through lots of shootings and other crap. I wasn't sure which we'd end up in. I'm happy to see us in neither." She wandered across the sidewalk between two parked cars.

Then she turned her back to traffic—not that there was any (fortunately), and craned her neck upward.

"Niko, you say?" she asked.

Lo nodded, then realized she wasn't looking at him. So she wouldn't see the nod. "He said Niko's Village," Lo said.

"Well, we landed beside it," she said.

He turned and peered. A squat red brick building with a colorful rainbow arch over the door had the words *Niko's Village* stenciled in gold on the arched plate glass window. A wooden sign—also done in rainbow colors—was nailed to the door. The sign read *Everyone Welcome* but in smaller print said, *But please knock first.*

Lo glanced at Dallas, who looked at him and shrugged as if to say, *What have you got to lose?*

Nothing, he supposed. Although part of him was regretting coming here already.

He walked over to the door and knocked. Something clicked, and the door opened ever so slightly. He pushed it open the rest of the way, and as he did, he finally understood why they ended up in the alley.

This building was warded against all magic. No one who was not the designer of the wards could pop in or out. Everyone with magic had to be invited.

A triangle of light appeared on the ground as the door opened, but Lo couldn't see inside. He waited until Dallas was beside him before stepping through.

The interior was slightly darker than outside, but significantly cooler. The sweat chilled Lo's skin, and left him feeling just a little dirty. Dallas wiped her forehead, then wiped her hands on her jeans. She shifted her shirt from hand to hand as if she was trying to decide whether or not to put it on.

The front area was a waiting room unlike any Lo had seen in the Greater World. To the left was an area with a big fat red gate, and behind that gate were toys, child-sized furniture, and a thick green rug. He smiled to himself; Niko couldn't seem to stay away from holiday colors, even if he wanted to.

Along the back wall of that gated area were shelves filled with books. It looked like someone had tried to segregate the books by age category, and had failed, mostly because the books were scattered on the shelves, a nearby table, and the rug. A little girl sat in the middle of them, a blond ponytail on the top of her head making her hair stand up like a tiny paintbrush with the wrong bristles.

She was reading out loud to a nearby stuffed monkey, and occasionally shoving the book in its face, apparently so it could see the pictures.

Directly in front of Lo was a thigh-high counter, with a laptop precariously balanced on one edge, and an actual computer—several years old—gathering dust on a credenza nearby.

A woman stood up from behind the desk, cradling some folders. "Hey," she said, in a way that was intended as a greeting, "Niko said some old friends would be dropping by. I guess that's you…?"

Lo made himself smile. "I'm the old friend," he said. "I'm Loth—Lo Johanssen, and this is my friend Dallas Demaris."

"Yeah, he's expecting you." The woman inclined her head toward the dusty computer. "Through that door."

Lo hadn't even seen the door until she indicated it. That made him wonder if it required a magical invitation just to see the door as well. He glanced over his shoulder to see if Dallas was following.

She wasn't. She was looking at the little girl, as if entranced.

"Dallas," he said quietly.

She started. He moved his head just like the woman had, and Dallas nodded. She came up beside him, walking one half step behind as they threaded their way around a surprising amount of furniture behind that desk.

The woman held the door for them. Lo went through first, feeling that same tingle he had felt as he opened the main door to the Niko's Village. This area was warded as well, and more so than the area out front.

Lo had stepped into a working office, with some chairs pushed against a wall, a table covered in paperwork, and a bookshelf crowded with more paperwork. A laptop sat on top of some of the paperwork, but it looked unused. There were, however, dozens of half-used yellow legal pads, and a small ton of yellow legal paper scattered around the room, all of it covered with big bold writing in black.

The room had two windows that were covered with stained glass made in the form of a logo made from the words *Niko's Village*. Light did stream through the glass, but there was no seeing in or out.

A door that Lo hadn't seen opened, and Niko North stepped through. He looked different than he had years ago. Thinner, slightly older, with a little less glamor than S-Elves usually had. He was taller, too. His blond hair needed a trim, but his bright blue eyes were the same. When they saw Lo, they twinkled as only eyes belonging to a member of the Claus family could.

"Lothario," he said, coming forward.

Lo extended his hand. Niko took it, and pulled Lo forward into a hug, surprising him. The Clauses weren't known for their demonstrativeness.

Lo and Niko broke apart a second later than Lo wanted to, and Niko's gaze fell on Dallas.

Before Lo could introduce her, Dallas stepped forward, her hand extended, but her body slightly shielded from any hug by remaining slightly behind Lo.

"Dallas Demaris," she said. "Thank you for taking the time to meet with us."

Niko gave her the family smile, the one that made everyone feel good whether they wanted to or not.

"My pleasure," he said warmly, taking Dallas's hand.

Lo felt a moment of panic that she would like Niko better, and then Lo shook the feeling off. Niko was married now; he was not competition.

And then Lo let out a small breath. He had no idea where that thought about competition had come from. He had no claims on Dallas, and Niko had never been competition before. It was all just a little crazy.

But then this whole trip was.

As if hearing Lo's thoughts, Niko turned to him. "You wanted to see what was going on in Chicago. I could take you to shelters—"

"I've been to shelters," Lo said. "You said there were kids with no fixed address."

"Technically," Niko said, "kids who spend the night in shelters have no fixed address either, but you want to see something that most families try to keep hidden. So we're going to have to do a little Ghost of Christmas Present stuff."

"Ghost of Christmas Present stuff?" Dallas asked.

"He means porthole viewing of current lives," Lo said. It was a technique that the early S-Elves used as they were setting up the company, but he didn't feel like telling her that. He didn't want to go on a side track.

"It's different in the summer," Niko said. "There's a lot of illegal camping. The winter is what's heartbreaking. Kids sleeping in cars under a lot of blankets. The parents usually run the car's heater once an hour, if they can afford that much gas. And occasionally, we lose an entire family during a snowstorm because the exhaust pipe gets clogged and they don't realize it, filling the car with carbon monoxide."

Niko spoke of this as if it were something he had gotten used to. How did anyone get used to such tragedy? And should they?

"I can take you both," Niko said. "We'll see a bit less—"

"I don't need to see it," Dallas said. "I just arrived at the North Pole from Southern California. I volunteer at homeless shelters when I can. I know what's going on."

Lo had no idea she volunteered like that. He squinted at her. That explained some of her emotion when she discussed what was happening with the children.

"She's your outsider," Niko said to Lo.

"Yes." Lo said, feeling that edge of panic again. He had asked her to come with him, which meant being beside him while he saw...whatever it was. But he hadn't been clear, had he? He had just asked her to come with him to Chicago.

Dallas put a hand on his shoulder. "I can come along if you need me to."

He didn't know her well enough to say he needed her. Or maybe he was feeling just a tad macho. Or unwilling to admit to fear in front of Niko.

"No, it's okay," Lo said, not sure what "it" was or why it was "okay." "I'll go with Niko."

"I can have my wife show you the foundation," Niko said.

"That was your wife out front?" Lo asked.

"No," Niko said. "Raine's at work. But she'd be willing to come here if I asked her."

"That's okay," Dallas said. "I'll be fine waiting."

"Well, Deborah will answer some questions. I just don't want to tell her where you're from," Niko said.

"Your wife knows where you're from?" Lo asked.

"I'm not going to lie to the person I'm married to," Niko said, as if the idea that his wife knew nothing was abhorrent to him. It probably was. "You ready?"

No, Lo wanted to say. But he had come here to learn, and he was going to learn.

"I guess so." The words didn't sound as hardy as they had in his head. He patted Dallas's hand on his shoulder, then moved away slightly so she wouldn't get caught up in whatever spell Niko cast.

"I'll wait out front," Dallas said.

"No need," Niko said. "There's nothing proprietary in here."

"Yes, but there's no couch in here either," Dallas said, with a slight smile.

Niko smiled back. "Fair enough. You can find your way back, right?"

As if it were miles away.

"Of course," Dallas said.

"Well then," Niko said to Lo. "Let's go."

CHAPTER 18

*B*efore Lo could answer Niko, Niko snapped his fingers and the two men faded away. They didn't even vanish. They *faded*.

Dallas hadn't expected that. It was an elegant spell, something she had never quite seen before.

She had heard of porthole spells, but she thought they opened doorways in the air, not that they took the participants somewhere. But it made sense, given the fact that Niko had said it would be hard to accommodate both of them. If he were using a window sort of spell, accommodating them both would be easy.

She glanced around the messy office. There was nothing she needed to see here, no investigating she needed to do. It was obvious that Niko was a mage or an elf, without a lot of technical ability, because his laptop sat on top of papers, instead of front and center on some desk.

Now that the men were gone, Dallas felt uncomfortable even standing in the room. She felt uncomfortable being in Chicago. Her job was to take care of the machine, not Lo.

She let herself out of the office, and headed back to the front of the building, past the loose furniture, and even more papers than she had noticed before.

The woman at the desk, whom Niko had called Deborah, smiled at her. From what Niko had said, Deborah did not know she had a guy in line to be the next real Santa as her boss.

"I'm to wait out here," Dallas said, and marveled at the words that had just come out of her mouth. They made her sound like she was an assistant to Lo, instead of his equal or maybe even his superior.

Dallas rounded the desk. The little girl behind the gates turned toward her, and smiled. She had the bluest eyes Dallas had ever seen. They actually twinkled.

Dallas gave her a small wave, and the girl waved back. Then she grabbed another book, slid it toward herself, and dragged another stuffed animal—this one a bright red elephant—next to the monkey. She arranged the toys, put a pillow behind her back like she had done it before, and began to read.

"Let me guess," Dallas said quietly. "That's Niko's daughter."

Deborah nodded. "It's so obvious, isn't it? They have the same smile."

"They do," Dallas said. "I take it she's here often?"

"Every day until she starts preschool. Which, he says, he's dreading."

Dallas wanted to ask about the mother, but wasn't sure how. "So this setup is for her?"

"Can't you tell?" Deborah asked, then waved a hand dismissively. "Of course you can't tell. You don't know her. She prefers red and green. Christmas colors, her mom says with a laugh. We can't get her into pink no matter how hard we try."

"The daughter, not the mother," Dallas said almost to herself.

Deborah laughed. "Exactly. Not that we're trying to raise a girl-girl, or anything. But I've never seen a child so wedded to a color palate."

I'd wager it's not unusual at the North Pole, Dallas almost said, but didn't. If Deborah didn't know, then Dallas didn't want to give her any strange ideas.

"We?" Dallas asked. "You're involved in raising her?"

Deborah shrugged. "Everyone here has a hand in it. She's darling, but she's strong-willed. Which, Niko says, comes from his side of the family. Now that they're expecting another, I have no idea what they'll do."

Again with the unclear antecedents. Dallas knew what Deborah was talking about, but almost asked for clarifications.

Still, continuing this conversation without guidance from Niko was probably a bad idea. Dallas had no idea what Deborah knew and what she didn't.

Dallas moved to the edge of the couch, sitting on one of the arms. From that position, she could see the little girl and Deborah, as well as the door.

Dallas had no idea how the men would return—they wouldn't just pop in (or fade in) if Deborah had no idea that Niko had any magic. So they might walk in from the front, or they might simply just amble here from the back, as if they'd been there the entire time.

"I'm told Niko's Village only operates in Chicago," Dallas said, because if she didn't do something, she would go stir-crazy.

"Right now." Deborah grabbed a stack of papers and moved them into another pile. "But Niko is hoping that Mr. Johanssen will be able to bring in a big client with a lot of reach."

So Niko still hoped for help from Claus & Company. Who could blame him? Imagine if that organization did more than hand out presents to "deserving" children? Imagine if they actually used their reach for bigger things.

"Well," Dallas said, "Niko is showing Lo the need for that kind of help right now."

Deborah nodded, her smile tight. Then she put her hands on top of the nearest pile of papers.

"I'm not supposed to say much, but, Ms. Demaris, this is a *great* organization. We're always searching for funding—I mean, all charities are— but Niko is so compassionate, and he can convince anyone to give, and it makes the giver *happy*. But even though we're just focused on Chicago, the need is so great. Niko likes to focus on children, but between me and Raine, we showed him—"

"Raine?" Dallas asked.

"His wife. She's great, if a little strange. She's a writer, you know."

Dallas didn't know. She didn't know anything about them.

"Anyway," Deborah said. "We showed him that a child's environment and upbringing are as important to their well-being as their access to comfortable clothes and a good night's sleep. That's why we've branched out, partnering with a lot of organizations here in Chicagoland, so that we combine our fundraising and our outreach, and if we can do that with a group that has what is to us unlimited funds... oh, Ms. Demaris, you have no idea what that would mean to all the children."

Dallas liked the passion. And she wondered where Deborah got the idea of unlimited funds.

Dallas wasn't even sure how funds worked at the North Pole. There had to be access to money, but probably not in the way anyone expected. Niko might have said "unlimited funds" or seemingly unlimited funds as a way of explaining the magic.

"I have an idea," Dallas said. "I'm not with the same organization as Mr. Johanssen. I'm supposed to help him—"

Take a magical machine and make it work worldwide in fewer than six months. Her heart constricted in panic. What was she doing here again? She certainly hadn't been hired to make small talk with a mortal in a small charity on Chicago's North Side.

"—um, help him figure out how to take his company's considerable reach into the twenty-first century. Then he remembered Niko, and asked him to help as well."

"I know," Deborah said. "Niko's very excited—"

"Mama," the little girl said, and Deborah stopped.

She held up a hand, then said sideways to Dallas, "That child always seems to know when her mother is on the way."

Apparently, then, the little girl had her fair share of magic. Magic that early on was more common for S-Elves than it was for mages.

At that moment, the main door opened, and a slight woman who was far enough along in her pregnancy to look like she might topple forward at any minute pushed her way through the door.

Heat came in with her. She rubbed a hand over her forehead, and said to Deborah, "You want to tell me why I thought doing this twice was a good idea? And in the summer to boot?"

And then the woman patted her mounded stomach.

Deborah smiled. "Because you and Niko make beautiful babies."

"Oh, don't say that too loudly," the woman said, glancing at her daughter. "It'll go to her head."

Then she turned to Dallas, and extended her hand.

"I'm Raine Wilkins, Niko's wife."

Dallas took her hand, which was a bit sweaty and warm from the outdoors. "Dallas Demaris."

The woman—Raine—looked around. "I thought there were two of you...?"

"Niko and Lo had some things to discuss," Dallas said, hoping Raine wouldn't ask about anything else.

"That makes sense," Raine said.

The little girl was at the edge of the gate. She had dragged the elephant with her.

"Mama?"

"Hey, punkin'," Raine said. "You keeping everyone on the straight and narrow?"

"I been readin'," the little girl said.

"Quite intently too," Dallas said.

"Yeah, that's my gene pool," Raine said. "Words, words, words. Fortunately she got her looks from her daddy."

"Daddy doin' magicks," the little girl said, and Dallas felt her heart jump. It took all of her self-control to keep from looking at Deborah.

"That's what she calls her father's work," Deborah said.

Dallas nodded. "It probably does look like magic to her."

Raine gave her a sharp look, and then grinned. "You're exactly right."

She went over to the gate, and crouched awkwardly. Dallas had no idea how Raine would get back up.

"You show me what you've been reading," Raine said to the little girl.

At that moment, the men walked out of the back. Niko was half a step ahead, so Dallas couldn't see Lo's face. There was no twinkle in Niko's eye, though. But, when he saw his wife, he walked over to her and helped her up. Then he picked up his daughter. The little girl really was a dead ringer for her dad. She had his face shape, his blond hair, and his bright blue eyes.

She put her arms around his neck, pressed her face against his, and then reached across and patted her mother's cheek.

Dallas felt a moment of...well, it wasn't envy. But maybe it was rightness. Most of the time, when she saw children, she saw them in extremis. She worked with children's charities, she gave money to shelters, and she did what she could to make sure that children were taken care of.

She rarely saw a happy family.

Lo was standing slightly behind Deborah. He wasn't looking at Niko or his family. He was looking at the floor. Dallas's heart twisted. She wanted to walk over to him and put her arms around him, but she didn't know him that well. She had no idea if he would accept a hug from her or not.

She didn't want Deborah to see him like this, though.

Niko must have seen something on Dallas's face, because he gave her a sad half-smile.

"Let's have an early dinner and talk," he said to her.

Early dinner. She had no idea what time it was here or back at the North Pole. She was a bit hungry, though, even though that'd had that big meal at lunch.

"I'm not hungry," Lo said. He sounded odd. Not at all like the man she had met, the one who had spoken so strongly and confidently around that machine.

"I think we need to return," she said to Niko. "We'll take a rain check on that dinner, if that's all right by you."

Niko's smile faded, and Raine looked almost angry. Then Dallas remembered what they had told her; Niko had been looking forward to seeing someone from home.

His wife had probably never met anyone from the North Pole besides Niko.

"I promise I'll bring him back," Dallas said. "We just have to process..."

She let the words trail off. Niko nodded. Raine looked up at him, with a questioning expression. His daughter buried her head in his neck.

Lo walked past Deborah, keeping his face averted. As he got close to Dallas, his gaze met hers. His eyes looked hollow.

She stood, and put her hand on his arm. He stiffened. He didn't shake her off—that would have seemed odd and rude—but he didn't touch her in return. She let her hand fall off him, and she flanked him.

"We'll be in touch," she said to Niko.

"Yeah." Niko's tone said he didn't believe it. He looked bleak as well. His wife's mouth had become a thin line, and she almost vibrated with fury.

Dallas didn't blame her. Everyone from the North Pole seemed to have neglected Niko, and now, Dallas and Lo showed up, used Niko's expertise, and then decided to leave immediately.

She wished she could explain more, but the presence of both a mortal and a child made explanations impossible.

Lo opened the door, and stepped outside, continuing down the sidewalk without stopping. Dallas had to stop to pull the door closed.

The heat was oppressive, the humidity more so. Even from here, she could smell that garbage mixed with the exhaust from passing cars. The city had an underlying hum that she didn't like, which was probably unfair, since she lived near Los Angeles, the car capital of the world.

Lo stopped at the intersection, half a block past the alley where they arrived. He put his face in his hands, hunched forward for a moment, then dropped his arms and squared his shoulders.

He turned, just as Dallas reached him.

"Let's go home," he said, and she wondered, given the defeat in his voice, if she had won the battle and lost the war.

It would be so much easier for Claus & Company to continue the way it always had. Sometimes people, when faced with the reality of the world, retreated to their little corner.

Maybe Lo was one of those people.

The very idea made her heart sink. But all she could do was give him a sympathetic smile.

"We need to go back to that alley so no one sees us," she said.

"I suppose," he said. "I also think it doesn't matter. Who cares if someone disappears off the streets of Chicago?"

That question came from what he had seen, not from any sense of reality.

"Your friend Niko lives and does business here," she said gently. "Someone will care."

Lo nodded, then stalked toward the alley, as if the idea of going anywhere close to Niko's charity offended him.

She followed, uncertain what to say or do. Well, not entirely uncertain what to do.

She had to take Lo back to the North Pole.

What happened after that, she couldn't even guess.

CHAPTER 19

*A*fter the fifteenth child, Lo had lost count. The children seemed to come from everywhere. If Lo hadn't known that Niko was taking him all over Chicago, Lo would have thought Niko was taking him all over the world.

The children spoke dozens of languages, some so rapidly that it had taken Lo a moment to adjust. Everything from Spanish to German to Polish to Russian, along with Arabic and Hebrew, and languages that he recognized but hadn't really been tutored in.

And of course, there was English. Chicago English, with its long vowels and flat consonants. The language of despair and panic and sheer terror didn't need vocalization, though.

It was in the way the kids hunched their shoulders, or stood protectively near whatever parent they had left, or cradled a younger sibling.

As Dallas led Lo back to the stinky alley, he wasn't really seeing the brick buildings or the cracked filthy concrete. He was seeing all the faces, almost as if they were on some kind of instant replay.

The kids hadn't been able to see him or Niko. That was how the spell worked. Lo and Niko just watched what had happened, was happening or would happen. Niko took Lo to various places that had existed on this day. Some of those places were in the near past—kids waking up in the back of cars, buried under blankets and clothing and a family's entire worldly possessions. Others were in the near future—kids sitting next to their siblings in a soup kitchen or whatever those places were called now, pushing some unappetizing corn and chicken in gravy around with a battered fork.

Lo had no idea how many places he and Niko had gone, how much, exactly they had seen. Kids sleeping on benches. Kids showering in a Y, parent standing guard, shaking out the clothes the kid had just taken off because the kid only had one outfit that fit.

Niko explained some of it, how hard it was to penetrate the vastness of the problem because a lot of intact families were homeless now. A lot of kids were on their own as well, cruising the streets, making money in unspeakable ways.

Lo had asked to focus on the under-ten set, though, the ones who would still maybe believe in Santa Claus, and even that broke his heart. Or maybe because they were under ten they broke his heart. Kids spending the day guarding their even younger siblings while their parent went to work. Kids foraging garbage cans for food. Kids...

"Lo?" Dallas put her hand on his arm, again. He wanted to shake her off. If she hadn't talked to him, he wouldn't have come here. He wouldn't have seen...

"We need to go now," she said.

He blinked. Amazing how that alley had faded for him, despite the heat and the oppressive odor. He focused on Dallas's face.

Her eyes were filled with compassion, which he did not want. Her mouth was a thin line, which still looked good on her, despite all that had happened today.

He hated that he found her attractive. He hated talking to her, hated being here, wished he could still be banging around his machine, trying to make it work.

Even though it was inadequate.

And the word "inadequate" was inadequate. Such a small word for such a big miss. He hadn't realized just how far the world had passed the North Pole by.

And the world shouldn't have passed them by. Elves and mages went into the Greater World every single day. There were outposts all over the world, places where sleighs got repaired and rooftops got visited and Santas were supervised. Places where the image was maintained and certain members of the Claus & Company family who had an extra dose of charisma ended up talking to the press or whatever the image consultants did these days.

"Lo?" Dallas's voice was gentle. "We need to leave."

He nodded. They did need to leave. They were long past leaving. They should have left before they even arrived.

He half-smiled at the thought. He clearly wasn't thinking clearly. Part of his mind was still dealing with those children, with all of that misfortune. (Could it even be called "misfortune"? Wasn't that word as inadequate as, well, "inadequate" had been?)

He tried to pay attention to what Dallas was doing. She had placed one hand gently on his arm, and she was saying some kind of spell, one he wasn't familiar with—and suddenly, he was very, very cold.

She hadn't taken him back to the machine. She had taken him to the doors outside.

The promised storm had arrived. The wind swirled around them, filled with ice pellets and snow so thick that he could barely see her.

The sweat on his skin froze almost instantly, but the cold woke him up, made him remember where he was and why he was here.

Which was probably what she had intended.

"Let's go inside," she said and took his arm, pulling him in the exact wrong direction. That was how people died in snowstorms—although they didn't die here, mostly because almost everyone at the Pole was used to snow and storms and weather like this.

She wasn't. She didn't belong here. She had brought the real world with her—not the Greater World, but the world he had long forgotten about. The one where people suffered, not because they worked too hard or they had a demanding S-Elf for a boss, but because they didn't have opportunity or because they suffered from discrimination or they didn't have enough money to feed themselves.

He felt...overwhelmed and exhausted. He almost felt like it was all his fault. He had missed this, and now he was tasked with fixing it.

"Come on," Dallas said, still pulling.

Lo hadn't budged. He started to say, *That's the wrong way*, but the words didn't come out of his mouth. They got stuck in his throat, which had closed up with something like tears.

He swallowed, then managed, "That's the wrong way." The wind blew the words away as soon as he spoke them, but Dallas turned toward him. She seemed to hear him.

That's the wrong way.

It wasn't just about getting into the building. He had been going the wrong way for a long time now. The entire North Pole had.

And the Old Men in Charge either knew it or had closed their eyes to it. And no one else seemed to want to do anything either. If, indeed, they had seen it.

And Lo wasn't sure he wanted them to have seen it. Because if they saw it and did nothing, then they didn't belong at the North Pole. They didn't belong in Claus & Company. No one did.

Oh, behind that sadness Lo felt was a very, very, very deep anger.

He finally understood why the machine kept falling apart. It had been trying to accomplish the wrong thing.

Dallas stopped beside him. Her eyelashes had ice on them, which was a bad sign.

He tucked her hand in his arm, and led her across mounds of snow. The snow slid into his shoes, instantly melting against his still-hot feet, sending shivers through him. He marched her to the patio outside the machine building, although the patio was covered in snow too. The heaters under the pavers weren't working; that's how strong this storm was.

The wind buffeted Lo and Dallas sideways, almost pushing them to one of the doors. He grabbed the metal handle with his bare hand, and had a half-second of regret: his hand was wet, and he was afraid his skin would stick to the metal.

But it didn't, whether through luck or magic or some ambient temperature that was slightly too high to adhere wet skin to cold metal.

The hot air from the machine room blew across at him, carrying the scent of machine oil and hot ball bearings. The smell of home.

His eyes teared up (again, dammit) and he willed the tears back as he pulled Dallas inside the building.

The wind assisted. It blew him and Dallas inside, along with snow and ice pellets, and somehow, she let go of his arm and managed to pull the door closed.

The sound of the wind instantly faded. He hadn't realized until that moment that he had conflated the sound of the wind with the constant hum of Chicago. They had seemed like one consistent sound when they had been many sounds, sounds he was unfamiliar with.

He was shivering now. His inadequate clothing was wet, and his shoes were soaked. He couldn't go back into the snow to get clothing from his home. He had backups here, but not for Dallas.

She was in as bad shape as he was. She was obviously cold, from her blue lips to the ice on her eyelashes to—well, he wasn't going to be that guy and look (again) at her torso with the obvious indication of cold along her chest.

Somewhere along the way she had lost that shirt she was carrying. It was probably back at Niko's or buried in a snow drift.

"We have to get you into warm clothes now," Lo said. He could magic something from her cottage, if he could remember how to do such simple spells. He probably hadn't done them for a decade or more. "I have some things here that might fit you."

"No need," she said, and ran a hand from her collarbone down her torso, across her hips and down her legs to her ankle. As she touched each part of herself, her clothing swapped out, so fast he couldn't see the change.

She went from wearing a wet T-shirt and soaked jeans to a regular flannel shirt and black jeans. Her feet were bare, though.

"I assume you have shoes for me," she said.

"You need socks," he said. "The shoes are over there."

He pointed at one of the shoe closets, then he said, "I'm going to change."

He walked away before he could do anything else or before she could offer to magic him. He didn't want her to touch him any more than she already had. He didn't want to think about what she had made him see, and he didn't want to think about her and how pretty she was, even when her lips were blue, her teeth were chattering, and her eyelashes had turned white.

He was thinking about how pretty she was only as a way to avoid the problems she brought with her. He couldn't face those.

But he was going to have to.

He was going to have to face it all.

CHAPTER 20

*S*ometimes it seemed like Lo had forgotten every bit of magic he had ever learned except what he needed to know to keep the machine running. Dallas supposed that was possible; she had just never seen it before.

Or maybe he was so overwhelmed by what he had seen in Chicago that he wasn't thinking about spells or magic or anything quite logical enough.

Dallas wasn't sure she had ever seen anyone so devastated. He clearly understood what was going on, and it had had an impact on him. What he was going to do about it was something else entirely.

She was physically uncomfortable. Her face and hands were frozen, but her torso was too hot. Her bare feet were the only comfortable part about her, but she worried about walking on this ancient flooring.

The machine looked even more dodgy than it had before, as if it knew that she had taken Lo away from it. She glared at it.

They had entered the building near the middle of the machine. This part had tubes and an old logic board, and some primitive screens attached to one side. It seemed like every time she looked at the thing, she saw new pieces, other things Lo had cobbled together.

He had pointed her to a different shoe closet than she had seen before, and then he had walked away from her. She was clearly meant to stay behind.

He probably needed some time to gather himself together. She wanted to walk with him, more to soothe him than to talk with him.

But, if she were being honest with herself, she wanted to talk with him too, to prevent him from making the wrong choice after all he had seen.

Part of her—a very large part of her—was afraid he'd dig in even more, say that what those kids needed was a bit of joy and let's figure out how to expand the address lists—and then nothing would get done.

Or maybe he didn't have the ability to do anything. Maybe it really did all rest on the Old Men in Charge.

She let out a small sigh and padded across the warm and slightly slick wood floor. Steam from the machine coated everything, even the floor. It was amazing there was no mold or rot here. Maybe the cold counteracted that.

Or maybe it was all magic.

She really did have no idea how it worked. It was becoming clearer and clearer to her that the kind of magic she was used to, the kind that her friends in Los Angeles practiced, wasn't what was practiced here at the Pole.

She reached the shoe closet, and the doors eased back on their own. As they did, water dripped down the side. Maybe the steam had become a bit more intense while Lo was gone. Maybe the machine was breaking down even faster than they all expected.

Her stomach clenched. Maybe Lo had been right; maybe he shouldn't have been as far away from the machine as he had been all afternoon.

She wiped a hand over the nearby bench. It was damp as well, so she spelled it dry, hoping that her spell didn't counteract some other spell. Then she sat down, and touched her feet, covering them in a pair of runner's socks.

The shoes glistened behind those doors, as if the shoes were half alive as well. Maybe she was tired; maybe that was why she was seeing life in everything.

She grabbed a pair of black shoes, figuring she was going to get everything she owned dirty over the next few days. Then she slipped them on, and closed her eyes for just a minute.

When she had come here, she had expected a fight to get the machine out of the hands of whoever ran it. She also expected some of the culture clash.

She hadn't expected the emotional ride she'd had. From fighting with the Old Men in Charge to seeing Lo's face this afternoon, her emotions were getting a heck of a workout.

And it bothered her on some deep level that Lo's upset disturbed her as well.

She ran a hand over her face, and turned, only to see Lo standing a few yards behind her. At first, she thought he had been watching her. Then she realized he still had that thousand-yard stare, the one he had acquired this very afternoon.

"We're going to need some food," she said to him.

"Yeah." He turned his head, focused on her, and she felt the power of that gaze but she couldn't judge his mood. Angry? Sad? Devastated? He was closing down bit by bit, and she couldn't see past his barriers.

She had been able to see past earlier, or maybe the emotions had so overwhelmed him that he couldn't hold them back.

"We put the desserts in the break room," he said, "and I've got some snacks in the break room. Go find something for us, and I'll double-check the machine."

Go find something. As if she worked for him. No please, no nothing. Yet, she didn't mind. Because he really did seem only half there.

"I would like a real meal," she said.

"Me, too." He gave her half a smile. "But I don't want to eat it here. And I can't leave the machine untended, not at the moment anyway. I need to make sure everything is as I left it."

Which it probably wasn't, given the layer of moisture.

But she nodded anyway, not minding that he'd sent her to forage.

She'd found the break room once before. It was past the second machine room, down a narrow hallway, and through a door that should have led into a closet. The last time, she'd had to tug on the door to get it to open.

This time, it opened for her. She wasn't sure if that was because the machine had accepted her (had it?) or because she now was considered an official part of the North Pole (was she?) or because someone had put her into the Claus & Company system (was there a Claus & Company system? She had no real idea).

The break room was small and claustrophobic, as 1950s as the last section of the machine. There were no windows here either, just like Niko's office (which suddenly struck her as strange). The small refrigerator wheezed—it seemed like every machine in this part of the Pole wheezed—and the microwave was one of those gigantic monstrosities that had been invented in the 1980s. She was amazed it still worked, although she wasn't certain it still worked.

And she wasn't going to try it. She grabbed two apples, figuring they'd be easy to eat and they would hold her and Lo until that promised dinner.

She wasn't quite certain why he was being so mysterious, but she had a guess. And she wasn't sure if that guess was self-serving or not. After all, she wanted him to discuss changes to the machine.

As any good magical machine inventor knew, machines did not like hearing their futures discussed, particularly when that future might include a shutdown of the machine itself.

By the time she returned to the Machine Room Three, the air wasn't quite as damp, and the water no longer beaded on everything.

Lo stood in the doorway between the third and fourth rooms. He was weaving his hands back and forth as if he was doing some kind of martial arts very badly.

But she knew what he was about: he was doing some kind of spell, using some very, very old tricks. She preferred spells that were verbal. His, apparently, had some kind of movement component.

Which made sense, given the fact that his work with the machine itself had become so intense that he hadn't learned modern spellwork.

Not that every mage increased their spellwork ability over the centuries. Some mages stayed with the spells they had learned young. Only a handful continued to develop.

She was one of that handful, mostly because she loved technology so very much. She always wanted to incorporate it into everything that she did.

She waited until Lo was done moving and had opened his eyes. She didn't want to disturb the spell.

His gaze met hers.

"Apple?" she asked, and then smiled. She knew that a woman offering a man an apple, in some mythologies, had sexual connotations.

"Temptress," he said, obviously thinking of the same thing. "But, yes."

She tossed him the apple and he caught it easily with one hand. He took a bite, and some juice ran down his chin. He cleaned it off with one thumb.

"I only have two things to do," he said, "and then we can get dinner."

"Where?" she asked. "Because I'd like to talk."

His smile faded. And she hadn't realized until that moment that he had seemed more relaxed since their return.

Since he had started working on the machine again.

Maybe they were more intertwined than she had thought—and that wasn't necessarily a good thing.

"We do need to talk," he said. "So I was thinking my place."

She almost asked if there were listening devices in his place, and then realized just how ridiculous that question was. She was in Santa's Village at the North Pole. First of all, there would be listening magic, if there was listening anything, and secondly, they wouldn't spy on one of their own. Although they might spy on *her*.

Not that she wanted to return to that warm and overly tchotchke'd cottage.

Then Lo smiled—as if he had forced himself to smile. "And that has nothing to do with the apple you just gave me."

Was he flirting? Bantering? Trying to flirt? Trying to lighten the mood?

She hadn't expected it, given how sad he had seemed earlier. She appreciated the effort—and she had known that it had taken an effort.

"Noted," she said with a matching smile. "I'll be in Machine Room One when you're ready."

"Machine Room One...?" he asked with a bit of a panic. He still didn't trust her with his machine.

"It's all right," she said. "I'm just killing time."

That wasn't strictly true. She wanted to see one element of the machine. She wasn't even sure she could see it, but if she could, it would be in the earliest parts of the machine.

She bit into her apple, which was crisp and sweet, making her think of fall. Well, she'd hit three of the four seasons in just the last few hours. Now all she needed was a budding tree, and she would complete an entire year in an afternoon.

The thought didn't make her smile, though. She almost felt like she was going behind Lo's back.

But that visit to Chicago—and Lo's visible reaction—had gotten her thinking as well. The problems with the machine didn't just extend to the machine. They were endemic to Claus & Company.

That was clear, given who Niko North was, and the way the family had abandoned him. The very idea that the S-Elves had let one of the family in line to be the next Santa just vanish from their ceremonies and their roles disturbed her more than she could say.

Did they even know that there was a new generation? That Niko North's daughter already showed signs of budding Santa-ism, with her preference for Christmas colors and the way she had given those stories to her stuffed animals?

Probably not, and Dallas wasn't going to tell the S-Elves. She wasn't going to tell them much of anything, really.

She needed to think.

There were redundancies throughout Claus & Company. The sleighs stashed all over the world. The employees who checked out chimneys and did Santa marketing. The tech division of the toy building.

What she wanted to know was whether the machine was necessary at all.

She wasn't sure how she would figure that out. She certainly couldn't ask Lo about it. He would get defensive, and she really didn't blame him.

At this stage of his life, getting rid of the machine might actively hurt him. He certainly seemed better now that they had returned to the machine itself.

The original machine room smelled a bit like mildew this late in the day, although there was no steam here. The temperature was lower than it had been in the other rooms as well.

Dallas stepped inside.

Now that she saw how the entire system worked, she knew she had to return to the beginning to get her answers.

And the beginning was right here.

PART V

THE HEART OF THE MACHINE

CHAPTER 21

*L*o finally stitched together the holes in the machine's magic that had sprouted up just that afternoon. He had been worried that leaving the machine alone for an extended period of time might cause problems. And by alone, he meant without him anywhere nearby.

When he went to his cottage at night, he knew the machine would be just fine. His magic and its magic were linked enough that the machine could find him (or the magical part of him) if need be.

But he hadn't even been in the vicinity. He had been thousands of miles away, in the Greater World. And then he had actually gone to a magical portal made by someone the machine didn't know.

Given the holes in the machine's magic that appeared while he was gone, the machine had panicked. It had known he had left the North Pole, and it had pinged him, trying to find the connection.

It couldn't, and there had been a meltdown.

He wasn't quite sure what that meant. Dallas would know. She worked with a lot of magical machines. She probably even had a word for it.

His repair had taken him longer than he expected. He had thought he would only need a few minutes, but it had taken over an hour. He hoped Dallas didn't mind.

He made his way back to Machine Room One, feeling a bit more like himself. Working on the machine calmed him. It didn't soothe him; it focused him, took him outside of himself, made him think about something other than the day he'd had, the things he'd seen.

The lights were up in Machine Room One, something he hadn't done in years, maybe decades. Cobwebs hung like big shawls from the ceiling. He hadn't even realized that spiders could live at the Pole, but they clearly did. And if they were here, so were other bugs.

He didn't want to think about that or what it meant for the older wood in this part of the machine. He had enough to worry about.

He squinted in the brightness. The machine looked different than usual, probably because of the change in light. Some parts of the machine looked older than a few centuries. Those parts of the machine looked like they had existed since the dawn of time.

Some of the wood had darkened with age and too much moisture. He had a hunch if he touched some of the poles holding the outside of the oldest part of the machine together, those poles would crumble in his hand.

He had been fighting so hard to keep the machine alive, he had neglected the smaller parts of the machine, the frame itself.

The amount of work frustrated him. He really couldn't do it alone, and if he and Dallas didn't come up with a solution…

He sighed, the faces of the children he'd seen today, the *despair* on the faces of those children, crossing his mind, almost as if they had been magicked into his mind.

And maybe they had, for all he knew. Maybe someone (Niko?) was trying to make Lo feel guilty so that he would force the Old Men in Charge to change.

One thing Lo did know, however, was that Dallas hadn't manipulated anything. Dallas hadn't known Niko. She hadn't even known that Niko existed. So the two of them couldn't have conspired to show Lo any of those children.

And that—more than anything—had convinced Lo that the machine, the North Pole, Claus & Company—they were all failing in their mission.

But he had no idea how to achieve that mission or if the mission was, in the words of Dallas, so last century.

Speaking of Dallas, she had said she would be waiting for him here, and he didn't see her. Her parka hung from a peg near one of the doors, and a grayish cable knit sweater that had once been white hung from another peg.

But those were the only signs that Dallas had even been here today.

He wandered around the outside of the machine, looking for her. Something banged nearby. He had never quite heard a sound like that. It didn't sound organic to the machine. It sounded like someone bumped something or adjusted something that didn't want adjusting.

He walked toward the noise, then crouched, finally seeing two long jeans-encased legs ending in a pair of dusty black sneakers.

"Dallas?"

There was another bang, a curse, and then she slid out from underneath the machine, her entire body flat on a mechanic's creeper he had forgotten that he had.

She raised up on one elbow, and looked at him, comically, he thought, since half her face was buried in soot. The other side of her face was dotted with soot, so she looked uneven. Delightfully so.

She peered at him like she had never seen him before. Then she slid to one side of the creeper. Its wheels on the opposite side rose ever so slightly, showing how unbalanced it was.

"Do me a favor," she said. "Get on this with me."

The creeper was at least a hundred years old. It had wheels and a wooden base, but that was it. He had mechanic's creepers in the other room that had come from different decades. One, given to him by the Elf-gineers one Christmas, had a thick cushion, so that lying on it for all hours seemed easy. (He never used it; he was afraid he would fall asleep on it.)

This creeper tilted more as she moved.

"What do you want me to see?" he asked in a tone that (he hoped) would remind her that he knew more about the machine than anyone.

"There's a gap," she said.

His heart pounded. How much more could he take today?

"A gap?" In the machine? He would have noticed. "It's probably intentional."

"Humor me," she said.

He suppressed a sigh. He'd been humoring people all day, and it had left him emotionally bereft. Maybe that was why he walked across the floor and put a hand on the top of the creeper, easing the empty side back to the floor.

She scooted some more, smiling at him, her teeth white against the soot on the right side of her face. He didn't quite smile back, but he almost did, something he thought a victory, considering how he had felt since he had seen those children.

He crouched down, and slowly slid next to her.

Her body was warm and soft against his. He really didn't fit on the creeper, not with her beside him, and she didn't really fit either. The creeper had been made for just one person.

Half of him hung off it, and half of her did as well. Still, they managed to crab-walk the creeper back underneath the machine.

He understood how she had gotten so covered in grime. He clearly hadn't been down here in years. There was more dirt down here than he had seen maybe in his lifetime. The wheels of the creeper sprayed some of it on his back.

He had to work to keep his free arm off the floor, which looked greasy as well as grimy. He had to be aware of his other arm as well. It was pressed between his torso and Dallas's, and he was painfully aware that her T-shirt was both damp and too thin. She wasn't wearing a bra or any kind of undergarment, and he could feel the warmth of her flesh against the skin of his upper arm.

He found that ridiculously erotic. He was going to blame the emotional day for that reaction, even though he knew he was blaming the wrong thing.

He made himself focus on the machine. It looked different underneath, partly because light was filtering through gaps he hadn't realized were there. The gaps made a latticework of thin wood. The latticework looked deliberate and rather pretty, but it didn't seem to be functional.

The area that Dallas was pushing him toward was almost hollow. The remaining wood looked so thin he could see light through parts of it. He was afraid to touch it. This part of the machine had become extremely fragile.

And it shouldn't have been. It was the center of the oldest part of the machine, the core he had built the machine around. But there was no core here. He had built the entire machine around a bit of magic—an abacus that he had found in a thrift shop in London and had adored—and the abacus was gone.

"Do me a favor," Dallas said for the second time.

The loudness of her voice startled him. It also vibrated parts of the machine, and more dust rained down on them. He closed his eyes just in time, feeling the dust land on his eyelids. With his free hand, he wiped the dust off, then sputtered to keep it off his lips (so that he wouldn't open his mouth and swallow it).

"Slide up into that empty spot, would you?" she asked.

At first he thought she meant slide the creeper into part of the machine, but the bottom part of the machine got thicker here, and formed something like a barrier to the other parts of the machine. He could get through if he wanted to, but he didn't want to, and he didn't see the point.

Then he saw what she was looking at. She was looking up, into the latticework and beyond.

Parts of the latticework seemed wider than other parts. He wondered what she could see from her venue—not that she was in that different a position than he was. Maybe she had seen something when she had been here before.

And maybe she had knocked some of it loose. He had heard her bump something and curse, after all.

She glanced at him. There was more dirt on her face than there had been before. Both sides looked even now.

She inclined her head upward, as if she finally understood that he initially missed the point.

He peered through the latticework. The light filtering in here seemed thinner and whiter than it had outside of the machine. The latticework itself looked fragile, more so than anything else he had seen that evening.

If he slid up there like she had told him to, he had no idea what he would knock loose.

"I'm afraid I'll break something," he said, by way of refusing.

"I don't think it'll matter," she said. "It looks broken already, at least to me."

There was something in her voice that he didn't quite understand, as if she was holding something back.

"There's a missing piece to the machine," he said. "There—"

"Yes," she said. "I can see that."

But she couldn't see it, not really. She didn't know how important that abacus had been. It had glowed when he first found it, back in the corner of that tiny London shop. He had known, right from that moment, that it was possible to build a machine using numbers—ones and zeros—something that would have computational strength, and use magic as well.

He had bought that abacus and cradled it to himself as he left that store. The abacus had been both the impetus for the machine and the heart of the machine.

And now, the abacus was gone.

Maybe that was why the machine was cranky. Maybe that was why it wasn't working right.

Maybe…

Oh, he didn't know. But he did know that maybe, just maybe, that was why he felt lost when he looked at the machine.

"Maybe the pieces shifted," he said, more to himself than to her. That would make him feel better. If the abacus was there, just in a different spot. And he really needed to feel better. "Maybe—"

"Please," she said. "Just do me that favor."

The third request for him to slide into the machine. To inspect the latticework up close.

He wasn't sure why that was so important to her. He had the sense that she really needed him to make that one move, and he couldn't quite understand why.

He also had the sense that she wasn't going to explain it to him. He could ask, he supposed, but what was the point. Either he sat up and inspected the machine more closely, or he forced her to slide the mechanic's creeper out of the machine.

And he didn't want to slide away. He wanted to see what, exactly, was going wrong.

Dallas was looking upwards, her entire head, neck, and torso covered with soot now. His probably was too. And it smelled faintly of old wood down here. Old rotting wood.

He sighed, not really wanting to do what she asked. He didn't have the energy. He didn't have the *emotional* energy. He had been too tired for too long.

Besides, he had no joy left in him. He hadn't for years now. Much as he loved the machine—and he did love the machine—it had drained him.

And much as he loved the North Pole, he didn't feel like he was a part of it. Not anymore.

"Lo," she said quietly. "Please...?"

He couldn't handle the request either. He didn't like to be pushed, and he'd been pushed all day. Or rather, he had pushed himself. Doing things he didn't normally do, thinking of things he'd rather not think about, seeing things he would never be able to unsee.

But Lo and Dallas were both on the creeper, and he wasn't going to get out of here without her unless he used some kind of magic spell, and he didn't want to do that, not this close to the inside of the machine itself.

So he pushed up, gently, careful to make sure that his head didn't scrape any part of the machine. The gap in the wood seemed wider as he got closer to it.

He had to twist slightly so that his shoulders wouldn't brush against the opening. But he managed.

Soon, to his surprise, he was sitting upright. The gap threaded a little farther up, and then it closed off. The light was coming in the sides of the machine, not through the top.

It looked familiar here, even though he hadn't done work on this part of the machine in so long he couldn't remember the last time he'd touched it.

But he remembered building it, piece by piece, back when the wood was new and smelled of fresh wood shavings, and each part seemed precious and important to him. He could almost see his younger self, figuring out how the pieces worked together, how each junction he made, each little joist, each little part of the frame, seemed to make the machine stronger.

He had framed the abacus, leaving it and its beads and strings in what was then the very center of the machine. The abacus had added color and a bit of clarity. The beads had been red and white, designed to move left to right, and the strings had been taut.

The frame had been wood, and if the strings had rotted away, and the beads had fallen, then he wouldn't be able to see the wooden frame at all.

Although he was looking for it, as he was scouring his memory for any pieces of the abacus he had found over the years.

The floor in this part of the building wasn't exactly even, so the beads would have rolled toward the door.

Given the level of neglect that the dirt indicated, though, he probably hadn't looked at the walls in decades. The beads could be lined up against it, and buried under a pile of dust and silt and whatever else that dirt was made up of.

He almost leaned his forehead against the latticework, then stopped himself. He wanted to reach a hand up through the opening, and touch what was in front of him, but he didn't dare.

He barely fit here as it was, so he leaned in a bit closer.

Some of the wood looked familiar—not as part of the abacus, but as something he had found, something he had believed would work well with the machine.

There was a time when he would scour the earth for beautiful pieces of wood. He would travel to faraway places, finding the wood that would best suit the machine, or maybe even represent a culture the machine rarely touched.

As time passed, and the North Pole grew, Lo would visit the elves, to see what kind of woods they had found. Eventually, he stopped visiting, though, because somewhere around the machine's growth into Machine Room Two, he stopped using wood altogether and moved to metal.

Metal was nice and functional and good for the machine, but it didn't have the beauty that wood had. Nor did it make him feel like he was creating something important.

Metal didn't have the rich smell or the fine texture. And metal required oil, which had a scent that he had to get used to, a scent that (back in the day), he wasn't sure he liked at all.

But Lo had thought it necessary. By the expansion into Machine Room Two, he was working on the machine every day, all day, trying to keep up with demand. He didn't have time to travel, and he certainly didn't have time for beauty of any kind.

He definitely didn't have time to search for the "right" kinds of materials, to linger over the machine and think about what was not only best for it, but what would make it seem even more beautiful than it already was.

It had grown into a Franken-machine, rather than the lovely bit of magical crafting that it had started as.

He had forgotten what it was like to enhance the machine rather than repair it. He had forgotten the joy he had taken in building it, in helping the pieces blend their magic into something beyond them, how the machine had once been *grander* than anything that existed, rather than lesser than the mobile phones modern people kept in their pockets.

Tears pricked his eyes, and he had to take a shallow breath to calm himself down (again! Jeez, he was so emotional right now). He had loved this machine once, more than he had thought he could love anything. It had been the center of his existence.

It was *still* the center of his existence, but only as something that needed help to be less ramshackle than it was. It was long past its prime, long past the beauty it had once been.

Part of him was ashamed to show it to anyone, and an even greater part of him was embarrassed that Dallas, of all people, got to see into the machine's nooks and crannies. She understood its failures. She saw mistakes in its gaps.

He wondered what she wanted him to see here, besides the thin delicate wood, the broken connections, the missing abacus. She probably wanted to use this part of the machine to convince him that the machine was dying.

It wasn't dying. But it had certainly lost its purpose.

And it seemed as unhappy as he was, as joyless as he felt.

How could a machine that dispensed joy give away anything that it didn't already have? It had run out of the very thing that made it work.

No wonder parts of it were getting thin. It was pulling joy out of its frame, out of its body—old joy, joy that had once existed—so that the machine could continue its mission.

No wonder this part, the center, where the most joy had been, had become so thin as to be nonexistent.

Maybe that was where the abacus had gone: maybe it had sacrificed itself to the constant manufacture of joy.

That very thought made his heart constrict. He let out a small breath of air, and watched bits of dust (particles of wood?) slide off some of the nearby latticework and rain down on Dallas.

To her credit, she said nothing. Or maybe that was by design. Because, after all, she had sent him here.

She wanted him to experience the entire interior of the machine. The missing center of the machine. The way that it had fallen apart.

He closed his eyes for a moment, bracing himself against whatever she was going to say. He could almost hear it: *The machine has lost its way. It has no purpose any longer. It shouldn't be that hard to replace.*

Except to him. For him. And he didn't matter either. She could build a new machine, one that would handle the lists better than this machine ever could. One that would be able to maintain all the addresses as well as the floating addresses. One that might be able to find a way to get children as lost as those he saw today to a place like Niko's Village that could provide them with the right kind of assistance.

Lo opened his eyes, repressed a sigh so that he wouldn't see more dirt fly off this ancient and once-beloved part of the machine, and then he slowly sank back down to the mechanic's creeper, trying to set his expression so he didn't seem impatient in advance with all the proposals Dallas was going to throw at him.

She remained on her back, although she had her hands tucked under her head, giving it some support. She had been watching him up there, but he had no idea what she had seen. His expression had changed a few times. He had blinked hard, and closed his eyes, and sighed audibly once.

But he hadn't done much else.

He settled in next to her, wanting to lean into her soft skin. But he didn't. Because he was also braced for her words, and he knew they wouldn't be soft at all.

"Are we done down here?" His words weren't soft either, or rather, his tone wasn't.

Without waiting for her answer, he braced his feet against the floor and pushed the mechanic's creeper backwards. His half of the creeper moved, but hers didn't—at least, not right away.

Then she caught up, and they shot out from under the machine. He had to slow the creeper down with his hand, placing it flat against the wooden floor. This time, her end of the creeper kept moving while his stopped.

The net effect was to turn the creeper so that he was facing the back-side of the machine, which looked even more forlorn and forgotten than the inside of the machine had.

"What did you want me to see?" he asked, his tone lacerating. He had reached the end of his rope, emotionally. He didn't want the coming attack, but he wasn't going to be able to avoid it. And he needed to hear it, so better to hear it now, while he was already overloaded than to hear it just after he had gotten his equilibrium back.

The creeper had stopped entirely. Dallas sat up. The back of her T-shirt and jeans were clean only where the creeper had been. There was a creeper-sized image on the half of her clothing that had been closest to Lo. The rest of her clothing was as filthy as her face, neck, and torso.

"Well." She wiped at her eyes with one of her thumbs, then stopped to look at the additional dirt she had scraped off. She half-smiled, as if the dirt amused her. "I didn't really want you to see anything."

"What?" He didn't have time for games. He was done with games, maybe forever. And that would not go well with Elf-gineers who had to work with him in the future—if, indeed, there was *any* working with him in the future.

Dallas shuffled and pushed just enough to get him to sit up, and to sit on the opposite side of the creeper from her. It felt like they were about to play a game of teeter-totter, especially as the creeper seemed to adjust itself beneath them.

She moved just enough so that he could see her face and, he supposed, she could see his. The skin around her eyes had been wiped clean, the brown looking pale against her amber eyes. Her hair no longer looked amber, though. It looked like someone had run black shoe polish through it.

"I wanted to see something," she said.

"Well," he said, mimicking her tone. "Did you see it?"

"I more than saw it." She smiled. The smile made the dirt crease into her laugh lines and crinkle beneath her eyelids. "I felt it. Didn't you?"

Games. It was all a game. Why couldn't the magical be straightforward? It would make his life so much easier.

"Just tell me what's going on," he said, sounding even more tired than he felt.

Her smile faded into a look of concern. He didn't like the compassion any more than he liked the smile.

"I've been looking for the heart of the machine," she said.

"Yeah." Those damn tears prickled again. He willed them away. "It's gone."

"No, it's not." She touched his arm. He looked down at her dirt-covered hand, feeling like he'd never seen anything like it.

Her words weren't making any sense. "Yes, it is," he said. "I looked for it, and I guess we used it up. There's nothing left."

"I think you're right about overuse," she said. "That's clear, now that I understand what's going on."

He sighed and pulled his arm away from her touch. He felt the loss of her warmth, but didn't move back.

"I don't understand what's going on," he said.

"You wouldn't." She shifted ever so slightly. The creeper wobbled. He put the tips of three fingers onto the floor to stabilize the creeper, even though he wanted to get off of it and just walk away.

"I know the machine better than anyone," he said tiredly.

She nodded. "But I've seen enough magical machines to see patterns, and I knew I needed to find the heart of the machine to figure out what was going on. I wasn't sure I'd find the heart, but I knew it had to exist near the beginning of the machine, so that's why I went into Machine Room One."

"And now that you've realized that the heart is missing, you can fix things." Was he sounding bitter too? He wasn't sure he cared.

She spoke softly, calmly. "I'm not sure I have to fix anything."

"Great. You've given up. After all this." He braced himself on the hand closest to the machine and started to stand up.

She grabbed his free hand. "No, wait. I'm not being clear."

"That's right," he said, not sitting back down, but not standing all the way either. "You're not."

"It's you, Lo," she said. "You're the heart of the machine."

He frowned at her. "What? How could you possibly know that?"

She tugged him down. He nearly upended the creeper, but somehow managed not to.

"That's why I had you slide up into that empty space," she said. "The space moved to accommodate you. You didn't hit anything, did you?"

"No," he said, frowning just a bit.

"What you didn't see," she said, "was that the wood strengthened, and the machine leaned toward you when you leaned toward it."

"Next you're going to tell me that it's alive," he said.

"Well, it is," she said. "All magical machines are alive, on some level. This one more than most."

He couldn't really process what she was telling him. Or why that was good news.

"Whether I'm the heart of the machine or not," he said. "It doesn't matter. And we already knew that magical machines are partial to their builders."

"But some move beyond their builders," she said. "Rarely are they so intertwined that their builder is part of them."

His frown got worse.

"The machine was falling apart just from you being gone for a few hours this afternoon," she said. "You had to repair a lot of damage, didn't you?"

He hadn't told her that. "So?"

"So," she said, "having you far away from the machine when it's in crisis made it panic."

He couldn't help himself: he glanced at the machine. It did seem closer than it had a few minutes ago. But then, the mechanic's creeper had moved and Lo had had assumed a new position and this was all... strange. Just strange.

"I have live here then, for the rest of my life? Making sure the machine stays cobbled together?" That sounded worse somehow.

"No," she said. "No, it's simpler than that."

He looked at her. Her eyes were sparkling. There was no reason for her eyes to be sparkling, was there? What was making her so happy? *She* wasn't the heart of any machine. This didn't have an impact on her life.

Just on his.

"How can it be simpler?" he asked.

"You can change out any part of the machine," she said. "You can bring in new pieces or rebuild so that we're using modern tech, as long as you center the machine. As long as you believe in it. You'll be fine."

Lo glanced at the machine. He didn't want to be fine. He wanted the machine to be fine.

"That's how all of these disparate parts work together," she said. "Because you put them in place. That's why you haven't been able to have a good assistant, because they're not the machine. You're the machine, Lo. You are."

"So, I'm trapped here," he said, more to himself than to her. Trapped, in this room, constantly trying to repair something that will never be fixable.

"No," she said. "You can build—or I can build—a whole new machine, one that will work for Claus & Company. Or you can revamp this machine given what you learned today. That's up to you. If anything, this frees you. Learning this will make it possible for you to move on, if that's what you want to do."

He blinked. Something shifted inside him, something that recognized what she was saying.

He could leave? He could do something else with his life?

What would that something else be?

He let out a small breath. He didn't want to do anything else. He loved the job he had been given hundreds of years ago. He loved handing out joy.

What upset him was that no longer worked. What he thought of as joy, an important dollop of joy, was meaningless in this world filled with homeless families and sad children and despair.

"But joy doesn't matter anymore," he said.

"*What?*" She looked stunned. She leaned forward and caught his hands. Her touch was gentle, but her face wasn't. "Who told you that?"

"You said joy wasn't enough, that we've been giving children instruction in how to be greedy, not in enjoyment, and the kids who needed us most are the ones we didn't even see." He managed to keep his voice level, even though he wasn't sure how.

"Joy is always important," she said.

"But that's not what you said." Now he sounded like a petulant child.

Her hands tightened on his. "I had no idea that the machine was supposed to hand out joy. And it hasn't been doing the job that it was supposed to do, remember? It's been breaking down."

He shook his head, feeling confused. Niko had said that a fleeting moment of joy got people through horrendous days. That had to mean something, didn't it?

"Why would the machine be breaking down?" Lo asked. "It should have been continuing to function at the same level, just missing the increased population. The joy should have been there."

"Maybe it is," Dallas said. "I've never been in a situation to see it."

That didn't sound right. He knew the joy was leaching out of the mission. That's why marketing was taking over, why the Old Men in Charge seemed grim these days, why the North Pole wasn't the place it had been when he first moved here.

"The joy hasn't been there," Lo said. "Not the way it was. Otherwise children wouldn't have learned greed."

Dallas squeezed his hands one more time, then let them go. She gave him a rather sad look.

"Have you felt joy recently?" she asked.

He leaned back, then nearly toppled off the creeper, catching himself with the flat of his hands. He had to slide toward her to keep his balance.

Recently? He hadn't felt joy in...years, maybe? A satisfaction in his work, yes, until the machine kept breaking down. And then panic. And sheer overwork. And exhaustion.

But joy?

"No," he said. He would leave it at that.

"It's your joy that the machine's spreading," she said. "And it's been searching for more joy, but it only knows how to share your joy. That's why this part of the machine looks so frail. The machine had to find more joy so it took the joy you once had in creating, the joy you imbued each piece with, and gave it away, just like you had designed it to. That's why the machine is falling apart, Lo. Because it can't find any more joy."

He let those words sink in. His joy. He hadn't built the machine to find other joy. The machine was dispensing *his* magic, not anyone else's.

Oh, sure, the gifts had their own magic. But he made the lists, he was the one who made sure that the joy was distributed properly. His joy started the ball rolling, as it were, and then the gifts followed. Each provided part of the mix that would end up being the right amount of joy for each child, so that there would be enough joy to share.

Only he had run out of joy, so the machine—heck, the entire North Pole—was running on a deficiency.

"Okay," Lo said, not sure what he could do about this. It was his fault, but he wasn't sure how to make the repair. If there was a repair to be made. "After what I saw today, I'm not sure there is any joy to be had."

In anything.

He pushed off the creeper. He had to get out of the machine room. He had to be by himself, just for a little while.

He had to let all of this sink in, before he figured out what to do next.

CHAPTER 22

*D*allas nearly toppled off the mechanic's creeper as Lo got up and walked away, through a path around the machine that she hadn't even known existed.

His voice had sounded flat and dead, his eyes were filled with sadness.

She grabbed the creeper and held in place for just a moment, sitting still, letting herself think.

Normally, she didn't have to deal with people when she was dealing with a magical machine. The machine was what it was, usually an amalgam of its community, not of one person.

She should have searched harder for the heart of the machine. Had she known that Lo was the heart of the machine, she wouldn't have taken him to Chicago, maybe wouldn't even have argued as vociferously about the machine's failures.

Because the failures were his failures. At least, that was how he had perceived it, and he wasn't exactly wrong.

But *failure* was the wrong word. He had worked so hard, he had given so much of himself, he had nothing left to give.

And now, she had piled on, rather than make things right.

If she had known exactly what she was dealing with, she would have...

Oh, she had no idea, since she had never faced anything like this before. Nothing at all.

She couldn't repair the machine without repairing the man.

And she had no idea how to do that.

With a sigh, she stood up, and slid the mechanic's creeper back to its cradle on the far wall. She dusted off her hands, and realized that doing so didn't make any difference whatsoever. She was covered in dirt from the machine itself.

She made her way to the break room, where she washed off her face, stunned at the amount of dirt that covered her. If the machine, which Lo cared about, was this neglected, imagine how neglected he was.

She leaned forward, thinking. The man had dedicated his entire life to dispensing joy to children. And now, he learned that he had run out.

Somehow she—he—they—Claus & Company—*someone*—needed to replenish his joy.

She didn't have the capability of doing that. She wasn't a joy-giver or a people-pleaser. She knew machines.

And she knew one thing: she could complete her task without Lo.

She could install a new machine of some kind or another, probably something very modern. It would do much of the work of Lo's machine, or maybe even more of it.

But it wouldn't dispense joy. She would have to tell the Old Men in Charge about that, and they would have to find some excess joy that they could siphon to the machine.

Or they would have to make up that loss of Lo's joy with something else.

She leaned against the break room sink, feeling a curious reluctance to do anything. Going to the Old Men in Charge felt like a betrayal of Lo.

Setting up a new machine felt like a betrayal of Lo.

But setting up a new machine was the easiest and quickest way to get Dallas out of the North Pole.

Which was what she had said she wanted to do, from the moment she got here. Heck, *before* she had gotten here.

To do what was best for her, she needed to set up a new machine.

But was that best for Claus & Company? The organization seemed to have lost its way on so many levels.

Not that she needed to care. Not that she *should* care.

But she did care.

And most of all, she cared about Lo.

She peered into the reflective surface of the ancient refrigerator. It wasn't quite a mirror, but it would do. She was startled to see how messy her hair was, how it looked like she had drawn a face into a pile of black dirt that was, apparently, the rest of her.

Despite herself, she let out a small laugh. She was ridiculously dirty. She couldn't remember the last time she was this dirty.

And that meant Lo was too. She was so concerned with his emotions that she really hadn't looked at how the rest of him was doing.

She wanted to run after him, urge him to slow down, to take care of himself. But maybe he was doing that, as he gave himself time to think.

Although they had both been discussing dinner. And she was hungry. He probably was too, underneath.

She dried off her hands, then walked out of the break room, wondering how she could find Lo without expending any magic. She was loathe to use magic near the machine—too much could go wrong.

She would go back for her sweater and parka, and then step outside, before using any magic at all.

She had pushed him too hard. And she didn't know him well enough to know what his breaking point was.

She wasn't even sure she would recognize a breaking point, not with a mage.

With a machine, yes, but a mage…no.

And then she stopped.

He was the machine. She had been approaching him like he was another person—which he was—but he was also the machine.

And what would she do with a machine that suffered from these problems?

She would find the heart of the machine, and reinstall it. Then she would power down the machine and let it rest while she built something that took the pressure off of it. She would modernize it, and she would make sure that it never got this depleted again.

She needed to separate Lo from the machine—not exorcize him from it—but take the pressure off of it. Off of him.

They needed a secondary machine. Something like this one, but a machine that all of the Elf-gineers could work. Something that would survive beyond Lo.

Suddenly, her mind was full of plans. She knew how to fix this. She *could* fix this.

Or at least, fix the machine. The problem she was sent here to solve.

Not the problem that had developed, with Lo.

The trouble was, she cared more about Lo than the machine. Or Claus & Company. Or all that the North Pole represented.

Which was odd, because in all of her years of working on magical machines, she had never paid much attention to the mages working around those machines. She hadn't really cared.

There was just something different about Lo.

Something that pulled her, drew her in.

Something she cared about, more than she could say.

CHAPTER 23

The wind had died down. The snow now fell like it usually did here at the North Pole, big lazy flakes, the kind that showed up in every Christmas movie ever made.

Lo used to love snow like this. When had he stopped?

Or *had* he stopped loving it?

He tilted his head upward, felt the cool wet flakes land on his too-hot skin. He used to do this as a child, so long ago that it barely was worth thinking about, and then he would open his mouth and let the snowflakes in, as if the sky was feeding them just to him.

He smiled at the memory. It was visceral, despite being old, and for a moment, just a half second, he felt a little dollop of joy.

"Huh." He brought his head down, noted that the snow that had landed on his skin had melted and dripped onto the snowbank he sat on, creating little black ice pellets.

Just a few weeks ago, he would have stood up and gone back inside, to clean himself off, but now he touched those pellets, marveling at their different shapes, at the way that the snow had returned to water, picked up the despair (*dirt*. He meant *dirt*) that was covering him, and then deposited it on the snow around him.

Yes, he could still see that dirt, but it had transformed into something else, something new, something with an odd beauty of its own.

He wiped his face with his hand, noting for the first time that his hand was bare. He had left his gloves inside, along with his coat.

He had to leave the machine, even though, Dallas told him, he couldn't leave the machine.

Or, rather, the machine couldn't leave him.

Or something like that.

He wiped his wet hands on his jeans, feeling the cold prickle through him.

He hadn't stopped enjoying the cold. He loved it so much more than the stifling heat he had experienced that afternoon in Chicago. He loved the snow and the cold and the weird weather that always swirled around the Pole.

The weather had its own magic as well, because it was the magic of expectations. Everyone who had ever heard of Santa's Village in the North Pole expected snow, year-round. Those expectations actually created the snow, year-round. And usually it was this kind of snow—the fluffy, picture-perfect kind.

That storm they had returned to earlier wasn't an aberration, but it was something he thought of as real weather, not expectation weather.

The snowbanks hid him from the rest of the village. He supposed Dallas could see him, if she looked out the right windows.

She seemed to think her news was good news, and maybe it was. But he had a lot to process. *He* had lost the joy. He had been supplying it to the machine and everywhere else, which he hadn't expected.

And losing that joy—he hadn't even noticed when it happened.

When had he stopped looking up at snow flurries, watching them come down in their lazy swirly pattern, that always looked to him like little live creatures leaping to earth, anticipating some kind of grand adventure?

When had he stopped noticing that the snowbanks were all different heights, and the cold wind felt good after the warm steam bath of the machine rooms?

When had he looked at the holiday lights that filled the village year round and enjoyed how the colors changed with the seasons? Granted, the changes were minor—a light green with pastel red in the spring; white, grass green, and sunrise red in the summer; an almost Kelly green, reddish-orange, and silver in the fall; and then full-on Christmas colors throughout the holiday season. He smiled at that corrective thought, realizing he had noticed the changes, but he hadn't *seen* them. He hadn't taken a moment to look at them, to note the seasonal change, to appreciate the way that the inhabitants of the North Pole enjoyed their community as well as their jobs.

Lo didn't know when he stopped eating on the benches outside the food cart. Instead, he'd buy a bratwurst on a hard roll, and eat the sandwich as he walked to the machine room. Or maybe, he'd grab some pierogi, asking for it in a round container with a fork, shoveling the food in his mouth without tasting it as he headed to fix something.

Sometimes, someone—usually Rafn—would leave a full meal ready to cook inside Lo's cottage, with big instructions on the refrigerator, counter, and sometimes even on the coat hangers inside the door, reminding Lo to eat.

Lo was so focused, he wouldn't think about food. Even when he ate it, he wasn't thinking about it.

He wasn't enjoying it.

The first meal he had enjoyed in a long time (months? years?) had been the lunch he had with Dallas before they went to Chicago. That seemed like days ago.

And then he was only enjoying the meal because he was sharing it with her.

He swiveled slightly, and looked through the swirling snowflakes at the building in front of him.

Sharing it.

He hadn't shared anything in a long, long time. He had lost friends here—death was inevitable, even among the long-lived elves and mages—and he hadn't made any new friends.

Instead, he had wrapped himself in his work, not noticing when others had befriended him.

Lo had stopped paying attention to everything except the work. He had been so wrapped up in the machine, in the problems that surrounded him, that he hadn't been able to find his own little dollop of joy each and every day.

And that, more than anything, was the problem.

He sat on a snowbank, staring down the path he and Dallas had walked not three hours ago. When they had come back from Chicago.

He had lost himself then, in despair and anger and hopelessness.

And then the inside of the machine, the loss of the abacus—he now knew why it was gone. He had taken so much joy in that abacus. He had loved it, and it had been the very thing that made him smile whenever he saw it.

He couldn't remember the last time he had seen it. He couldn't remember the last time he had looked for it.

He couldn't even remember the last time he had taken joy from the machine.

Somewhere, the machine had become a burden. He still loved the machine, but he didn't like the time he spent with it, didn't like the work, even though he knew it was necessary.

Dallas was right, but not in the way that she had thought. He wasn't the heart of the machine. He had *become* the machine. He had done everything expected of him by rote, with no emotion, taking action, doing work, running on a schedule dictated by the outside, each day the same, each moment the same.

That was why Dallas's presence seemed so disconcerting to him. She immediately aroused emotions in him. She had made him step out of cocoon he had wrapped himself in. The cocoon of a machine.

His heart leaped.

She was right and she was wrong. They could fix the machine. He didn't have to abandon it, and they didn't have to keep it running for minor things.

He could make it more organic, not less, but it would take help.

Technical help.

He stood. The slight breeze chilled him now, but the snow still looked pretty. The snowbank he had been sitting on had a black impression of his backside and thighs, with just a touch of black around the base from his shoes.

His footprints coming to the bank were already filled in.

He ran a hand over his hair, feeling the damp and the goo from the machine. He could see himself, reflected in the glass windows of the building, a blurry grayish-blue figure that seemed almost unrecognizable.

He walked back toward the building, and as he did, one of the doors opened.

Dallas had been watching him.

That would have angered him just a day or so ago, but now it relieved him. He needed her help.

And more than that, he wanted her help.

He hoped she would appreciate the change.

He certainly did.

CHAPTER 24

*L*o looked like a crazy man. His hair was plastered against his head, dripping dark liquid, almost as if he had tried to dye it, but the dye was leaching off. His shirt was wet and black, and his jeans had black handprints along the front.

His face was clean, though, the cheeks ruddy, and his green eyes more alive than she had ever seen them.

The air coming in the door to the machine building was deliciously crisp. The snow was falling evenly now. It was a pretty snow, a classic snow, and it encased him as if it were guiding him inside.

Anything was possible, she supposed.

"I'm sorry," Dallas said. "If I had realized you were the heart of the machine, I would have approached everything differently."

He shook his head slightly as he stepped inside. Snow swirled in with him. She closed the door behind him.

"Tell me something," he said. "Do you believe that joy can save the world?"

"What?" she asked.

"Outlook, optimism," he said. "If you believe something can be fixed, then you look for a solution, right? Even if you're in the middle of it."

She frowned, trying to follow his line of thinking.

"It's a different focus," he said. "It's still giving joy, but…"

He swept his hand toward the snow. She had no idea why.

"We can't fix anything you showed me today," he said.

"I know," she said. "Unless Claus & Company helps Niko North."

"Which Claus & Company should do, and we're going to talk about it, and there needs to be a lot of changes." Lo ran a hand through his hair. More water dripped off it, leaving a brownish-black puddle on the floor. "But our mission is about giving just a bit of joy, and back in the day, before commercialism and everything, a gift was the best way to do that."

Her heart clenched. She didn't think Claus & Company should stop dispensing joy with gifts.

"It's not a bad way," she said.

"It's not the only way." He smiled at her. The smile was gentle. She hadn't thought he would smile at all today. "There are a lot of other ways to inspire and educate and focus and…"

He let his voice trail off. Then, to her surprise, he wrapped an arm around her, and half-hugged her. She almost turned into the hug, but stopped herself just before she did.

They were still colleagues, after all. They were working together, not…Oh, she had no idea what they were.

He released her, and turned her toward him. His eyes looked clear for the first time since she had taken him to Chicago.

"I know I'm not making sense," he said. "I'm figuring this out, and I need your help. We keep the machine. We make it accessible to all the Elf-gineers. We actually make joy magic a separate part of it, and we… oh, I don't know, exactly. We inspire children, and give quiet comfort to children, and…we'll have to talk to everyone. This isn't something easily solved."

She nodded. She was beginning to see that.

"But," she said, "everyone says we need the machine working before Christmas."

"We do," Lo said. "We can do that. We can cobble this machine into something that will do the job for this Christmas. We'll keep this machine, because it needs to stay. But we also need a new machine, a revised machine and that's going to take a long time, and I can't build it alone."

He was asking her to help him, asking her to stay here, and create something big and vast, something they couldn't entirely envision right now.

Her heart rate increased. She was actually nervous.

"I repair machines," she said. "I don't build them."

"Well," he said, "it would be something new for both of us."

She frowned at him. "What happened out there in the snow? You seem different."

He glanced at the door. The white flakes were coming down harder now. It was impossible to see the snowbank where he had been sitting, alone, for nearly fifteen minutes.

She had watched him, worried, but he seemed all right. He seemed better.

"Nothing happened out there," he said. "It was in here."

"Huh?" she asked.

"You got through to me," he said.

"Niko and I," she said.

"No," Lo said. "You. And your optimism. You think we can fix the machine. I had lost that. I had lost almost everything except the dogged focus on work."

She shrugged. She had always been optimistic. That wasn't new. "Other people are optimistic."

He shook his head. "Not like you. You stop and look at things. You see them. And you gave me hope. I don't think I've had hope for a long time."

Then he raised an index finger, moving it slightly. He was almost smiling.

She liked this mood on him. It suited him.

"Hope and joy," he said, bringing his middle finger next to his index finger, so that they became a pair. "They're part of the same coin."

"And optimism, and the belief that out of darkness comes light," she said, which was, to her, the true meaning of the season.

He nodded, clearly pleased she had understood. Then his smile faded and he took a deep breath, as if he was going to ask her something important.

"I don't know how long you were supposed to be at the North Pole," he said, "but this would take—"

"Years," she said more to herself than to him. This would take years.

Years away from her beloved beaches, and warm summers. Years buried in snow and cold and too many Christmas lights.

Years, spent working with people who wanted to make change, rather than bulldozing her way into a situation and forcing them to do something that they never wanted to do in the first place.

"Years," he said, studying her. "Is it fair for me to ask you to contemplate a project that big?"

She smiled at him. "Probably not," she said. "But I'm contemplating nonetheless."

Then he hugged her, and she hugged him back, even though he was chilled and damp and smelled faintly of grease. She probably did too.

She liked how he felt in her arms. That was new. She hadn't liked holding anyone, particularly colleagues. Particularly attractive colleagues.

He said into her ear, "I promised you dinner."

"You did," she said.

"Let's have a grand dinner," he said. "And let's talk about the future."

"All right," she said.

They stayed in the hug, though, neither of them moving, not for the longest time. And it felt good. It felt natural. It felt right.

Just like the decision they had made.

It felt like they were standing on the edge of a future, one she didn't entirely understand, but one that seemed worthwhile.

One that seemed worth the risk.

One that would cause a life change—for everyone.

Including them.

PART VI

THE CREATOR(S) OF THE MACHINE(S)

CHAPTER 25

The wind off the ocean wasn't quite as warm as Dallas had hoped. But the sun was heavenly. Her bare feet dug into the sand. The water met the sky somewhere far from her, looking all blue and sparkly and inviting.

Malibu was just as pretty as it had always been. And she loved it as much as she always did.

It really was one of the best places on earth.

But she had never expected to stand here, on a secluded Malibu beach in January, surrounded by people (and elves) she hadn't even known one year ago.

She felt slightly ridiculous in a red and green dress one month after Christmas had ended, but everyone from the North Pole wanted a traditional wedding.

Traditional, in the post-holiday season, was a beach wedding, with holiday colors, and The Big Guy presiding.

He was crouched with a gaggle of S-Elves, all of them talking to Niko North, his wife, and his little charming daughter, who looked prettier than the bride, at least in Dallas's opinion.

Of course, Dallas never really thought that much of her own looks. Nor had she ever expected to be surrounded by twinkling blue-eyed S-

Elves wearing red and green Hawaiian shirts, khaki shorts, and flip-flops, and baring too much skin.

Lo came up behind her and wrapped his arms around her waist. "Thank you," he said.

She leaned against him. "What did I do this time?"

"You mean besides marrying me?" he asked.

"Yes," she said.

"Oh, I can't really count the ways," he said.

Her smile grew. She hadn't realized how lonely she had been when she lived here. Nor had she realized quite how empty her job had become.

She learned a lot of that, as she and Lo struggled to keep the old machine working just enough to get through the holiday season.

Now, on a table near the bright red punch, were design specs for not one, not two, but fifteen new machines. Dallas figured they'd probably end up with five of them, not all fifteen, but she wasn't certain.

She had been distracted since the day after Christmas. Planning the wedding had taken some focus.

Thinking of herself as a woman who had fallen in love had taken some adjustment too.

She turned in Lo's arms, and touched noses. Her relationship with Lo was complicated. It wasn't romantic in the traditional sense. They were both a bit too mechanical for that. He once told her he felt like a machine, or had, over the years.

And the comment had made sense to her, since she had gone places to fix machines.

At the Pole, she hadn't fixed the machine at all. She had fixed Lo, not by tampering with who he was, but by helping him remember who he was.

And in doing so, she had found a new chapter in her life.

She kissed him, and behind them, a bunch of Elf-gineers ooohed.

"Get a room!" one of them said.

"No, they should build a room," another said.

"I think they're going to," said a third.

Elf-gineers. Magical machines. Living in snow.

Her life was very different than it had ever been before.

She leaned back ever so slightly, and said to Lo, "You know, I think I should thank you."

"For what?" he asked.

She waved a hand toward the ocean, the bright blue sky, the warm sun, the beach, and her new colleagues and family. Other friends—her mortal friends and some mages from California—had come to the reception the night before.

She and Lo decided not to mix myth and reality for the Californians.

"I should thank you for challenging me," she said.

Lo chuckled. "I think we challenge each other," he said.

And there it was. The essence of who they were. Intellectual, nerdy, and focused on building things.

Like rooms.

And machines.

And futures.

She kissed him, as that slightly cool breeze continued tease at her dress.

This was more than a dollop of joy. This was joy personified.

Not something to experience every day. But something everyone should experience at least once in their lives.

With someone who understood them. With someone who shared their interests.

With someone they loved.

AUTHOR'S NOTE

Every year, charities ask for donations during the holiday season. As this novel points out, though, the need is great year-round. I know many of you simply can't afford to donate money, but there are other ways to help out. If you have an hour or two per month, you can volunteer. If you don't have the time to volunteer, then hesitate before you throw out food or clothing or blankets. There are many organizations that will pick those items up from you or give you a donation location. Even one can of soup, near its expiration date, will help someone have a good warm meal.

While there are many great national and international charities, I'm not going to list many here. I support St. Jude's Children's Hospital, which gives children life-saving care for free, as well as Able Gamers, which helps people who are bedridden or unable to socialize much due to their disabilities get access to equipment for online gaming. Online gaming is often the only social interaction these folks can get.

Mostly though, I donate to local charities, from the food bank to the animal shelters. The local charities have lower overhead costs. You can also see what they're doing in your community, which charities are effective and which ones aren't. The local food bank always needs donations, and homeless shelters can use blankets, pillows, and lots of socks.

Don't forget the Toys for Tots drives, the Thanksgiving food programs (here in the US) and the giving trees mentioned in this novel. Participating in those will help children get the dollop of joy that Lo and Dallas discussed.

Finally, donate sideways. By that, I mean participate in events and programs that also give money to charity. WMG Publishing participates in Storybundles every year, because Storybundle gives some of the proceeds to charities. I also participate in a lot of runs and walks for charity. Those are a great way to meet people and to make money for some local cause. Here in my hometown of Las Vegas, you can participate in most charity run/walk events by walking a mile or by actually running. Even if you don't finish, your entry fee will go toward the charity that helped sponsor the event.

If you look at the need just in your local neighborhood, the task of solving it all is overwhelming. But if you donate a bit of time here and a can of soup there, you're making the kind of difference that will help more than you realize. You don't have to be Niko North to help others. You can do it with a tiny bit of compassion, well placed, whenever and wherever you can afford to.

Thank you reading this far. I know you didn't buy a holiday book to have someone remind you to donate. But since one of the main threads in the novel is charitable giving, I figured I should say something here.

Again, thank you.

All the best,
—Kristine Grayson

I value honest feedback, and would love to hear your opinion in a review, if you're so inclined, on your favorite book retailer's site.

Be the first to know!

Just sign up for the Kristine Kathryn Rusch newsletter, and keep up with the latest news, releases and so much more—even the occasional giveaway.

So, what are you waiting for? To sign up go to kristinekathrynrusch.com.

But wait! There's more. Sign up for the WMG Publishing newsletter, too, and get the latest news and releases from all of the WMG authors and lines, including Kristine Grayson, Kris Nelscott, Dean Wesley Smith, *Fiction River: An Original Anthology Magazine, Smith's Monthly,* and so much more.

To sign up go to wmgpublishing.com.

ABOUT THE AUTHOR

Called "The Reigning Queen of Paranormal Romance" by *Best Reviews,* bestselling author Kristine Grayson has made a name for herself publishing light, slightly off-skew romance novels about Greek Gods, fairy tale characters, and the modern world.

She writes historical mysteries as Kris Nelscott, and she also writes in a variety of genre, from literary to science fiction to romance, under her real name—Kristine Kathryn Rusch. She has won dozens of awards for her writing

As Kristine Grayson, she also edits the romance volumes of *Fiction River: An Original Anthology Magazine.*

For more information about her work, go to the Kristine Grayson www.kristinegrayson.com and sign up for her newsletter.